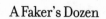
A Faker's Dozen

A Faker's Dozen

Stories

MELVIN JULES BUKIET

—

W. W. NORTON & COMPANY

NEW YORK • LONDON

"Squeak, Memory" and "Splinters" appeared in the *Paris Review*,
"Paper Hero" in *Southwest Review*, "The Suburbiad" in *Princeton
University Library Chronicle*, "The Swap" in the *Reading Room*,
"Filophilia" in *Conjunctions*, "But, Microsoft! What Byte Through
Yonder Windows Breaks?" in *Agni*, "The Two Franzes" in the
Massachusetts Review.

For information about permission to reproduce selections from
this book, write to Permissions, W. W. Norton & Company, Inc.,
500 Fifth Avenue, New York, NY 10110

Manufacturing by Quebecor Fairfield
Book design by Barbara Bachman
Production manager: Amanda Morrison

Library of Congress Cataloging-in-Publication Data

Bukiet, Melvin Jules.
A faker's dozen : stories / by Melvin Jules Bukiet.
p. cm.
Contents: Squeak, memory—Splinters—The return of Eros to
academe—Paper hero—The suburbiad—The swap—Filophilia—
But, Microsoft! What byte through yonder windows breaks?—
Tongue of the Jews—The two Franzes—The war lovers.
I. Title.
ISBN 0-393-05816-6
PS3552.U398F35 2003
813'.54—dc21   2003053956

W. W. Norton & Company, Inc.
500 Fifth Avenue, New York, N.Y. 10110
www.wwnorton.com

W. W. Norton & Company Ltd.
Castle House, 75/76 Wells Street, London W1T 3QT

1 2 3 4 5 6 7 8 9 0

To Jennifer Lyons

Contents

———

A Faker's Dozen

Squeak, Memory

IT WAS 1973, THE SUMMER OF WATERGATE, BUT MY MIND WAS not on politics, but literature. While the parade of unreliable narrators told their stories on daytime television to be followed by their nightly commentators, I read, mostly Russians, mostly classics: Tolstoy, Dostoyevsky, Chekhov. I didn't really enjoy Chekhov, those lonely doctors, shabby and sentimental. I preferred the grandiose passions of their fathers, and thought I understood them.

There was a girl—there were still twenty-year-old "girls" then. How long ago was it, oh, about as many springs as she was young that summer. You can always count on a thief for a fancy prose style. And you, the one with the degree, you already think you know where I'm going, you've already overleaped the transition from the blunt forms of Czarist fiction into the heady flamboyance of the twentieth century.

It was actually Andrei Biely who led me to Mr. Nabokov. Usually it's the other way around, but I was an autodidact without benefit of tutelage, and relied upon one volume to pull me to another. I haunted the used bookstores of Fourth Avenue, inhaling the must from Dauber and Pine's basement as if it were motes in the rose window at Chartres. Even then the grand street was a shade of its glorious past, but there were remnants of the glory. I found a dog-eared Grove Press edition of *St. Petersburg*. The title called to me and even more so the quote on the back, declaring this book one of the four great works of the century, along with *The Metamorphosis, Remembrance of Things Past* and *Ulysses*, so I bought it for a dollar, but what really thrilled me was not the unknown masterpiece, but its unknown advocate who dared to place it in the same pantheon as those other monuments—as if he defined such realms. The arbiter's name was Nabokov.

I had heard of *Lolita*, but only after reading the author's extravagant, arrogant blurb for the esoteric symbolist, Biely, did I dredge his own lurid best-seller out from the disorganized bins in front of the Pageant, several blocks and a half dozen other venerable antiquarians away from Dauber and Pine, and fell in love—with the author as well as his heroine. How could I not when he penned the best parenthesis in literary history, describing a character's tragic demise "(picnic, lightning)." After several wrong guesses, I made it a point to learn how to pronounce his name, moving from Nah-bah-kov, accent first on the first, then on the second, and third on the last syllable, to Nuh-boak-off, accent dead center.

I found a photograph taken of him sitting on a stone-balustraded terrace in the Alps, a delicate *kirschwasser* at hand, a butterfly net angled against his rattan chair. He was wearing thick loden shorts with a button-down shirt. In this first image, I saw no shoes, but had an image of immense, puckered knees.

First I saw him in my mind, and then in the flesh.

I was walking the streets of the city that summer, map in hand, determined to cover every block on the magic island before Labor Day. Don't ask why. It was the literal-minded youth's manner of making the city his own. Sometimes this led me to inspiration, more frequently to a mathematical rigor. I learned the best pattern to cover the most blocks without overlapping footsteps, the snake, river to river, east to west, down a block, river to river, west to east. Later I strode in 100-block straight lines down the avenues. I took in brownstones, warehouses, office towers, imagining the lives led there as I avoided dragging my march-sore feet to soak in the bathtub in the kitchen of my girl's apartment on West Fourth near where it intersects West Eleventh, where the grid gets tangled and you can't pursue a simple snakewind.

That day, July 15, as the proceedings were broadcast from Washington to every television in the nation, I was on Madison Avenue in the thirties when I was yanked from my plan to cover Turtle Bay by a familiar profile not twenty feet away. It was Mr. Nabokov himself (despite our subsequent intimacy, I will never be able to refer to him as Vladimir, emphasis on the first or second syllable, let alone the sweet diminutive Vlady). I recognized him as much by stature as profile. He was a heavy man—made substantial by vocabulary—and had thin hair swept back off a high, sweaty forehead. It was summer, and Nixon was sweating too. The novelist had smallish eyes and a prominent nose and presidential jowls that I could not see at first, since he was angled, keeping a watch on a Checker cab—there were still Checkers then—taking a too-tight right turn in order to pick up a woman holding a small dog. Perhaps he was thinking of Chekhov, whom he admired.

Then he crossed the street. Maintaining a subtle distance, I followed, although it took a few moments for me to realize that I was following. "Hey," I said to myself, "this is a creepy thing to do. This is what G. Gordon Liddy did." Then I relaxed and enjoyed my transgression.

I assumed that he was heading for the Morgan Library, to

examine the antique etchings in the mansion that may have reminded him of his family home confiscated by the Revolution sixty years earlier. But he passed directly by the stately porte cochere. We continued northward against the pedestrian traffic flowing southward from Grand Central Station. I was astonished that people did not recognize him, pester him, adore him. I turned to make certain I was not the lead sheep for a flock of acolytes and nearly lost him. He wove with an elegant, even mincing, gait through the commuters' rough oceanic flow. At Thirty-eighth Street, he paused to examine a hot-dog-and-pretzel salesman, inhaling the scent of the New World. But despite the apparent randomness of his path, I was sure he had a destination.

Perhaps he was in New York for a meeting of a genealogical society or to confer with a lawyer suing the Soviet regime for restitution of stolen property, an estate roughly the size of Connecticut, or to make a presentation at a symposium on the sexuality of verbs. Or perhaps he was en route to a lunch date with his publisher, some bushy-haired thug who planned to berate him for not repeating the succès de scandale of *Lolita*. The man clearly had a reason for being on this block in this unseasonable city.

There was a bookstore on the corner that specialized in travel writing, its window full of Baedekers and memoirs. Perhaps he required some esoteric volume on Micronesia for research into a new project, *Pnin in Tahiti*. By following I might anticipate his next novel. But he passed the store without so much as a glance.

He veered off the avenue at Thirty-ninth Street, where the buildings rose in height, and I hurried and nearly bumped into him. He was stationary in front of a different window, that of a shoe store with a slim brown awning—perhaps to catch me off guard. I think he sensed my presence all along, but was too generous, or too removed, to take offense, and the sinister bend in his path was meant to allow me to pass ahead gracefully and leave him be. Instead, I pretended great interest in a sign designating local parking regulations, as if the low-slung sports car at the curb belonged to me. I noticed that the meter had expired, so I fished into my trousers and found a dime and gave it another half hour, and leaned against the hood I felt I had rented for half a circle on the tiny municipal timepiece of sorts.

But the master's absorption in the wares of the shoe store seemed genuine, and then he entered. I was close enough to feel a draft from within. Since then I've learned that shoe stores always turn the air-conditioning way up, so that sweaty socks do not create unpleasant odors to offend other customers.

A salesman not much older than myself but with a tired manner appeared, to join him on the inside of the front window. Words were exchanged.

The fellow took a pair of wing tips from the window, but Mr. Nabokov shook his head and gestured several inches to the side, moving his finger in an arc that bisected the window and my stomach like a surgeon's blade. I could have told the clerk which shoes such a man preferred, an oxblood cordovan, with cylindrical laces like spaghetti rather than the more common flat linguini style. They were comfortable, elegant, Italian.

Suddenly I was keenly aware of my own footgear, a pair of Converse All-Stars that had seen better days. How long ago, oh, you know that one. A lace had broken and I had made an awkward knot between grommets that kept it from tying snugly. There was a tear in the side and, worst, a worn spot in the sole. I was standing in a slight depression in the asphalt in which a pool had gathered and the water was seeping in and wetting my socks. It was the third day I had worn those socks and they were stiff. The puddle was a cooling lubricant to my chafing toes.

Mr. Nabokov held the sample and flexed it to make certain it had the suppleness he required to cushion his great bulk. It was a left shoe, as were all the samples. I wondered if Mr. Nabokov knew that the right foot is usually larger than the left, the reason why stores always use left shoes for samples, to fool people into thinking their own feet are minimally more tasteful than they really are. Of course, he knew everything; he would factor that into his decision and did not require my advice. Appreciating the texture, he nodded, and lowered himself ponderously into a row of chairs linked together like those in a movie theater as if he had hemorrhoids.

The clerk then knelt at his feet—I would have exchanged positions with him in a flash—and placed the novelist's rather small hoof into a contraption that measured it. The thing resembled a silver tray with sliding extrusions, ridged to simulate toes, that came from the top to the black marking that read 7½, while another bar slid in from the side to determine width. The result was unusual; his feet were wide, perhaps splayed from Alpine hikes in search of rare butterflies. By then I knew his hobbies, habits and obsessions. Now I knew his shoe size.

Then the clerk disappeared into the back room to fetch the requested shoes while Mr. Nabokov peered about the store, at the other styles of left shoes on display together with wooden stretchers and other accoutrements of the trade. The store also sold umbrellas, but it wasn't raining; it was humid.

The clerk returned, and knelt again to insert Mr. Nabokov's foot into the merchandise. Thus shod, he paced back and forth in front of a mirror set upon the carpeted floor. He looked out the window at me, and I patted the car proprietarily while a man in a suit rushed toward me down the block.

The man looked at the meter, perplexed, and then at me. Distracted, I missed the next phase of the transaction, but when

I looked back Mr. Nabokov was at the counter, reaching into his vest pocket to extract a wallet whose Florentine leather was as luscious as the shoe, and then came the moment I was not waiting for. Apparently spontaneously, he plucked a pair of shoelaces from the spindly, multiarmed rack on the counter beside an enormous brown cash register. I might have guessed he would purchase an extra pair of laces; the man was fastidiously prepared for any contingency a traveler might face. I was caught with a hole in my sneakers, wading in a puddle, prepared only to make rubbery squishing noises for the rest of the afternoon. There was only one problem. The laces were yellow.

I was so shocked at this whimsy I forgot the fellow whose car I had usurped, and hardly heard as he cleared his throat and said, "Excuse me."

Bright, beaming sunshine yellow.

I heard the ring and authoritative chunking open of the cash register.

"Please get off my car."

Lemon yellow.

"I'm going to call the police."

Crayola yellow.

FORTUNATELY, Mr. Nabokov left the store. He was cradling a rectangular box presumably containing his old shoes, since he was sporting his new ones, enjoying every step, dancing a one-man quadrille between sidewalk squares, composing a line in his furrowed forehead, something about a chessboard.

"Take your lousy car." I sneered, and gratuitously kicked the fender of the steel perch I had been evicted from, as we moved farther north, past the railroad terminal, toward the hotel.

It wasn't the Algonquin, which I would have expected from

my callow early readings, but an anonymous hostelry on the same block, also named for an Indian tribe—in those days there were still "Indians."

Pretending that water was not cascading back and forth in the cavity below my instep like a tide, I sloshed past the liveried doorman as if I belonged, or maybe my parents belonged, and I, the impoverished prodigal, was visiting them for a good meal and a handout designated to pay the rent but destined to be squandered in used bookstores. My first thought once past the sentry was that the state of the air-conditioning he guarded was far from the shoe store's. The lobby was nearly as sultry as the street. It had a few sickly palms in pots.

Mr. Nabokov made a side trip to the thick mahogany receptionist's desk to check for messages—in those days messages were written—but there were none in whichever empty pigeonhole the clerk cast his bored glance upon. If there had been, I was ready to note the room number, but there wasn't. I was already plotting how I might call in from the lobby phone booth in order to see which slot he placed a faint blue "While you were out . . ." slip into, but then Mr. Nabokov moved toward the elevator.

It was an old-fashioned glass enclosure topped by a semicircular position indicator with a working arrow without a tip, and it was protected by an art nouveau gate operated by an elderly man, who was either a midget or looked like one, sitting on a stool behind the large brass lever that controlled the elevator. He wore a rumpled brown uniform and matching cap clamped low over his brow. The fellow saw me and paused, to avoid a second trip, but I quickly feigned interest in the sundries stand, examining a *Time* magazine with John Dean on the cover. Nonetheless the operator's wait was well timed for purposes of saving his own labor because a well-dressed woman entered the elevator a second before his left arm, elongated by decades of singlelimbed exercise, stretched to pull the gate closed. Then I rushed for the stairs that spiraled around the vehicle as it rose. At each floor, I glanced at the position indicator atop each closed entry door. At each floor, the arrow was still ascending. I was out of breath, but determined. I was dizzy, circling, rising and circling only several feet below the elevator, and could hear its chains clanking. It stopped on six, and I halted several feet below, directly behind the cab, gasping for breath, looking down at all the flights I had climbed and the wet sneaker prints evaporating in my wake. The woman got off.

Once stopped, it was hard to recapture my breath, but I followed again as the elevator recommenced, and the woman stared at me as I brushed past her in my eagerness to match the elevator's pace. We passed seven and eight and then, thank God, it stopped again on nine and Mr. Nabokov alit. I peered from behind, while the operator continued upward alone in response to an urgently blinking light that summoned him to twelve, the penthouse.

Mr. Nabokov, who did not lodge in the penthouse, walked down the hall, its carpet thinner than the shoe store's plush, and stopped in front of the third door on the right. If I was correct in my estimation of direction, Room 918 would not have had a street view, but one to the rear, from the hotel into an air shaft between it and another ninth floor in a building fronting on the next block. He shifted the box with his old shoes from one arm to the other and removed the key from his trousers pocket. I heard it click, and saw the door swing open, revealing a glimpse of an unmade bed and a plaid suitcase. Then it closed.

I was steeling myself to knock, to introduce myself, and perhaps kneel. I walked to the door, and stopped. Brass numbers were glued onto the ersatz wood-grain surface glued to the steel that the hotel's original portals had been replaced with in

order to comply with city fire regulations, one askew. A yellow
shoelace was strung around the knob.

THERE WAS A BAR OFF the lobby of the hotel, but it was more
of an extension of the lobby than a room of its own. It was a dark
alcove, suitable for assignations and mediocre salesmen. I ordered
a scotch; it was the most continental drink I could think of, and I
tried to look as if the bartender did not need to request identification from me, as if I were used to drinking by myself in Midtown hotel bars on Tuesdays in July. The television in the corner
showed Senator Ervin, full of righteous indignation.

Did Mr. Nabokov purchase the shoes merely to justify purchasing the laces? That yellow strand was obviously a symbol,
but of what, and to whom? Or was it some aristocratic Russian
custom, gone with the monarchy in all but his own personal
etiquette? I ransacked my recollection of his books in search of
a clue.

Of one thing I was certain, it was not an affectation. Neither
was he here for a publisher, nor did he say to the members of the
genealogical association, "I'll be in the Hotel Mohawk, on Forty-
fourth Street, in the room on the ninth floor with a yellow
shoelace draped over the knob." Was this a message left for a
salacious schoolgirl by her Humbert?

Three scotches stiffer, I decided to return to the ninth floor
and confront the mystery. I thought he would do no less. This
time I took the elevator, despite the smirk of the operator.

As soon as he let me off onto the stained carpet lit by dim
fixtures, I knew that something had changed between the thickly
impastoed walls during my sojourn in the bar. In front of Room
918, there was a pair of shoes. The great man had left them for

shining, but they were his brand-new cordovans, which did not require shining. They fairly glowed with their own pale fire. Nonetheless, my first inclination was to expedite the great man's request, to take them down to the bar and caress them with the cocktail napkins embossed with a cartoon of a martini glass and an olive on a pike. Then I thought of peeing in the shoes.

It was a moment of high giddiness, the liquor speaking, I told myself. But what would he think? Perhaps that the color of the congealed urine was like butter? Or that the texture of the ruined leather now resembled the flakiness of a butterfly's wings.

Or would he fail to think in images, and merely fume with outrage at the vulgarity—or delight in the vulgarity—of American culture? Or would he remember a day back at the homestead when, four years old, say, and already quadralingual, he peed in his family's butler's boots, and chuckle at the reminiscence of how the man had to wear them anyway, squishing around for afternoon tea as if he were a child in water-sodden sneakers much to the young Vlady's (I mean Mr. Nabokov's) barely restrained hilarity.

Then I noticed the really remarkable thing; the shoes were there, but the yellow lace was not.

IT WAS BACK to the bar, shattered by the strangeness. I scribbled frantically on the napkins I would have used to shine the shoes if I had made that decision. I sketched diagrams and charts of the series of events. First shoes; that made sense. Then laces. Then the lace on the door. Then the lace off the door and the shoes in front of the door. I made arrows back and forth, like the arrows atop the elevator. Perhaps he was a spy—there was still a U.S.S.R. then—and this was an elaborate code meant to convey information.

I tried to recall if the lace had been looped around the knob in a particular knot, the shape of a double helix connoting biological research or coiled in representation of a hydroelectric plant or tied into crisscrossed ovals for uranium. I flailed myself for my lack of perception and analytical capacity. I considered returning upstairs, but was terrified that I might find no shoes, and laces again, and began to question my own sanity.

"Another?" the bartender said.

I thought I had had enough.

"This one's on the house," he said.

I didn't know that this was standard procedure. It's called a buyback, and occurs after the third round, if the customer has tipped well. I hadn't intended to tip well, but had miscalculated in my confusion. Ignorant of my generosity, I thought he recognized me, admired me. So I accepted his gift, as graciously as a Nobel Prize. I started to make an acceptance speech, but he was called to the other end of the bar by the woman whom I had last seen on the sixth-floor landing. She must have changed out of her uncomfortable heels and taken the elevator down while I was pondering the situation on nine. I think she winked at me. I gulped the drink and fled, leaving no tip.

Much as I wanted to exit onto the street and return to my grid, I was compelled upstairs one last time. I knew my behavior was suspicious, but I was beyond caring. I think the elevator operator would have called the house detective if he gave a damn. I couldn't tell if it was me or him who smelled of scotch. The cage came to a shuddering stop at nine.

"Watch your step," the man said.

I did. The difference in levels was so minuscule I could barely discern it, and I wondered if he was sarcastic. I might have ripped that dumb monkey's cap from his head, or thrown him down the shaft.

The cage lingered while I inspected the safety certificate framed beside a standpipe with a hose like an endlessly elongated shoelace for a giant's seven-league boot. It was expired. I was about to turn to check on the elevator certificate too, me, Mr. Probity, when the vehicle was summoned, probably by the woman downstairs, disappointed in the bar's booze or the company.

As warily as if I had been invited to a beheading, I tiptoed down the hall, studiously keeping my eye on the doors on the odd-numbered side until I was about even with his door to my blind side.

I didn't know what to expect when I turned: a lace without shoes, a pair of shoes without laces, an open door with a potbellied genius demanding to know why I was dogging him, a jar of live butterflies, Vera or an autographed copy of *Lolita*. In any case, I knew, knew in my belly, that I would not be faced with a blank door.

It was the least dramatic of these alternatives, the shoes, alone, again, as if the lace had been my mistake, a mirage. For a second I wondered if I was not mad, but simply wrong, if the man I had followed was not Mr. Nabokov at all, but just a salesman, in town for a convention and a little shopping and maybe some hanky-panky, and if the shoes were not new, but overdue for a shining. It was a service of the hotel that anyone would use, like the shampoo in the complimentary miniature tubes. But the shoes *were* new and they were beautiful.

Before I knew what I was doing, I had slipped off my sneakers and tried on the left shoe, fully aware that my left foot was a tiny bit smaller than my right. I didn't pace the corridor to make certain of the fit. I didn't ask the clerk or the genius for another size. I slipped on the right. And then, dear reader, I fled. I honestly can't say whether it was because I didn't have a box to place them in, or in shabby recompense, but I left my wet sneakers in front of the door without the shoelace.

I didn't dare face the elevator operator and took the stairs three at a time, slipping on my new shoes' barely scuffed soles, but on six, as I rounded the corner toward five, I could have sworn that I saw another shoelace, lime green, Crayola green, hanging from a knob several doors down the corridor.

The palmed lobby was different in my new shoes. And the city was different in my new shoes. I tossed my idiotic map of the grid into a garbage can on the corner of Sixth Avenue, and headed downtown. Already my feet ached a little, for the fit was imperfect. My feet were larger and narrower than his.

The real problem came later when I arrived in the West Village. I walked up four steep and creaking flights to my girlfriend's apartment without leaving a single wet footprint, and I wasn't happy when I turned my key in the lock. Vanessa didn't read and she didn't steal, not even shoplift.

Nixon resigned later that summer.

Splinters

———

HALF AN INCH LONG, AN EIGHTH WIDE, FLAT AS parchment, sharp enough to pierce and pain anyone of mother born, the gray section of wood sat upon an ecclesiastical purple matte between a gold-leafed garland of frame. The catalogue copy with its photograph on the cover read: "Documented, Authenticated Piece of the True Cross, First Sale in Two Thousand Years."

Other religious artifacts were grouped together in Barkeley's annual theological auction: silver kiddush cups that had belonged to Sigmund Freud, African fetishes, a ruby-studded Buddha, an original papal bull, a sheaf of correspondence between Reinhold Niebuhr and Teilhard de Chardin lamenting the discovery of Peking man and celebrating the birth of Niebuhr's daughter and several mosque-sized prayer rugs from Mecca. Assembled over the year from many sources, the estimated value of the collection was nearly seven figures without calculating in the priceless designation of the True Cross.

The regulars in Barkeley's grand salon fidgeted nervously. Some reknotted their rep ties, others foraged through Florentine handbags that bulged as if their material's breadth were presumed to be a reflection of their material depth. These people were accustomed to paintings and furniture, rare stamps and coins, property, jewelry and even golden records and pop memorabilia. They laughed when John Lennon's sweaty T-shirt went for sixteen thousand dollars the year before. But no one was laughing now. There was something about this round that made them uncomfortable in their familiar seats, and the characters Lot 78 brought into their domain under Barkeley's domed rotunda were too unsavory for their elite tastes. The odors in the room had clearly not been atomized.

First there were the priests. Traveling in strength for mutual protection from modernity, four of them represented the monastery that was relinquishing its claim to ownership (perhaps *caretakership* was a better word) of this universal treasure in return for a substantial check that stood for another kind of faith. It was their first time in New York or, for that matter, for most of them, out of Sardinia, and they belonged in the elegant surroundings as much as a flock of crows. Dressed in black robes, they were balanced on the opposite side of the room by several Hasidim, who might have been residents of the temporal city, but had never been seen in Barkeley's tony precincts. Wearing jackets and fur-trimmed hats, their beards brushing the glossy cover of the catalogue, the Orthodox Jews were there for the sixteenth century Torah, and an intricate model of the golem of Prague.

At least a portion of the rank scent drifting among the audience came from a Cypriot gentleman who unwrapped a crinkly wax-paper package containing a liver sandwich and munched contentedly in the front row, while a pale man, Scandinavian Lutheran to judge from his gaunt, albinoid features, sat on the aisle, his long feet extended like crutches. Together with others in the room from more exotic locations beyond identification, they might have inhabited a Middle Eastern souk more fitly than parlor society.

Barkeley's had always been international in stature and tenor, but the usual foreigners came in discrete waves, the result of historical trends. Japanese tycoons bought art in the eighties and German industrialists invested in precious coins when their economy boomed, while Australian land barons in the grip of subequatorial social inversion contended against each other for Chippendale highboys to furnish their vast outback ranches. More recently, the newly prosperous Mafia leaders of Russia had been spotted purchasing letters or documents signed by delegates to the first American Continental Congress. Only time would determine if their investments were wise or whims.

Unlike these waves, the olio on hand for the theological auction was simultaneously too diverse and too concentrated for the regulars to type—not a United Nations but a Divided Faiths. Whereas the Japanese and the Russians seemed to wish to purchase respectability along with objects of value, and the Germans and the Australians had the grace to aspire to Barkeley's definition of class, this crew's concerns only coincidentally overlapped the house's. Their raucous jabber, like a mob down at the docks buying spices in bulk lots from the Levant, showed their uncouth manners. Worse, their criteria for judgment were not temporal, but eternal.

A rotund Nigerian man in a porkpie hat idly flipped through the catalogue's introductory essay, "The Ecstasy of Faith in an Era of Faith in Ecstasy," by Dr. J. Rittenour, Professor of Comparative Religion at Hunter College, extended monograph for sale at Barkeley's office.

The Hasids glanced with irritation at a middle-aged woman in a green blouse who sat next to them. They did not raise their eyes high enough to perceive her coppery red hair or the gold chain that dangled against the pale freckled flesh inside the V of her silk shirt. In the Hasids' homes, as indeed their entire world, the sexes were rigorously separated, but this was neither their home nor their world. They might as well have been in Rome, and had no choice but to do as the Romans. Even if they were inclined to move away, they couldn't; by then every seat in the cavernous room was filled.

One man in the back row tapped impatiently, waiting for the object he had come for to be brought to the rostrum. His name was Mark, and so far as he knew he bore no relation to the apostle.

A LINE OF CREDIT for the man in the back row had already been arranged, its cap deemed "upon discretion of bidder." Since such designations were rather unusual, his presence had been brought to the attention of the auctioneer through a coded mark on the seating chart that showed the locations of likely ringers.

Forgetting, or choosing to ignore, the years in which his credit was not so excellent, Mark took his distinction in stride. Son of a White Plains dry cleaner, urged but never convinced to believe in a vague suburban Judaism, the sacraments of which were lox and pastrami, Mark had been a mediocre student at Boston University during the late 1960s, where the tastes of the era had led him from drugs to loud music to science-fiction novels about robotic dystopias and time warps. Indeed, it seemed a dystopian time warp when his father simultaneously shook his hand and informed him that the bucks stopped upon receipt of a diploma. Reiterating his dogma once more upon being introduced to Mark's faculty advisor, whose academic gown could have used a good cleaning, the graduate's father said, "I've bought all the books I'm going to."

Summoning the range of worldy skills he had mastered in four years at college, Mark thereafter clerked for the better part of a decade at a used record store in Somerville until he found himself thirty, married, baffled and balding, and returned to science fiction in his spare time, first for escape and then for sustenance. Scribbling nights in the basement of the house he couldn't remember buying, but vividly detested—its proliferating weeds, stuttering boiler and mortgage—he produced a novel about a world where people were born at thirty and grew younger until they died at birth. Lo and behold, it sold.

Whatever small talent Mark brought to knocking off conceptual, postapocalyptic thrillers, he was fortunate that there seemed to be an insatiable appetite for the genre, which he could, in his own small way, satisfy. His books were brought out by a second-rate San Francisco publisher. They paid him well enough to keep at bay his insufferable and by now, thank God, ex-wife and unpleasant daughter, but not so well as the pirated editions he saw one day cheek by jowl with the UFO section in a New Age bookstore in the Berkshires paid someone else. There, as if captured in one of his own alternate universes, Mark scanned a volume that was unmistakably his long since remaindered *Journey to Eternity* condensed, divested of superfluous plot and rebound with a glowing light on the cover.

Two days later, his attorney from the divorce had filed an injunction against further distribution of the volume as well as a demand for royalties. The latter never did materialize, but the injunction was granted and a new version of *Journey* incorporating the editorial revisions of the spiritual pirates was mailed to a cynical New York literary agent who understood the lure of faith. Republished yet again, the book began to sell under Mark's own name, and, no longer confined to the secretive realm of the plagiarized, it soared from specialty to mainstream bookstores. Under the category of "Inspirational Literature" it simply refused to stop selling, no matter the belated savaging of critics who hadn't deigned to notice it the first time around.

Had *Journey* been the stuff of the author's own soul it might have proved a difficult act to follow, but since Mark was a hack from the get-go, he was able to tailor his vision to a new suit, and came out with four more *Journeys* in quick succession, each one lodging as fiercely as Mont St. Scipelli on its rock on the bestseller lists, and that was just the beginning.

"LADIES AND GENTLEMEN, please take your seats," the auctioneer announced, and began the patter that would carry them through the long afternoon. In rapid succession he disposed of kiddush cups and Judaica, letters, rugs and bronzes until he said, "And now, for the lot you've all been waiting for . . ."

PLAYING WITH HIS NAME, the king of spiritual prose realized that the letters reconfigured also spelled Karma, well nearly, so he eliminated *Journey*'s Western orientation, retooled the essential core for a different market and tapped into yet another vein of transcendence. This way he gained readers—or, more accurately, adherents—from Back Bay to Bombay.

A writer not so much by as of inspiration, the reminted Mark Karma asked his agent why they bothered to cut in the publisher. He was a brand name; he didn't need any cute animal on the spine to sell his books. He opened his own publishing house and took in other authors under the one eye imprint. Then he cut out the agent.

Unconcerned about the dubious verification of high literary culture, Mark hired preachers, signed them to the kinds of overreaching contracts he had once been subject to and sent them off to hustle their wares on the road, renting some of the same auditoriums he remembered from his rock 'n' roll days, selling cartons, truckloads, of books and T-shirts and lunchboxes so the believers' children could "take their faith to school."

He purchased a chain of suburban newspapers and some radio licenses and turned them into the print and broadcast venues that *Time* magazine lambasted in a cover story on "The New Religiosity." Allegations of anti-Semitism were hurled at the magazine for referring to The God Network's founder as one "whose head, viewed from the rear, resembles a poppy seed bagel with an unusually large hole."

"Not inaccurate," Mark said, as he searched for more lucrative investments. Why pay the satellite company a transmission fee, he asked his new lawyer, and began negotiations to put his own artificial comet bearing the one eye logo into the astral plane. Then he fired the lawyer who worked by the hour and bought an in-house attorney all for himself. Eventually he needed an entire crew of attorneys, all dressed identically in three-piece suits and vests and ties bearing the one eye emblem.

"DO I HEAR fifty thousand dollars to commence the bidding on this remarkable relic from the foundation of Christianity?" The auctioneer caught the eye of the man in the back row. "Yes, I have fifty thousand dollars."

SECTIONS AND SEGMENTS of the cross ranging in size from the tiniest chip to enormous planks were treasured in abbeys and monasteries as well as national libraries and private, aristocratic vaults from Lisbon to Istanbul. One huge chunk was in deep storage at the Hermitage, while others were scattered in priestly redoubts as far afield as São Paulo and Cambodia, where a society of Jesuits brought one as their group talisman in the seventeenth century. The joke, attributed to Twain after his European tour, but probably as old as the hills, was that if all these pieces were set together they would form a cross as large as a clipper ship. Healthy or sacrilegious skepticism was the only proper scholarly attitude toward relics.

"I HAVE AN opening bid of fifty thousand dollars. Do I hear one hundred?"

DESPITE RATIONAL DISDAIN, however, these relics had exercised an undeniable fascination for more years than science had been the cult of the West. The relics fell into several categories. First there were the man-made artifacts, such as crucibles and shreds of holy garments, but others were organic, the more gruesome the better. Bones and shriveled organs commanded the highest veneration, but toenails of prophets and teeth of saints, locks of hair and, in one case, a nose, were also worshiped in any church that maintained a claim to antiquity or authority. Nevertheless, in the hierarchical realm of the sanctified, there was nothing to compare with the pieces of the cross itself, and within the realm of cross pieces, there were none to compare with the one from Mont St. Scipelli.

MONEY POURED in so swiftly that the Karma Corporation had a difficult time managing its cash flow. Mark purchased other companies, which also gushed income. From publishing and broadcasting, he moved to real estate to railroads and provided venture capital for other innovative young entrepreneurs, until all that was worth Mark's time was to invest in national currencies.

"After all," he said, "the dollar has one eye too."

Fortunately, this limited vision didn't stop him from shorting the dollar on the Capetown exchange and nearly breaking the Federal Reserve when the notes plunged—at least partially because of his action.

"BACK TO YOU, SIR. Yes, I have one fifty. Do I hear two hundred?"

THEN CAME THE more difficult question—what to do with his money? Not charitably minded, not particularly hedonistic, the man needed a hobby. He began to collect, not houses, not horses, not paintings; well, some paintings. Not Renoirs of sentimental bourgeois in the garden, and surely not the vulgar expressions and abstractions of his contemporaries, but Titians, Giordanos, El Grecos, portraits of cardinals, saints and then, the font of visual artistry in the West, paintings of God in His many incarnations.

"The deity's been good to me," he said.

WITHOUT A DOUBT, the particular splinter on the cover of Barkeley's catalogue had been in the possession of the Scipelli brotherhood since the early tenth century, when Julian Despasse, illegitimate son of Henry, Comte de Navarre, Knight Hospitaler, brought it back from Jerusalem. Perhaps he was intending to convey it to Malta, several hundred treacherous nautical miles to the north, but felt mortality boiling inside his swollen blood vessels and delivered it instead to the monastery that sat on a jagged outcropping of volcanic rock on the seaward edge of Sardinia in return for the funeral he required three days later.

Julian's second, unwelcome and invisible gift—plague—

mated the monastery before it ran its decade-long curse. The end of the epidemic was attributed to the .... curative powers of the piece of the cross its original victim had brought, although perhaps it was blame rather than gratitude the segment of wood deserved.

ART WENT AN INCH in the direction of satisfying Mark's own inchoate yearnings. He bought madonnas and crucifixion scenes, and then, after a moment of inspiration, he set his two eyes upon the objects which inspired the artists. Discreet inquiries about the Holy Grail and the Ark of the Covenant were sent abroad, but the best research revealed those objects to be merely legendary. The only things from the age of faith that indubitably existed in the modern world were the relics. Mark was almost shocked when a Madison Avenue antiques dealer offered him St. Peter's left sandal and intimated that an ankle bone might also be available.

"You mean you can buy this stuff?"

"With all due respect, sir, you can buy anything."

"Well, of course. I should have known."

And he plunged in. At first, he bought his share of ankles and fingernails and teeth, and toyed with the idea of attempting to reconstruct Jesus, but was brought up against unfortunate biological lacks—tissues did not endure so well as bone. Besides, the sacred body parts were tainted by the very humanity of their origin. It was the spiritual object nonpareil that lured him. It was the cross.

BEFORE JULIAN HAD rescued the precious relic during the Crusades, it had been kept safe by an Islamic clan that had received it from an Essene tribe they had obliterated several hundred years earlier. Yet even under the reign of the infidel, the wood had been cherished; in fact, it was the fame of the splinter of Haroun Tell that led Julian to lay siege to its keeper's castle. The siege lasted seventeen months until the besieged had exhausted all the water in their cisterns, all the blood in their horses and all the meat of their dead. Then when they opened the gate, Julian and his men marched in, and demanded that the heathen leader bow to him. So the Turk abased himself before his captor, and Julian's sword neatly severed his befezzed head.

Alas, Julian was not a visionary. If the conqueror had saved the bloodied repository of Allah consciousness, he might have been able to sell it as a relic to the Arab world and create a new touristic industry, but instead he threw the wide-eyed, olive-skinned prize to the dogs.

THE BIDDING—TRANSLATED via large-screen monitors into all the major currencies in which the bidders were likely to be proficient—escalated swiftly. The Cypriot threw up his arms in disgust at a quarter of a million and stormed theatrically out of the room, but peeked back in. A further round, to three hundred, priced out the taciturn Swede who had been a prominent bidder at the early rounds. Likewise the three-hundred range eliminated all but three bidders, two in the room and one on the phone.

Rumor swept Barkeley's as to the identity of the bidders. A Saudi sheikh was apparently one; at least he was nodding intently, either bidding or napping. Allegedly the phone was connected to a foundation established by Christendom's wealthiest peer, the owner of a chain of athletic shoe stores in California. The third was clearly a Jew, in the back row.

Mark was slim. He wore corduroy pants and a vest that

smelled faintly of tobacco. Sporting a short ponytail with the remains of his hair, he looked rather like the student he had once been, but he had the deep-set eyes and sweeping curve of nostril that made him instantly identifiable to either fellow Jew or Jew-hater, as he waved his fan with the number 18 upward again and again, making 325 into 350, 425 into 450 and on.

LEAVING A GARRISON behind to be devoured in turn by heat and disease, Julian boarded ship back to the civilized Christian world he had set off from a half dozen years earlier. All he bore was the precious splinter and a faint swelling in his groin. Flea-bitten and infected, he was welcomed at the harbor of Mont St. Scipelli when he displayed his gift and buried in a sarcophagus in the same nave as the cross itself, a signal honor.

Despite the historical fact that everyone who touched the piece of wood from its first presumed user forward died, the cross was enshrined behind the Sardinian altar. There it remained, the pride of the monastery for a millennium as medieval pilgrims flocked to behold and benefit from its mystical emanations. According to legends as well publicized as the flacks of the era could do with their primitive means, sans fax, the limp walked after viewing the cross, and the dumb spoke. The blind, vouch-safed a precious touch, saw, and a thousand other healings for every ailment from leprosy to infertility were claimed for the cross of Mont St. Scipelli.

THE AUCTIONEER paused to wipe a linen handkerchief across his brow. The bidding had slowed to $25,000 increments, and he thought it was a moment to build suspense to compensate for subsiding momentum. "Do we know," he asked, "how rare and special, how utterly individual a commodity we have here?"

SADLY, COME MODERNITY, the glamour of the thing began to wane.

Early on, other relics appeared at less inaccessible venues, making the arduous journey to the island fortress less necessary. Disdain their competition as the Scipelli fathers did, make sly insinuations that other fathers in other cellars steeped their ersatz relics in sacramental wine to simulate the patina of blood, their scorn had little effect on the appeal of their rivals. At less guarded moments, the Scipelli brothers might even admit to jealousy of a thorn in the abbey directly across the waters, a day trip by mule from Naples. On the other hand, the faithful who made the seaborne passage were usually better-heeled than the peasants on mules, and therefore more likely to leave some portion of their fortunes to the monastery that inspired them. Scipelli remained one of the richest castles in Christendom for centuries, until faith itself began to lose its appeal.

AUCTIONS HAVE PATTERNS, and different people use different strategies. Some bid by regular steps and then jump to frighten the competition. Others lay low, cagily silent until all but one other bidder is out, and then enter the fray, hoping to shock and dispirit the one who felt the prize within grasp. As for Mark, he just kept his hand up, and intended to keep it there until everyone else put theirs down.

The representatives from the monastery murmured among themselves. Even the goatish sheikh would have been preferable, but their hopes centered on the anonymous phone connection. They hovered breathlessly at every pause from the Barkeley's employee on the line to California. They had done what was necessary, but they dreaded the consequences. A Jew had not entered their calculations.

Abominably, satanically, wealthy, the shaggy, shabby mogul in the back row might buy it for vengeance, to fling the trauma of his tribe into the ocean, or, worse, take it back to the Holy Land to donate to some Jewish museum for display among that stubborn tribe that refused to acknowledge the Lord who sprang from their blood and gave his own blood to redeem the irredeemable. For all anyone knew, he might simply drop the priceless piece of wood that bore the stain of divinity into a pulping mix at one of his factories and truck it out on a spool the size of a sequoia trunk to be printed upon by one of the hundred papers he owned: tawdry headlines today, spread under birdcages tomorrow. The same newspaper that chronicled the sale of the cross might actually contain it, and no one would be the wiser.

It was an atrocity, an outrage. But it was too late to remove the item from auction. The brotherhood had signed a contract with Barkeley's. Once the minimum upset bid (confidentially, pricelessness was defined in the papers as $50,000) had been reached, the sale was to be considered final—unless they bid themselves, and paid Barkely's ten percent commission. That commission alone was now past their grandest expectations of the entirety.

DIDEROT. ROUSSEAU. Even if the enrollment of the church remained steady, the ardor of its parishioners' passion diminished, and by the advent of the enlightened eighteenth century, the descendants of the pilgrims to Mont St. Scipelli were reluctant to make the difficult trip. Still the worst was yet to come. First there was Darwin and railroads, then Marx and psychology, each like a rabbit nibbling at the verifiability of doctrine, and then Hitler, and the bombing of the monastery by benevolent Yankee Flying Fortresses. The sedentary fortress had been used as an Axis command post in the latter days of World War II in a last-ditch effort to retain the Mediterranean and mount a southern naval offensive.

Now the time had come to heal the physical wounds of the war and the gradual deterioration of centuries. Roofing and repainting were dreadfully overdue. More importantly, if new acolytes were to be enticed to devote their lives to Scipelli's mission, it was vital to replumb the premises and purchase computers, perhaps replace the straw sack mattresses with Sealy Posturepedics since the days of mortification were history. Finally, after much painful deliberation, the sad time had come to send the monks' blessed glory and one clear asset off for auction.

WHAT BARKELEY'S auctioneer in a silver-striped waistcoat did not know was that the seedier religious artifacts dealers on five continents were already well acquainted with Mark since he had already purchased every other remnant of the cross that had come up for sale on the secondary market. Most of these relics were of clearly bogus provenance, but he didn't mind. His capital seemed endless, and though he was willing to haggle, he always, always, ended up with the merchandise. After all, what price was too great for something priceless? After acquiring a particular large section from a Moroccan gunrunner, he sat with his French representative over celebratory arrack in an Alexandrian hotel bar. The thing itself sat between them.

One sip too many of the pungent liquid, and the dealer confessed his suspicions. Perhaps he was hoping to steer his well-heeled client in the direction of more prime merchandise, or perhaps he took unaccustomed pity on the victim.

Mark just laughed. "It doesn't matter."

"But . . ."

Lifting up the object, Mark said, "Each of them has been the subject of faith, no? Perhaps it is the faith of the forger if no one else. But wouldn't Jesus say that the forger's—or sinner's—faith is more valuable than the saint's?"

"But . . ."

"Besides, who says the real thing was, well, real? Are you telling me that you believe?"

"Of course not."

"Good, then get them. Any of them, as many of them as you can. I want them all. I want IT." He idly plucked at the grime underneath his fingernail.

THE WOMAN IN the green blouse was the first to turn around. Staring was contrary to auction-house etiquette, but her perusal was so frank that it transcended gawking. It was not merely curiosity, but a form of judgment.

AND SO, THOUGH he didn't know it, the Cypriot, among others, scoured the Mediterranean basin on Mark's behalf, but fewer and fewer of the pieces of the true cross were left. Mark had purchased everything available, and when they were officially unavailable for a reasonable or unreasonable sum, he employed yet another, more delicate agent to hire a contingent of trustworthy thugs to scale walls, crack safes and remove the sacred splinters, leaving carefully fabricated forgeries in their place. Sometimes he later purchased his own forgeries to avoid suspicion. In this way, Mark had acquired the entire continental horde of wood chips, ranging from modest to more brazen timbers. Only Mont St. Scipelli's was untouchable.

Since one fright (lightning, fire) in the fifteenth century, a cadre of monks dedicated themselves to sleeping on the flagstone floor beneath their treasure through eternity. The Scipelli fragment was therefore as continuously well tended as Lenin's tomb. Mark pondered a guerrilla assault upon the monastery, but that spiritual castle that Allied planes were compelled to bomb into submission could be breeched by no less a force. Disdaining the common morality, Mark knew that even he could not wage unilateral war against one of the pillars of the Church. He had to wait, and bide his time—until modernity compelled an outright sale. But until that day, this day, arrived, he had much to accomplish, and did so. He waved his fan, turning 750 into 800.

ONCE PURCHASED or pilfered, the sections were shipped with extreme care, more care than insurance since loss was inconceivable, back to the Jew. Houses everywhere, at home no place, Mark chose the least of his dwellings to receive his wares. It was the one atop the Manhattan tower from the roof of which an antenna bounced the signals of The God Network into the heavens. Sitting on a white sofa in a white living room—he liked white; it dirtied so easily—he contemplated the glow of the city below, each corner an illuminated cross in the city of a million intersections.

One eye to his empire, he sat with his horde, some in elaborate frames, others in slim wax-paper envelopes, some under glass, some, like the infamous Hermitage plank that had required the assistance of the remains of the KGB to liberate, leaned up against the wall like a carpenter's scraps. An enormous glass conference table sat in the middle of the room. Carefully Mark set his collection upon the glass.

THE EXCITEMENT IN the room was palpable. The regulars had long since forgotten their disdain for the newcomers. They were united in their fascination with the process and their amazement at the result. Agape at the expenditure, which had not yet reached its limit, their eyes jerked back and forth from bidder to bidder to the Barkeley's employee holding up the eight-inch square that would be transferred after the bidding was over to one of those contending so fiercely for its acquisition.

Of course, from anywhere in the room but the auctioneer's pulpit, the splinter itself was invisible. Only its purple matte shone with the intensity of its contents. It was as if the furious bidding were for the frame alone, its substance an afterthought. Yet there, upon closer examination, sat the tiny piece of wood that several human beings were willing, avid, delirious to exchange for a king's ransom, so the others in the room assumed it must be worth something. In short, they believed.

TWAIN WAS WRONG; pieced together they would not make a clipper, a mere rowboat perhaps, or a four-pronged life raft on which to weather the harsh storms of this world's sea. They all sat on the long glass conference table along with the tools that had been delivered to the private suite at the top of the office tower as per the boss's instructions along with a crate of Elmer's yellow wood glue and another crate of epoxy wood filler.

For a moment, he felt like he had as a child in his family's Westchester basement, eyeing the rack of tools his father kept on a pegboard over the washing machine. Or perhaps the sensation was more akin to moments of struggle during the creation of his first *Journey* when he was attempting to place the words in proper alignment. Now, however, it was the greatest jigsaw of all time in front of him that would, he was confident, reveal a sum far greater than its constituent parts.

Humming tunelessly, the incongruous magnate in the grip of obsession painstakingly attached each to the other. He still didn't know why he was so consumed, but Mark had never especially questioned the path his life had taken; he merely set to the task, and did so now. Some pieces fit immaculately, clearly of a unit once upon a time, while other crude fragments had to be forced into blunt configuration with their peers. Mark overlaid one to the next, filling the gaps between two enormous rectangular arms with dabs of putty and filler.

Not a boat, but a cross, eighteen feet long, ten wide. Piece by piece came together over months of laborious trial and error, but in the back of Mark's mind he was always waiting for the centerpiece that would bind the two arms together forever. Now it was for sale.

UNACCOUNTABLY THE bidding went over the house's expectations, despite its coy word *priceless*. Price was on everyone's mind at

Barkeley's. Seven hundred became 750, 800 became 850 until the auctioneer paused dramatically and said, "Do I hear one million?"

Mark waved his card with the same mild irritation as if he were swatting a fly.

The sheikh turned around in his seat and made a salaaming gesture of respect as he ceased his nodding.

The auctioneer turned to the telephone. The employee taking the call wiped sweat from his brow and said, "Two million."

Mark didn't pause to blink. He said, "Three."

The voice on the other end of the phone was apparently silent. The assistant hung up.

The men from the monastery cringed.

"Three million," the auctioneer cried, lifting his gavel. "Going once, going twice . . ."

WHO MADE THE CROSS? In response, one might ask who was the best-known carpenter in Jerusalem?

It was radical speculation, perhaps, but the answer Dr. J. Rittenour suggested in Barkeley's catalogue was expected to create a stir in religious/archaeological circles by asserting that the cross was the work of Joseph, and the famous final cry of the creature or creator—whatever he was—depending upon its beam was addressed not to a heavenly, but an earthly father.

"Forgive them," he said, "for they know not what they do."

And then his head collapsed upon the internal beam of his breastbone.

"FOUR," THE WOMAN in the green blouse announced.

Every face in the room turned in her direction. For the first time Mark looked at the competition. She stood up and strode to the back of the room. "Every Christ needs his Judas," she said. "Or Judith. Here's my card." It read: Dr. J. Rittenour.

She left the room.

JUNKED AT THE site after the body was removed, the twin timbers lay askew, in a heap along with others that had carried less divine passengers. And how could one tell them apart? By the workmanship.

That night a barefoot child snuck among the trash, searching for a coin or necklace or anything of any value that might be bartered for a scrap of food in the marketplace. He heard the wailing of the mourners at the edge of the hill, and saw the flickering candles of those who were preparing the body for the interment from which three days later . . . maybe.

Perhaps it took a child to make the leap into metaphor. Considering the pain of the believers, he suddenly understood that more valuable than gold, to them at least, might be the physical embodiment of the memory of their Lord and the anticipation of their salvation. He pried at the huge timbers and then leapt back in pain.

Tentatively, he approached the cross again, but the second he touched it, the fire in his hand flared. The boy could not see in the dusk, but he could feel the jagged edge of wood emerging from the ball of his thumb. He pinched the wood between the long, filthy nails of his other thumb and forefinger, extracted it and fled.

PANDEMONIUM EXPLODED in Barkeley's as the echo of the auctioneer's gavel faded. Junior employees hurried to their positions to conclude the afternoon's business and stringers from newspapers rushed to phone in the unexpected story. The regulars huddled in stunned acknowledgment of the financial clout of faith while dealers jabbered among themselves and the brothers from Scipelli sank back in their padded seats, relieved yet as uneasy as their hosts had been at the start of the auction. They felt as if they had witnessed a miracle, and it did not feel good.

THE BOY CARRIED his prize to a small encampment south of Jerusalem, hard by the Dead Sea, as Julian would carry it forward a millennium in the future. There he traded it to the tribe for a melon and the believers tossed the holy item into a clay jug with some ancient—even then they were ancient—manuscripts and attempted to live the life their master had decreed.

MARK SAT AT home and looked at the card. He still sought the unlimited now that even the sky was ablink with his satellite. The only terrain left to conquer was the ineffable, the ethereal, the other, something beyond the atmosphere, something celestial. For a second he almost laughed to realize that he felt the same cravings that his inane books apparently satisfied across the globe.

He knew that she had bought the piece of cross for either of two reasons: to keep it, or to sell it to him. Barkeley's would take its commission on the four million, not bad for ten minutes' work, but the auction house was heretofore eliminated from any further transaction. Had the both of them remained in the room bidding against each other, they might have gone to five, six, seven million, who could tell? If he was willing to pay one more penny than she was, he would still have it, not in the auction room, but elsewhere.

———

THE KEEPERS OF the splinter by the inland body of salt water eventually died, but not before they told their children about their legacy. Those children in turn told theirs, who told the Turks who slaughtered them as Julian would slaughter their Turkish descendants ages into the future.

And all of their bones bleached in the sun and crumbed to desert dust.

MIDNIGHT, CONTEMPLATING his loss, the doorbell rang and Mark knew who it was. A person whose seven-figure check was good at Barkeley's had the wherewithal to detect his secret address. He dismissed his servants and buzzed in the woman with the green shirt.

"Call me Judy," Dr. Rittenour said. She didn't look like a woman with four million dollars to spend, but then again, neither did Mark appear to be such a man.

"Wine?" he asked with the sophistication that came naturally with vast wealth, and ushered his guest onto the terrace where the huge structure had been hoisted into a vertical position and secured with thin wires by the baffled, well-tipped superintendents of the tower. Side by side with the metal broadcast antenna, it was almost modest, but Mark flicked a switch which sent beams from three concealed spotlights and turned the cross into an illuminated vision. In the center of the vision, there was a gap, half an inch long, an eighth of an inch wide.

"Just as I expected," Dr. Rittenour said.

For the first time, Mark examined his competition—or was she his confederate? She was easily fifty, but her spiritual inquiries had kept her vigorous and she was clearly aware of how attractive she was. Her skin glowed in the reflection. The silk fluttered against her chest, her breasts unconstrained by any variety of elastic cross.

"Really?"

"It was obvious. Last November, the piece of the Omphalos cross was sold to a mysterious, unidentified party, and in April the piece of the Santa Hermina cross was removed from its crypt by undiscovered culprits, as was the Hermitage piece. Yes, I've been watching the gradual disappearance of the pieces of the cross for years. For one with an eye to the sacred, it was clear that they were headed for the same destination. The only piece that was left was Mont St. Scipelli's. That was the key. Wherever it was bound, the rest were to be found, and I rather assumed that they would now be in one piece."

"Elementary, Watson."

"Of course, the thing that is truly curious is that although one might hazard an educated guess as to the what of the matter"—and she gestured to the giant cross with admiration—"one still wonders about the why."

"I've asked myself that."

"And how have you answered yourself?" She swirled the dregs of wine around the glass and reclined on the terrace's redwood chaise lounge, placing one ankle over the other, toeing a leather sandal to the floor.

"I . . ." He was nervous. "I don't know." Met with silence, he repeated himself. "I just don't know. I suppose there's an emptiness that I'd like filled."

Dr. Rittenour extended one arm to the left.

He was at a loss to echo the moronic language of his books. "It's a need for something greater than myself."

She extended the other arm to the right and remained silent.

"I . . . I never got that at home."

Her voice lower by an octave, the professor purred. "Come to Momma."

WORDS, WORDS, in the beginning were words . . . ecstasy on the page.

From his secret adolescent readings of the sci-fi porn comix that satisfied his imagination as the cheerleaders of White Plains High failed to satisfy his body, Mark had found something cosmically, karmically, he might have said, vital in the notion of words making worlds on paper. Creating something from nothing. Yet even before the disastrous day his vice came to light he had the sense, so clear yet so far from verbalization, that there *was* a prior truth.

Then came the day when his mother discovered his cache, ineffectively hidden under his Sealy Posturepedic mattress. She showed the offending texts to his father, and the man who would later vow to never buy another book turned brick red at the sight of such language. "Filth," the dry cleaner cried when his son returned from school proudly holding forth a sign he had made in wood shop.

It was a rectangle of knotty pine, eight inches wide, eighteen long, notched at the perimeter, bearing upon its unevenly stained surface the chiseled-out word *The* followed by the family's surname with an elegant if ungrammatical apostrophe before the pluralizing *s*, and it was set upon a pointed stake.

"They're just . . . books," he stammered.

The explanation was so insufficient and Mark's father's rage so great. The man's chest expanded barely short of exploding like the primordial Big Bang. Finally, however, as sadly incapable of giving voice to his passion as his own offending offspring, he simply thrust out his arms and shoved Mark.

Boy and sign toppled backward, but the sign fell first, and the boy fell upon the sign, the stake of which pierced his temple as it was intended to pierce the quarter-acre greensward in front of the suburban ranch.

Mark's mother, absolute cause of his birth, proximate cause of his pain, shrieked and bundled the bleeding child into the family station wagon. She drove at warp speed to the local emergency room, where a sleep-deprived intern stitched him up and left a novice's pucker in the side of his head.

MARK KNEW WHAT Dr. Rittenour—Judith—meant; that he knew, that he needed. He was sick of answering other people's questions and satisfying other people's spiritual cravings. He wanted his own answers, and if God couldn't give him that, perhaps this one of His creatures might.

No further overtures were required. He unbuttoned his shirt, unbuckled his belt, kicked off his shoes. Wearing only briefs, he curled into her arms, surprised for a moment that they were not nailed to a ledge of wood and were capable of embracing him. "Forgive my father," he said, "for he doesn't know what he does."

"Forget him," she murmured, as she reached into her bag and grasped the tiny expensive item between her fingers.

HE FORGOT WHERE he was until he felt a pinprick on the temple, most vulnerable point of the body, beside his left eye, in the spot marked by the small indentation from his childhood, the incompetent surgical pucker half an inch long, an eighth of an inch wide.

A second later, the pucker was filled, the searcher's life and vision simultaneously complete. But for that one second, he saw the blinding illumination he had sought for as long as he could remember. The light of eternity flashed, the bite of eternity drew blood and both of his eyes rolled into his head, and he rolled off the professor, dead as God.

———

DR. RITTENOUR sat upright and replaced her shoes. Then she opened the large pocketbook she carried everywhere. She extracted an axe.

The Return of Eros to Academe

—

Philosopher Herman Stone—yes, he had heard the joke, in every possible permutation—known for his elegant linguistic analyses of the things he preferred to call "phenomena," swung his old Volvo across West Campus Drive in Lessmore, Mass., to avoid a swerving—and, if he wasn't mistaken, comely —coed on a bicycle. In the wild fraction of a second before impact, he did, however, discover abundant time in which to ponder a multitude of questions. Why a Volvo, and why West Campus Drive and why Lessmore? Not to mention why him, and why, catching a glimpse of the girl's lambent blond locks aflutter in the breeze—was the breeze a direct consequence of her own glorious transit or was it windy and should he have brought his muffler?—her?

First things first, as the wheels of the philosopher's own vehicle somehow refused to obey the commands of his wrinkled fingers. He had purchased the car used from the previous chair of his department, who had certainly not purchased it new. It occurred to Stone that he had never seen a new Volvo, certainly not in Lessmore. Or were new Volvos so outré that a factory hard by the Arctic Circle distressed them for the pedagogic trade, hiring Swedish graduate students to work on an assembly line slapping Greenpeace stickers onto the bumper and wielding heavy chains to whump and thump the vehicles until the finish bespoke Nordic integrity and North American tenure?

Secondly, the locus of his about-to-occur interaction: Stone lamented how generic a name West Campus Drive, Lessmore, Mass., was. It bisected guess which moiety of the university installation like a badly curved spine, for the purposes of automotive transport, and the professor sputtered out a wheezing giggle at the thought of East Prison Amble, More or Less, Di Minimus.

By that time he had run out of time in which to consider the third, and really engaging, question, because the Volvo had veered across the drive and upended a recycling bin, a bench and an, until that moment, free-standing kiosk wheat-pasted with layers of posters for foreign films and concerts by local bands with names that might as well be foreign films, The Triumphant Dodos being the current favorite allegedly attracting industry w.o.m.

Also, there was a boy under the bench. How unfortunate.

A small crowd gathered, and the girl on the bicycle waved as she cruised idly past. It was that unhurried splash of unwrinkled finger-flesh through space and time that struck Philosophy Professor Stone gaga.

THE SOLE CLAIM to fame of the lecture hall in Millstrom B was that it had once served as the set for a motion picture that took place during World War I—from there the scene shifted to the trenches, which might have been metaphorically rendered by the same miserable location. A certified antique, Millstrom B was—unfortunately landmarked, which prevented the university regents from tearing it down to make way for the humongous cement waffle envisioned by a renowned architect—older than Professor Stone by at least a decade, and showing its age from the sunken grooves in the marble stairs outside, eroded by generations of shuffling students—or did they crawl on their knees like Mexican penitents before the other professors?—to the chairs inside, their curved wooden backs idly dorm-key-carved with so many overlapping initials that they more closely resembled the walls of a Neolithic cave than seating in an institution of so-called higher education.

And yet, despite—or perhaps because of—its decrepitude, the professor always enjoyed the room as he entered from the back to descend between ranks of awed sophomores to the creaky stage to deliver his weekly lecture on the great minds to the great unwashed.

"Kant today," he announced.

"Sure you can, Prof!" a wit called out, secure in the knowledge that he could not be identified in the midst of his drug-addled peers.

Pause for recollection that this was philosophy, not pharmacology.

"Critique of *Pure Reason*."

Pause for books to be hoisted out of Danish knapsacks, random pens and pencils and Magic Markers, tubes of lipstick, key chains to clatter to the floor.

"Chapter fourteen."

Pause to flip through to a set of pages that ought to have been read and reread, crumpled and dog-eared, but were obviously— Stone could tell from the stage—crisp as a virgin banknote.

"Does the categorical imperative ring a bell?" If not, not. The professor cleared his throat and went on about acting as if one's every action could be extrapolated into a universal principle. He was about to give his favorite example, the one about the cat eating the mouse, but if all mice were eaten there wouldn't be any mice left for cats, who would then die, and be unable to eat more mice, which was logically inconsistent, and therefore amoral, presuming of course that one could impute moral qualities to the beasts of the jungle or, as the case might be, parlor, such as those in the boardinghouse in which he resided, but never called home, at least partially because he hated his landlady and her two cats, Muffy and Fluffy, an oversexed male and female that rutted with abandon and gave the overstuffed parlor sofa the perpetual scent of procreation. He was about to give that lecture when he stopped cold. A new student entered the room.

She was blond and had the utter, positively feline, nerve to wheel a bicycle into the hall. As the vehicle descended the steps toward the pit with a succession of rubbery thumps and metallic clangs, he felt his heart jolt with every step.

Immanuel Kant: the eunuch of Königsberg, advocate of pure reason, who spent his seventy-nine years living so reasonably he might as well not have lived at all.

Perhaps Philosopher Stone said something for the remaining forty minutes of the lecture, but when the bell rang, he couldn't remember a word and wondered what the students would have done if he hadn't. Then he realized: occupied whispering to each other, reading science fiction novels about worlds ruled by superintelligent cats and carving their initials into the backs of the chairs in front of them, they couldn't have noticed.

Fortunately, the girl wasn't able to wheel her bicycle back up the stairs until the other students had preceded her. Justice. "Ahem." Professor Stone came up from behind, purring like a brand-new Volvo engine.

"Oh, hullo. I'm so glad you weren't hurt."

"Miss . . . ?"

"Yes, you did."

"I don't understand, Miss . . . ?"

"What fantastic reflexes you have. I just wasn't paying attention. But you did miss me."

"For years," he sighed.

"What?"

"I missed you by inches, Miss . . . ? You are my student,
Miss . . . ?"

"Just transferred in from U.C., you see; that's a joke. There
were just too many parties. I mean, I came to college to get an
education, you know, not a baby."

She might have been speaking French, the only major
European language Professor Stone didn't know, the only one
without a major thinker to its claim after Descartes. Oh, Mon-
tesquieu, Voltaire, Diderot. Mere humanists. Political theorists.
Not thinkers, like his favorite, Kant. "Yes, yes." He nodded,
longish white hair—needed a trim, no, that was a euphemism,
needed a cut—falling into his eyes.

"Call me Trish."

"With pleasure."

THAT EVENING, in his dormered attic quarters on Pleasant
Street, a highly unpleasant street filled with the clatter of unpleasant children kicking soccer balls and riding bicycles until dark,
too distracted to read anything but *Candide*, Professor Stone
heard the doorbell ring.

Nobody ever visited the professor, but nobody ever visited
his disgusting landlady either. Besides, Miss Marsh always took
a "constitutional" at dusk. Just ten minutes earlier, she had asked
him. "Are you sure you don't wish to accompany me, Professor?
The winter air is so refreshing."

"No, no thank you," he had said, as he did most every night, refraining from pointing out that he despised the winter air, as well as the rank summer air, the loathsomely fecund spring air and the brittle autumn air, which only reminded him of Sweden, although he had never been there. "Besides, I have papers to grade."

"Just give them all A's." Miss Marsh chirped.

"No, no, I don't think that would be right." In fact, he never gave A's. Whether it was a principle or a judgment he didn't really know, and wasn't inclined toward self-analysis. A person wasn't a thing.

Stone ignored the bell, but the thing rang again, insistently, as if one of those stupid children had fallen asleep against it.

So, beslippered, berobed, *Candide* tucked under his arm, he padded downstairs to shoo the unwelcome intruder.

But the professor, though he did not yet realize it, was hip-deep in destiny stew. Aquinas—first-rate despite his faith—creator, intellectually speaking, of the uncreated divine watchmaker, was at work. Wheels within wheels meshed so intricately as to logically preclude random chance. Volvo and Schwinn wheels circled within the further wheels of solar systems and galaxies churning through space to place him in precisely this bathrobe under this splintered doorjamb where the misguided Miss Marsh had left a seasonal sprig of mistletoe in hopes of catching up her own divinely ordained match.

"Hullo," she said, hair the color of sunbeams.

"Oh, Miss . . . Trish."

"You remembered."

"*Ich can nicht anders.*"

"I love foreign languages, don't you?"

"All except French."

"Me neither, all those subjunctives."

Flustered—and naked as Candide under his terry cloth—Professor Stone choked out, "Can I help you?"

"That's what I'm in school for. I mean, this is really confusing. I read *Pure Judgment* yesterday and I'm not sure I understand how pure reason fits into the schema, because here . . ." She thumbed through the heavy, highlighted—it was a library book—tome toward a section toward the end where previous generations of thinkers had also gotten lost.

But all he noticed through the haze of pale fibers that obscured his vision was a bicycle leaning up against the porch. And then she was sliding past him, a blond shadow. And then she pushed herself up on tiptoes and pecked his cheek.

That was enough to summon forth Professor Stone's rectitudinousness of yore. "My dear young lady!" he humphed.

"One shouldn't ignore customs," she said sweetly, winking toward the mistletoe. "At a certain point customs become laws. I think it was Maimonides who said that. He was Jewish."

"I know."

"I know you know. That was why I wanted to ask you about this problem." And she was inside, and he was explaining. They were upstairs in his room.

"I love your space," she said. "By the way, he's okay."

"Kant is more than okay."

"Yeah, he's the greatest, but I meant the boy you ran over. I visited him in the hospital. His name is Brian, and he doesn't know anything about philosophy. You know what he's interested in, pre-law. I asked him if he meant nature, and he didn't get it. I mean, what else is pre-law but nature? What a dodo!"

"At least he's not extinct."

"No, I didn't mean that like in a negative way. He's in a band called The Triumphant Dodos. Everyone says that they're really hot, but I'm not interested in all that. You know what I'm interested in?"

"Philosophy."

"Oh, that too, but I meant sex." She removed her blouse.

SOMEWHERE, STUDENTS were highlighting library books, and somewhere, bands were practicing, and somewhere, old cars were hurtling into warm, dark tunnels as swiftly as their drivers could negotiate the perilous curves, but in the suddenly over-heated air under the dormers of the attic on Pleasant Street, Philosophy Professor Stone was saying, "Trish"—suddenly they were on a first-name basis—"this is absurd."

"Oh, stop joking, everyone on campus knows you don't do twentieth century."

"I meant the situation, not the ... um ..."

"Proposition."

"Precisely." Words fizzed through his head. Here in Lessmore, she was winsome. Here in Miss Marsh's resident home for forlorn academics, he was sinking into a swamp. There were eternal truths. On the other hand, customs become laws. What was she saying?

"If one should act as if one's actions could be extrapolated into universal principles, then if one is half naked, others should be half naked. Even if one shouldn't eat mice."

"Yes, yes, yes," he assented to the irrefutability of her discourse.

"I read Joyce two days ago, and couldn't stand it. All that relativism. I prefer universal principles, don't you? So if my body is exposed"—she whisked off a pale blue brassiere—"so should yours be. *N'est-ce pas?* Oh. I forgot, you don't like French." She gig-gled, and extended five fingers—Socratic, not Platonic—toward his robe.

Never in Philosopher Stone's forty-five years in Lessmore had he ever been more shocked by and less prepared for an intel-lectual experience. Words and names eluded his grasp, as Trish grasped the fraying cord that held his robe in fragile position over his essence.

Naked under the robe, Stone backed off, unaware that as his feet slid across the dusty, planked floor, the cord slid out from loop after loop into the eager hands of the girl without any cloth-ing whatsoever above her plaid skirt, unaware that the moment the cord slid from its final restraint, the moieties of his robe diverged, like the split between East and West Campus Drive, revealing . . . "Oh, my God!" he cried.

"Sir!" Trish reprimanded him. "This is philosophy, not reli-gion."

Stone bumped into the bentwood chair in front of his paper-strewn desk, knelt to pick it up and felt a hand caress his spine. He stood bolt upright and clutched at his robe. "Give me that . . . please."

"Oh, look, a kitty."

One of the repulsive beasts from below had padded omi-nously up the staircase and stood rubbing its back against the doorjamb under the mistletoe. "How Hobbesian," Philosopher Stone muttered.

"Oh, the kitty wants a kiss. Come here, sweet baby." Trish lifted the pale orange hairball against her chest and scratched its chin, and the creature's tail hung down between her breasts like the cord for a tatty brown terry robe. And while Professor Stone tried to reassemble himself, she continued to coo, "Life needn't be nasty, brutish and short. Just act as if all of your actions could be universal principles, kitty."

Just then, the door downstairs creaked open.

Stone groaned. "It's Miss Marsh. Now you mustn't leave."

"Who said I wanted to?" Trish replied, and dropped the cat abruptly. It scurried between her legs and through the door, which the professor leapt to shut.

Trish cornered him, and opened the hastily bunched robe. "Oh, gee," she said. "It looks just like Karl Marx."

"I . . . I never thought of it that way," Stone stuttered, looking down. "But then again, the angle of my perception may not be optimum."

"Take my word for it," Trish said, and reached down, her lengthy—was it possible to describe flesh as blond?—fingers . . .

The professor sighed and sat on the chair he had righted, chin raised, shoulders back, arms lank at his sides, begging reprieve. "Please, please, Miss . . . I can't."

Ignoring his complaint, Trish continued stroking as if the kitty were still the object of her affection and murmured, "Barring the factual inaccuracy of that statement," and stared Professor Stone in the eyes and, just before she strode forward, lifted her skirt—no more beneath it than his bathrobe—and descended upon his phenomenon, said, "sure you can."

A SEASON OF bliss.

Every day at dusk, when Miss Marsh took off on her fortuitously paced "constitutional," Trish appeared at the entry to Professor Stone's attic. Sometimes they played with the cats, and afterward they imitated the beasts, stalking each other across the dusty study floor, nipping at each other's necks and indulging.

Was it wrong? Did he care? Ethical philosophy had never been Stone's strong suit, but text was, and the linguistic analyses of his newfound endeavors led him to the most fertile vocabulary in the world.

An entire lexicon of slang had been prohibited from the professor's speech, but with Trish he discovered the power of things and the words that described them. Mixed with his own arcane jive, the result was a hybrid neither more nor less absurd than the commingling it described. "Come here, my Nietzschean nookie," he greeted her as the snow melted, and together they empirically investigated every possible avenue of being they could devise.

Trish was endless in her inventiveness, utilizing costumes and props beyond the ken of Kant or even the Kama Sutra. Stone's attic was transformed into a pit of debauchery and pornography as they recited and re-created favorite passages from *The Story of O, Lady Chatterly* and Krafft-Ebing's *Pyschopathia Sexualis*. More au courantly, they played out the tenets of Jeremy "the greatest good for the greatest number" Bentham by renting videos of *Deep Throat, Debbie Does Dallas* and other, esoteric products of Contemporary Californian Philosophy.

And yet always, despite the vast enterprise of physical human lore they explored, from the secret deviancies of Sumerian priests to the smut of the Internet, the man and his lubricious muse returned for their most passionate inspiration to those arched-back avatars of sheer sensuality, Muffy and Fluffy—even if Trish had to hold them upside down so that Philosopher Stone could determine which one was which.

Aberrant, you say? Not in the least. There was a glorious logic to Professor Herman Stone's life. For the first time in his sixty-three years, he felt the perfection, far from Platonic, of existence. And he could prove it too, for, from days clad in the public forum of Millstrom B to nights of nude abandon at 259 Pleasant Street, discussing Leibniz's monads and Schopenhauer's gonads, he and Trish remained loyal, above all, to the categorical imperative.

O TEMPORA! O MORES!

Perhaps it was inevitable. Trish was simply too lovely not to be noticed wafting in and out of 259 Pleasant Street, and, as the couple grew brazen, Stone's office on West Campus Drive. One night their caterwauling could be heard emanating from Millstrom B itself, and the next morning the air in the lecture hall was still rank with pheromones when the professor tried, with a straight face, to explicate phenomenology.

Envy, surely, motivated the gossip that bubbled up like lava as Stone skippingly exited the faculty dining room with a joie de vivre that none of the other sour faces over the stuffed cabbage served that day displayed.

"He should watch it or he'll get a heart attack," Perkins (Biology 101) said.

"But what a way to die." Pnimp (Slavic Languages) sighed.

Further sly and leering insinuations came from a slew of bitter adjuncts and instructors in Philosopher Stone's own department, avid to occupy the professor's besmirched office and title. But nobody listened to them.

Everyone, however, listened to Chancellor Hiram Wussterman, the former advertising executive who ruled the university like a Mississippi warden and raised the millions for the waffle that couldn't be built on the site of the despicable Millstrom B. No battered Volvo for him, Wussterman drove a sleek college-paid-for Jaguar, lived in a college-paid-for penthouse and played around with an international circuit of tootsies at college-paid-for administrative boondoggles from Moscow to Malibu.

So when Professor Stone received a memo requesting that he "visit" the chancellor's office, he knew that it wasn't to discuss epistemology. After a little ritual chitchat, Wussterman got down to business. "I've been hearing things I don't quite believe, Herman."

Nobody called Professor Stone "Herman," not even Trish. He wasn't about to be taken to task like a second-grader called to the principal's office for chewing gum. "Read the newspaper," he replied testily. "They happen every day."

"Things about one of this institution's most respected teachers and a student a third his age."

"Closer to a quarter."

"Herman . . ."

Professor Stone's teeth were grinding.

Wussterman was attempting mediation. "You've been a fine and valued member of this community for many years."

"Past tense, *Hiram?* Am I no longer a fine and valued professor here? Are you asking for my resignation?" Stone asked this secure in the knowledge that since rumor of his private life had become public, his classes had become the most popular on campus—with the exception of Lucy Tonakati's "Sitcoms of the Sixties: Gender Roles and Imperialism from 'Gidget' to 'Gilligan's Island.' " If the seats in Millstrom B had once been occupied only by hungover frat dolts and sorority fillies compelled to satisfy a requirement, now his course in "Heuristics and Hermeneutics"—he could alliterate as well as any lit-crit nitwit—was positively oversubscribed—as well it should be. For the first time in Professor Stone's career, he enjoyed his lectures. He was lucid and funny and the students loved him back. They filled every available seat and stood in the rear and sat in the aisles, taking notes—actually learning. Besides, they thought it was pretty cool that a guy of an age to be pricing caskets could

THE RETURN OF EROS TO ACADEME · 67

romp with the best of them. Fed up with P.C. drivel, yet terrified
of sex and disease, it was vicariously satisfying to them to know
that somebody was getting laid.

Wussterman continued, "The fact that this gets to me at all
means that you have been incredibly indiscreet, if not . . . well,
immature."

"Spare me the adages about old fools."

"Okay, shall I cut to the chase? Fine." Actually Wussterman
preferred the direct mode. Delicacy was for donors, not teachers.
"Sexual relations—even consensual—between faculty and students are strictly prohibited by the school's harassment policy. It
can lead to detenuring"—jeez, wasn't that the dirtiest word in
the academic dictionary—"and dismissal. It is inappropriate, to
say the least, and perhaps litigable on the student's or her parents' behalf. *You* may not wish to be responsible, but *we* must. I
want this stopped."

"I'll think about it."

"I just hope it's not too late."

AND THOUGH THE DOOR slammed on Wussterman with all the
authority that (nearly) unassailable tenure could muster, still, the
chancellor had had the last word. As Wussterman, like Niet-
zsche, knew, power was as potent—and incidentally aphrodisia-
cal—a force as sex. And as Professor Stone would learn, the
world outside the idyll inside 259 Pleasant Street was unfortunately real and therefore as subject to change as the life he had
lived—and would have argued was immutable—B.T.

"Maybe you reacted too strongly," a disconcertingly sober
Trish said as they lay in bed under the eaves later that night.

"I don't give a hoot," Stone declared, rather enjoying his new
role as the voice of wantonness and freedom. So what if he did

look a trifle silly raging while wearing the pair of fun boxer shorts that Trish had brought for him that said "Peekaboo" on the flap. He was wrought. "I'll quit; the pension's vested; we can move in together while you finish your dissertation."

Trish turned sideways and propped herself on an elbow.

"That should take us into a new administration, and blue noses like Wussterman will be history, hah!"

He already had her in graduate school, and studying for orals. He already had her in a house that together they owned, a house with a kitchen, as well as a bed, and a new Volvo in the garage because the old ones were so unreliable. He already had her taking care of him at the age when even his prodigious sexual vigor had waned and humor was just a memory. She was a sophomore, and without knowing it, he already had her old.

Trish looked at Philosopher Stone with a queer expression, and if he had been as adept at understanding people as he was at ideas, he might have noticed.

HE NOTICED THE NEXT evening, however, when Trish wasn't on the porch as the streetlights blinked on one by one in random order as their individual sensors took individual readings of minimally different shadings of dusk. Odd, Stone thought, that it seemed darker once the lights went on, and the lack of Trish's being was suddenly more palpable than any presence he had known—even hers. But the nonexistence of a thing could only be defined in relation to its prior being, if only in the mind—as a unicorn merged man's images of horse and rhinoceros—which meant that everything that ever existed still existed, if only in the past, which, since time was relative, existed as absolutely as the present, more so, perhaps, since it was no longer contingent, except, perhaps, on the perceiving mind itself. Fluffy was out on the porch mewing.

"I know, honey," he said, scratching the scruff of the cat's neck. "She's always here by now." He craned his own neck over the porch rail to peer up the street for a glimpse of Trish's celestial bicycle floating under the lights. He worried that she had been hit by a car driven by someone without his reflexes.

Fluffy cried.

"Okay, okay, baby. Here, I'll tell you what I'm going to do. I'm going to find Trishie. You wait right here, baby, and I'll bring Trishie back, and then we'll play cat games, okay?"

God, he was saccharine, but Professor Stone had never known any emotions until he learned the extreme ones of the last semester. Frantic with worry, he hopped into the Volvo and drove the route she would have taken from her dorm, an atrocious five-story bunker on North Campus Drive. He squealed to an uneven stop on the sidewalk and bumped over a trash can, sending yogurt containers and cigarette butts and letters from home and flyers for a local band flying.

Standing in the lobby, confronting a row of eighty-five identical mailboxes, it occurred to Stone that all of his interactions with Trish had occurred on his territory: Pleasant Street, the office, Millstrom B. He had never seen her room, and never been curious—except for yellow, tame stuff compared to the torrent to come. He scanned the mailboxes for her name and found it, Number 214, stuffed with university send-outs as if she hadn't checked it for months.

Upstairs, the hall reeked of marijuana smoke and dirty laundry. Number 214, seventh from the stairwell on the left, had an erasable white plastic board hung from a nail with a red marker dangling beside it on a piece of yarn which gave off a homey, knitting-sweaters-by-the-fireside feel. Various notes were scrawled on the board for Trish and her roommate, Delia. They read:

"D. Meet you in the Union. 5:00. M."

"To the residents of 214, Midterms. GAAAA! Guess who?"

"Stopped by. Nobody in. Later. Lori," with a heart over the *i*.

"Trish and Delia, You are cordially invited to a kegger at PKZ, Friday night, Yours, Tony the . . ." and a line drawing of a cartoon tiger.

And then, at the bottom, there were two final notes that suddenly made Philosopher Stone's spine feel as old and cold as a Siberian woolly mammoth's, the first a philosophical joke, "I fuck therefore I am," and the second, worse, though he didn't know why, and, somehow familiar, "Dodos Rule." He knocked on the door.

"*Entré*," a high-pitched voice called.

The room was smaller than Stone's attic on Pleasant Street and more crowded. Hardly an inch of the industrial gray carpet was visible between two regulation collegiate-issue cots and two desks and two chairs and scattered clothing, and the wall was plastered with postcards and posters as densely as a kiosk. Stone recognized some of the books he had lent Trish heaped on the floor beside the unoccupied and unmade bed: Pascal's *Pensées,* even if the author was a Frenchman, Heidegger's *Being and Time,* even if the author was a Nazi, and Segal's *Love Story,* even if the author was a Yalie.

"I'm—"

"I know who you are, for sure," the elfin, dark-haired girl lying on the bed in bra and panties interrupted. "I've heard your course is neat."

Neater than her room, for sure. Eyes averted from Delia's utterly unselfconscious display—were all college students like this? had they always been and had he simply failed to notice?

hadn't he once been a college student himself back in the serious days when undergraduates wore pants made out of wool?—he said, "Um, thank you, but I'm looking for Trish."

"So's half the world. Hasn't been seen since yesterday evening. Even her stuff's missing."

Stone didn't ask how anything could be missing in this spilled cornucopia of a room, or how anyone could tell. He backed toward the door, and before he shut it he heard Delia giggle, "Call out the Mounties," and turn about on her cheap bed to the creaking of springs.

Next he thought of calling Trish's parents, but abandoned that as a bad idea for many reasons. Instead, he drove back and forth—a mobile yo-yo—from East to West Campus until the halves of the institution welded themselves in his mind and finally returned—demoralized, but then again, he never was an ethical thinker—to the district of deteriorating Victorian gingerbreads around Pleasant Street. Careening around corners, the normally twenty-mile-an-hour professor was so heedless that, when he caught a glimpse of wheels on a side street, he jammed on the brakes and reversed direction straight for the unfortunate cyclist, who wobbled into a gentle trench that paralleled the macadam, but not before he could tell that she was nonblond, nonlithe, non-Trish. Alas, the professor was so blinded by his quest that he didn't recognize that the shaken, slightly overweight sportswoman climbing out of the ditch in his rearview mirror was his landlady, Miss Marsh.

Heart pounding—partially from the near fatality, more so from grief—Stone pressed on the gas all the way home, where he jumped the curb, missing a parked yellow sedan by inches and screeched to a horribly abrupt stop in the driveway of 259 Pleasant. There she was.

———

"WHERE WERE YOU?"

"I was helping Brian move."

"Who's Brian?"

"You remember, the nice boy you ran over the day we met." Trish shrugged to the yellow car at the curbside, which, Stone now realized, contained the shadow of a youth behind the tinted glass and a bicycle strapped to the roof. It was a new car of American manufacture.

"I didn't know he was nice. I thought he was a lawyer. Lawyers are never nice."

"Oh, he gave that up. A couple of months in the hospital gave him the chance to see what was really important in life. He's decided to forget pre-law. He's really a very natural creature, after all. Besides, The Dodos have signed a contract, and we're going to California."

"We?" Stone felt a weight descending.

"Oh, yeah, I was meaning to tell you. I've transferred back to U.C., you see."

Weakly, the professor said, "I hope that's a joke."

"Sorry, no." And she pushed herself up onto the very same tiptoes he had kissed so tenderly in the library stacks one glorious winter afternoon, and touched her lips, those lips, chastely to his cheek.

"If—" he started.

"*No!*" Trish screamed, and ran to the Professor's Volvo, and knelt down sobbing by the front right tire. He had squashed Fluffy.

THE PHILOSOPHER'S CREED: always face the truth.

"I have something bad to tell you," Professor Stone addressed Miss Marsh when she arrived wheezing up the mild incline from the street, pushing a bent-framed bicycle he had never seen before—or rather, once. He was prepared to pay whatever punishing reparations she demanded, move out, leave town, start over—all the plans he had intended to pursue with Trish—alone, terminally alone.

"That you nearly killed me. I know that. You really ought to be more careful. Maybe get your eyes checked."

"My eyes are as sharp as a teenager's," the Professor snapped, and immediately regretted his impatience, even if his point was well taken. He could see the dot of yellow—canary yellow, curious yellow, Trish yellow—rolling down Pleasant Street toward the west.

"Well, mine aren't," Miss Marsh replied. "Nor, I guess, are my lungs, or my legs. Despite my constitutionals. Who was I kidding? Fifty-five years old and acting like a student. I couldn't ride this thing to save my life." She laid the bicycle against the porch. "I didn't understand the gears and—"

"Miss Marsh," Stone interrupted, determined to get his confession and future life under way.

"Yes, Professor Stone?"

"I . . ." It was harder than he expected. "I owe you an apology."

"Nonsense, Professor. You are a man of great personal vigor, and you have your needs."

Then he realized what she was talking about, what she knew—in a way that Aristotle could never know, partially because he was dead—from the beginning, and the humane delicacy with which she had allowed him to pursue his muse. Those stupid constitutionals—what was the derivation of that term? how did it shift from an establishing political document to a stroll?—had grown in duration as his doomed affair with Trish had blossomed. This woman he had thought of with no more regard or attention than a thing was actually a person of consummate wisdom and generosity who, in addition to space, had also given

Professor Stone the most precious gift of all, time. . . . Was that a tear collecting at the corner of her eye?

"Yes, Professor."

"Fluffy!" he blurted.

"Yes, I know. But she led a good life. Sat in the sun. Had a lot of fun with Muffy and also with . . ." she didn't have to say who.

Fifty-five, a little stocky, lines as deep as her character etched around her rather striking gray eyes. God, could she surprise him.

And then, surprising himself, unaware of what he was going to say even as the words came out of his mouth, but certain, as truly as he was of any first principle, that it was necessary and good, the professor asked. "You know what I'm interested in?"

"Philosophy."

"Well, yes, that too. But I meant . . ." He leaned over her face, felt her breath, hot and sweet, and swallowed it.

"Herman," Miss Marsh purred.

Holding hands, they went upstairs. The hell with phenomena. Professor Stone was alive! The next morning, he gave Trish an A.

Paper Hero

—

"RUSHDIE REDUX, DON'T YOU GET IT?"

"No."

"Okay, I'll explain again." Randall tossed his hair back and languished against the bookcase as if his photograph were being taken. "Salman writes books."

"Since when are you on a first-name basis?"

Randall ignored his companion, a pale, freckled young woman sitting on the shabby, quilt-covered couch in the dim living room overlooking an air shaft. "They're published. That's nice. They win awards. That's nicer. And they sell, decently I presume."

"Nicer and nicer," Annie said, curling her feet demurely underneath her thigh.

Randall squinted at Annie's knees and paused to parse her syntax before continuing, "But still nobody out in the world really knows who he is. Until—"

"The envelope, please."

Randall took the gambit and mimed receipt of an envelope from some starlet in a split bodice. He removed an imaginary piece of paper, adjusted his glasses to relish the suspense and announced, "The winner is *Satanic Verses*. It's a massive, international best-seller. Nobody reads it, but they all buy it. Salman is the most famous writer on the face of the globe. Why?"

"Tell me," Annie cooed, a cross between a pigeon and a vulture.

"Because it's off the book pages. Not because it's loved; because it's hated. Because of the Ayatollah Khomeini, because of the fatwa. Because of the publicity."

"Do I hear a magic word?"

"What you write hardly makes a difference anymore."

"I've been saying that for years."

"I'll just ignore that."

"As so much else."

Busy formulating his theory, Randall was unfazable. "Look at what sells. Sports biographies. Celebrity tell-alls. Political scandals. They sell because they have built-in constituencies who read about these books when they're not on the book page. And the biggest books are those on the biggest page, the front page."

"Wasn't there a movie by that name?"

"And a damn good one, too."

"So?"

"So, how does one get on the front page?"

"Tell me, Socrates."

"Rushdie Redux. Just imagine. Author goes to Frankfurt Book Fair to hawk thrilling new novel about end-of-the-world doomsday conspiracy involving Islamic terrorists."

"Rings a bell."

"Two years it took me. Big shit. Author sits alone at bar in hotel lobby with thousands of other authors trying to separate their books from the other literary seaweed in the Sargasso."

"Nicely put." Annie yawned.

"Thank you. Where was I?"

"In the Sargasso."

"Right. Nothing's happening for our hero. Then a gunshot rings out. Islamic terrorists have received advance copies of book. Infuriated, they send out a team of veiled hit men to whack him."

"Only the women wear veils."

"What greater accolade for a book than to be taken seriously enough to kill for? Imagine it. Assassination attempt on previously unknown author at the largest book fair in the universe. Whammo, front-page news. Editorial outcry. Ad hoc committees defend his right to artistic freedom. Books fly off shelves. Conferences. Parties."

"Do I know this guy?"

Randall pushed the lock of hair back again and grinned.

PROBLEM NUMBER one: getting a gun. Randall goes to Harlem.

"There," he told the taxi driver as soon as he caught a glimpse of blood-red neon script that read, "Lenox Lounge."

Inside the dark cavern, a bartender the size and complexion of a mahogany tree loomed over the bar and aksed what he'd like.

"A black Russian."

"Sure you don't want a white Russian?"

Randall sometimes knew when he had been dissed.

PLAN B: TWO DAYS later, Randall went to the Bronx, by subway, to get in the mood, to the next likely venue he spotted, where he ordered a beer.

"What kind?" said the bartender. "We've got Heineken, Red Stripe, Dos Equis, Corona, Kirin, Guinness on tap. But our specialty is frozen daiquiris: pineapple, strawberry, banana. We're out of the mango."

"Make it a Bud, bud."

No mixed drinks or yuppie brews for this honcho. Randall wore black jeans and a T-shirt, rolled up to show his muscles, although the only ones he exercised regularly were his fingers, ten thin digits that played every other morning on a computer keyboard and whenever they could with a variety of brassiere clasps.

Randall sipped coolly and perused the other patrons, a ferocious lot of young men. He focused in on two revolutionary young Puerto Ricans circling a scarred pool table.

"Six off the four, side pocket." A second later, the white ball glided across the felt and clipped the green ball, which nipped its purple neighbor straight into the designated receptacle.

Hovering, imagining his picture taken against the gritty background, Randall commented, "Nice shot."

"Can I help you?"

"You might." Cagey now. "Buy you a drink?"

"Pedro?" the one stroking his cue in satisfaction nodded to his friend.

"You know I can't drink," Pedro pouted. "I'll bloat."

"Pedro can't drink. I'll take a Corona with a nice strip of lemon peel."

Momentarily uncertain whether he had the right guys, Randall obliged and sat down at a corner booth with his new friends. The shooter's name was Chico—perfect—and Pedro accepted a cranberry juice, and they hunched forward for the conference. Randall sneered to get in character. He was used to these deals, done it before. "I need a gat."

Pedro and Chico started giggling.

———

THIRD TIME, LUCKY. Downtown Manhattan, a pastry shop with an ornate terrazzo floor. On the recommendation of a friend of a friend, Randall explained his need to Mr. G., a beefy man in an ill-fitting suit and fedora. Randall could hardly wait to get home to write about him.

"Like this?" Mr. G. took a gun the size of a keyboard out of his breast pocket and laid it on the table.

Randall slammed a newspaper on top of the weapon as if it were a mosquito. He reached underneath the headline, "Freak Out in Corruption Trial," to touch the chilly metal grip.

A leatherette wallet flopped onto the newspaper. Thick fingers plucked it open to reveal a police badge.

"Christ."

"That'll be five hundred dollars."

AT THE AIRPORT, Randall picked up his boarding pass and checked his luggage through, all except for the heavy carry-on bag with a manuscript and his recent acquisition. He walked the long corridor to Gate 18B. Then: problem number two.

The passengers ahead of him—how many of these same people on the way to Frankfurt were publishers and agents?— were bunched together in front of the metal detector. Randall tossed his gun into the nearest garbage can.

TWO BLACK RUSSIANS after takeoff, Randall had cheered up sufficiently to flirt with the stewardess. "On the way to the fair"—he yawned—"blah, blah, been there before, the price one pays for being a famous author, oh, you haven't heard about *Strange Fire*, my new novel: Islamic terrorists, big deals brewing, hush-hush, movie rights, interesting female roles for talented unknowns, maybe you'd like to go out for a drink once we get to Germany?"

SIXTEEN HOURS LATER, alone in his hotel room for the first time since he and Jeanette—or was it Suzette?—shared a cab, jet-lagged and exhausted, mildly hungover and mildly guilty— Nanette?—Randall called Annie.

The phone rang too many times and she picked it up with a groggy "Hullo."

"Oh, the time difference."

"Meet anyone?" she asked. Her first sentence. Psychic bitch. Was she really in New York or the next room?

The next room—Christ! Suddenly nervous, Randall dragged the phone cord to the bathroom to make sure the stewardess wasn't at her toilette. Safe. "Um, not really. Just a couple of weeds in the Sargasso."

"And how goes the quest for ink?"

"I'm not sure you take this trip seriously."

"I take the cost of this trip very seriously. We could have bought a new couch."

"Ouch."

"Just another literary game."

"No games, hon. This is dead serious."

"Onward and upward in the arts."

Obscurely disappointed, Randall made kissing sounds into the receiver and set out to scout the terrain for his ascendance into the highest realms of public awareness. He zipped his pants and sang out, "Front page, here I come." But there was another problem: Valette had stolen his wallet.

———

THANK GOD FOR American Express. Even if Randall and Annie's account was overdue, accruing interest charges at nineteen percent, an hour later he had a new card along with sufficient cash to hail a cab which pulled up to the Frankfurt convention center, a vast structure built to the style and scale of an airplane hangar.

Inside, banners bearing the various international publishing associations' insignia hung from the exposed beams while booths as elaborate as the Taj Mahal were erected to dazzle and impress colleagues and competitors for the three-day duration of the fair. There were stacks of the new season's books, larger-than-life photos of best-selling authors, and thousands of snappily clad junior editorial types cruising the aisles, grabbing the logo-bedizened tote bags and umbrellas and other freebies distributed by the publishers eager to advance their own name into the communal consciousness.

An outsider wandering into the pandemonium might have thought that publishing was a prosperous business, when in reality this annual gala that always took place the first week of October was the one span of the year in which book people could pretend to each other that they were important. The whole damn industry lumped together didn't generate as much money as Nike's grommet division.

Paying the admission fee with his mint credit card, Randall debated what attribution to grant himself on the plastic tag about to be issued, and settled for the title of his book, *Strange Fire*. It could also be a publishing house or a literary magazine, and if it caught anyone's eye, he could explain that it was really the next big thing—given half a chance and a huge advance. "You know, Islamic terrorists, et cetera, et cetera."

But who among the swarm of editors, agents, scouts, foreign and sub-rights personnel had time for a rather handsome man with a manuscript burning a hole in his tote bag? The only way any of them would notice him would be if his face was staring at them from the front page of the *International Herald Tribune*. It would be the story they would all read, the gossip they'd crave, the buzz du jour—and that was all he wanted. He had three days to put it together.

SURELY, PEOPLE SHOT each other here: muggings, drug deals gone awry, domestic disputes. Frankfurt was a city; it had lowlifes, racketeers, corrupt policemen. So once again, Randall struck off for the dark side. He wandered fruitlessly until he finally stopped to have a drink at a dingy café on a side street on the edge of the red light district. He briefly contemplated the girl on the corner, but knew he had to save his money for more important things. Later, he'd have all the money in the world for whatever he wanted. He'd leave Annie the rent-controlled walk-up in the village. And the couch. Maybe a modest alimony. It would be vital to start proceedings before the income from *Strange Fire* gushed in. He knew how to be good. Even generous.

"Book fair?" the waiter asked.

Randall nodded, pleased that he had an identifiably literary look, forgetting that half the city was filled with visitors to this annual boondoggle and that the resident half delighted in their once yearly brush with international high culture.

The waiter continued, "I hear that Rushdie will be making an appearance."

Randall was disgusted. "Salman's everywhere."

"Salman?" the waiter raised his eyebrows at the presumed intimacy of Randall's reference.

"Of course I don't know for sure. But I've heard that he's more sociable now than ever."

"Perhaps not for much longer," the waiter whispered mysteriously.

Suddenly, Randall became aware of the waiter's dusky complexion. Suddenly, he noticed that the man at the next table was reading an Arabic newspaper. Suddenly, he realized that he had stumbled into a nest of militants, and that the infamous fatwa had never been officially rescinded.

Brain aflame, Randall realized that he had a potential scoop here over the West Bank Café bitter liqueur. The problem was that a journalist's fame lasts until the dog needs walking, while the novelist's lasts forever. Or a reasonable facsimile thereof. He didn't want to write about someone else; he wanted someone else to write about *him*. And Rushdie's assassination would obliterate all of his plans. First, the guy was more famous than Randall, and would therefore command greater attention. More significantly, Randall was planning only to be wounded, not killed. If both of them were shot, one fatally and one in the fleshy portion of his upper arm, poor Randall's fate would be that of the addendum. John Connally.

He had to save the author of *Satanic Verses* in order to preserve his own linear inches of hot type. Randall put on a conspiratorial tone and confided. "You, I mean *they*, would get the wrong guy. Rushdie's become a penitent. His next book exalts the Prophet."

It was drivel, of course, but say what you might about his writing, Randall could tell a story. Pretty soon, confusion turned to comprehension in the waiter's eyes. Yet the bloodlust remained unsated. Randall had to offer the fellow something else and then he had a true inspiration. Until this minute he had simply assumed that he would create his assailant from whole cloth together with an obliging police artist, but now he saw a way to provide neutral, credible witnesses who would confirm his story. The pieces fit together as neatly as a front-page layout. "The book you'll really hate is *Strange Fire*."

The waiter looked suspicious.

"The title comes from the Bible. It's the substance that the sons of Aaron, the high priest, brought into the sanctuary. Then God killed them for their sacrilege. The book is heresy."

"How do you know this?"

"Um, I work for the publisher, as a publicist. But I refused to handle this one, because I hate it too, because it desecrates our Lord."

"Our?"

Randall nodded soulfully just as the wail of a muezzin came from the roof of a small mosque that serviced the immigrant neighborhood, and the men at the next table fell to the rugs. Randall fell with them, praying as fervently as he ever had in the church of his youth. "Next year." He was thinking penthouse. And a quiet woman. But what if these guys took him seriously? No problem. Next year he could afford his own retinue of bodyguards. Hell, he'd be safe. They hadn't managed to get Rushdie, had they? Eternal vigilance was a small price to pay. Besides, everyone, even nonfamous authors, had to be security-conscious these days.

DAY TWO—ONE TO GO—at large in the fair, Randall's head swam among the exhibits. Book after book, a million books in sight, and none of them his. A thousand names and none of them his. He fumed at the schedule announcing the luncheon honoring the deposed dictator whose memoir just sold for three million, at the special autographing sessions with the anorexic supermodel, at the hum of deals being made and invitations being extended to parties he wasn't invited to back in the hotel suites. Finally, exhausted, he collapsed into a chair at one of the hospitality booths and sipped a vodka and tonic, mulling over his next step, when a familiar face sat down next to him. It was a legendary literary agent from New York, a tall, angular, impeccably dressed elderly man who wore enormous purple glasses that made his eyeballs appear to bulge. This was an opportunity with a capital O.

"Hello." Randall tried to summon the ease that Annie always seemed to have, shifting the 423 pages of *Strange Fire* on his lap.

The man glanced breastward to check Randall's name tag and asked brusquely, "Who are you?"

Nothing like cutting to the chase. Randall appreciated that. He might call the fellow in a few days. Hell, in a few days the fellow would be at his hospital room, offering sympathy at Randall's close call, trying to sign up the hottest author in town. "Author," Randall said, loving the sound of the word.

"Published?"

The question hit him like a dentist's pick hitting a cavity. And it was *always* the question that *everyone* asked the second he defined himself. A question that nobody asked Salman, a cavity that Salman never had probed. Hadn't they heard of manuscripts of genius buried in an attic trunk only to be discovered a hundred years after the author's death? Randall started murmuring, but he knew the contradiction in his logic: if all that was important was the work, then it didn't make a difference if he had the magic imprimatur of some dumb cute animal logo on the side of a physical volume.

And he yearned for that hound or bird or fish or whatever. Who wants posthumous fame? Fat lot of good it did Kafka.

And besides, no matter one's self-assurance, it would be stu-

pid not to acknowledge that most of the unpublished manuscripts of the world really were fit only to line the bottom of birdcages. So the question still hurt, and Randall couldn't help
himself from shifting into defensive mode. "Publishing is in a
downward spin. Chain bookstores that pander to mass taste lead
to corporate cowardice. Sometimes I think that good books don't
have a chance and that modern editors develop a professional
immunity to quality."

"No, huh?"

Randall's head sank onto his chest.

"But heck," the agent spoke with a glib, infuriating chipper-
ness, "it's a living."

An opening—slim, but Randall had to see if he could slip
through. He put on his most somber, authorly expression and
intoned, "I just hope that I keep on living. I've heard that the Ira-
nians don't look too favorably on this." He tapped the manuscript suggestively.

"Pardon me, there's Heidi Wadleigh-Falls. I should say
hello."

Randall swiveled to see a striking white-haired woman. Ms.
Wadleigh-Falls was a fancy-dancy literary critic—couldn't understand a damn word she wrote—turned novelist. She wrote intellectual potboilers usually involving professors swept into a realm
of phenomenological intrigue and kinky sex, a potent combination that transformed her from femme fatale of the Ivy League to
token brain of the jet set.

"But . . . what about my book?"

"Send it along, I'll have one of my assistants take a look."
The agent flipped a card out of his Florentine wallet with the dex-
terity of a riverboat gambler. It bore a Midtown address and the
embossed image of a bunny.

———

MULLING OVER his problems—he had a plan and a patsy, but still no gun and, worse, no confederate—Randall noticed that Mr. Bunny and Heidi Wadleigh-Falls had kissed and parted, and that the great author had sat down with her own watery gin. It was another chance, bound to lead to humiliation, but he steeled himself for the approach. "Excuse me?"

She peered up through bifocals. "Yes?"

"I loved *Critical Mass*, especially that scene where the Derrida character disembowels the pope."

"Oh, how lovely. Have a seat, you dear boy." Heidi patted the plastic beside her and Randall duly descended.

Unlike the agent, the author didn't bother to ask what he was doing at the fair. Probably because she knew the answer and didn't give a damn. It was up to Randall to explain himself. "I'm here to sell a book."

"Who isn't?"

"I mean one that I wrote."

"Your first?"

"Third," he confessed.

"Any luck?"

"Not yet, but I have great expectations."

"Poor lad, I can assure you that even if you do sell the hermeneutic opus it won't change your hegemonic life, but you won't believe me. You see, even if you do sell it you will, of hubristic necessity, fall prey to the heuristic law of ascending beefs."

"What?"

"Here's the way the literary life goes. First you say, 'Oh, God, please let me be published. Anywhere, I don't care, the *Zipadee-doodah Review* mimeographed in a basement.' Then you get that, and it's nice for a day. You show it to all your friends. But you get to thinking, and so you revise your request. You say, 'Oh, Go-od? What I really meant was a nice magazine, one with a little reputation, *Colossus*, say, or *Hopscotch University Review*.' Then, maybe you get that and you say, 'Thank You, God, but what I really, absolutely meant was glossy paper. If I could see my name on that slick beautiful stock with an ad for expensive vodka on the back . . .' You did say you were buying?"

Randall snapped his fingers for the waitress, a cute fräulein who reminded him of the traitorous Valette. Next time, he'd hide his wallet. "What then?" He was salivating.

"Well, it never ends. After the gloss, you say, 'One more request, God, cardboard. If you give me cardboard on either side of my words, I'll never ask for another thing, because I'll know that the sun has risen in the west.' "

"But the sun doesn't rise in the west."

"Precisely, Socrates. And you're never content. You publish books, but you want reviews. You get reviews, and you want sales. You get sales, and you want prizes. You get prizes, but you want one prize, the one those stuck-up, blond, socialist—" She broke off and peered around suspiciously. "Stockholm has spies everywhere, but you get the gist. Have another drink and get out of this business before it's too late."

"Will you help pretend to kill me?"

The great author leaned back and sipped. "That's the most interesting proposal I've received all day."

Randall needed help, and this titan of trade was the only person he had managed to meet. He had to convince her and he did have one true skill at his command. "I have an even more interesting proposal to make." Casanova Redux.

THAT NIGHT RANDALL and Heidi went shopping at the scummiest dive they could find. She placed a large handbag on the bar and ordered shots of rye, and Randall went to the bathroom. When he returned two minutes later, Heidi downed her whiskey and said, "Let's go."

"Where?"

"Back to the hotel."

It was fine for her to abandon the quest this easily. Her reputation was secure and, despite the law of ascending beefs, she couldn't complain. She could turn in the damn phone book and it would be purchased and published and adored. "Go if you want. But I've got to get a gun."

She opened the handbag and let him catch a glimpse of steel. "I just did."

"But how?"

"Never mind."

Instantly, Randall's thoughts turned elsewhere. The gun on her lap was like a red-hot coal. No matter her age. No matter her fame—well, maybe fame did have an erotic quality. Not with any of his many infidelities had he ever felt so aroused.

DAY THREE. Timing was everything. Randall and Heidi synchronized watches; she was five minutes ahead of him.

Randall called the West Bank Café and spoke to his friend the waiter. "Giza, it's me. Yes. It was extremely dangerous sneaking into the office at midnight. A guard nearly caught me." Remembering the writing school dictum "God is in the details," he couldn't help but embroider. "He was wearing a silver star. I think he was Shin Bet." On second thought, he didn't want to scare the fool. "Probably not."

"But you do have the manuscript?"

"Yes. Come to my room at the hotel at seven, alone, and I'll give it to you. Remember, seven—sharp." Giza had to be seen in the vicinity for the plan to work to its utmost. "Not a minute earlier. Not a minute later. Or the deal is off."

Randall had chosen the hour carefully. If something went wrong—particularly Heidi's aim—the hospitals wouldn't yet be filled with drunk drivers impaled on their own steering wheels, and the doctors not yet exhausted. Randall was nothing if not cautious.

Putting the phone back on the receiver, he looked across the bed at Heidi. "We'd better not be seen together."

Heidi sighed, "How honestly sad, but, alas, how horribly true," and she slipped into her silk blouse.

Randall saw her to the door, thinking that with a little luck he had just enough time to fit in the waitress from the hospitality booth before evening. It would relieve some of the pressure.

THAT AFTERNOON the international lines from Frankfurt were jammed with editors checking in on the underlings they had left to mind their various stores in New York and Tokyo and elsewhere across the globe. In five thousand hotel rooms, they sat on five thousand unmade beds confirming sales figures, gnashing teeth at reviews that hadn't come in, huffing and puffing and basically strutting to maintain stature. The lines were so busy that Randall, who tried to call Annie, couldn't get through and didn't try again.

AT FIVE MINUTES to seven, Heidi Wadleigh-Falls was stationed in the lobby where she immediately recognized Giza from Randall's description. The young man entered in a delectably furtive Levantine fashion; he obviously wasn't accustomed to Western hotels on this side of town. She strode straight ahead, bumped into him and cried out, "That's my pocketbook, you thug."

Giza recoiled, and Heidi glared at him just long enough to command the attention of the bell captain, but not long enough to have the boy apprehended. Besides, he quite neatly jumped into the elevator in full view of everyone in the lobby. Heidi herself made a beeline for the in-house telephone and called up, "The bird is rising." Then she waited for the next elevator.

Immediately, Randall himself called the operator and asked for security, trying to sound nervous rather than excited. "This is Room 825. I think someone is trying to break into my room, but I'm not sure. If you could send someone up . . . What, ten minutes? Fine." He had deliberately worded his worry vaguely enough to ensure a belated response.

There was a knock. From now on, there was no turning back. Randall opened the door, thrust half the manuscript into the stunned Arab's arms and said, "You'd better get out of here fast. I heard security was coming."

Giza fled toward the elevator, but ducked into the stairwell when he saw the same woman who had made such a fuss in the lobby two minutes earlier striding in his direction along the eighth-floor corridor.

Presumably nobody would correlate Giza and the gunshot to the second, but the rest of the action had to occur swiftly. By the time Heidi entered the room, Randall was already busily tumbling chairs and smashing lamps to make the premises look as if a fight had taken place. He was sweating from the effort, but managed to tap one final reservoir of rage at and envy of and desire for the whole publishing business to heave a heavy glass ashtray at the mirror over the dresser. Finally spent, he surveyed the devastation with satisfaction, turned and said, "Ready."

Heidi opened her bag and removed the gun. "I'm aiming."

She lifted the gun and pointed it carefully at Randall, who cringed for the sacrifice, practically dislocating his shoulder to extend it as far as possible from his more vulnerable parts. The angle looked right. She couldn't miss, but just to be safe he held the remaining pages of *Strange Fire* against his chest.

Randall gritted his teeth and braced himself. Then he gave the order, "Fire."

The gun went off and Randall fell to the bed, seeing the next day's headlines flash in his head. Heidi was a brilliant shot. Her bullet created a flesh wound that sent a spurt of blood onto the bedspread yet only tore a tiny bit of skin and sinew. Perfect. Randall watched the copiously flowing blood that would turn to ink, which would turn to gold. "Thank you."

"Anything for a story, darling." Heidi pantomimed a kiss and walked down the corridor, but Randall was too thrilled with the success of his plan to parse her syntax or observe that she exchanged bags with another woman who was walking in the opposite direction along the same corridor at seven o' six, sharp, peering at room numbers through gold-rimmed spectacles. "Third door on your left," Heidi said.

One more thing, Randall thought, and he took the last chapters of manuscript and flung them up into the air with glee.

As they came snowing down, there was a knock at the door.

Inconsequentially noticing that it was awfully quick for security to respond, he rushed to the door. He hoped they didn't actually catch Giza, but if they did, so what? The master of international intrigue paused to put on his game face.

A moment later, he ripped the door open and shouted, "Thank God you're here!" before he saw who it was and changed tone. "What are you doing here?"

"Hullo," Annie said, and fired.

———

MIDTOWN MANHATTAN, an elegant art deco office building with a prestigious piano showroom on the ground floor. Upstairs, occupying the entire penthouse, was an office with glass doors with a bunny etched onto them. Annie strode in as if she owned the place.

Immediately the secretary buzzed the corner office, and a moment later a tall angular man with large purple glasses hurried forth to clasp both her hands in his own cool limbs. "Oh, my dear, how awful for you."

"He was such a talent."

"I know, I know, but as literary executor of the estate, you can take comfort that *Strange Fire* will live on. We've just received the revised offer from the book club, and I must say it's quite generous. Quite. Meanwhile, Japanese, Hebrew and Swedish translations should be out in the fall. But you know," he said, as he ushered Annie into the corner office and signaled for a pot of tea, "I've been receiving an entirely novel set of calls."

"Yes?"

"People are interested not only in Randall, but in you, dear, all your suffering, and your life with the Great Man."

"Are they really?"

"In fact, Heidi Wadleigh-Falls has been looking for a project like this for years. She's bored with fiction and wants to do the biography of a strong woman who has faced great adversity."

"*Moi?*"

"You'll have to dredge up some very painful memories."

"Oh, that will be easy. I've been taking notes for years." Annie brushed her hair back and grinned.

The Suburbiad

SING, O BRAVE LARRY, TO THE FAITHLESSNESS OF CHICKS. Sing the distress that a merely honest man engenders in the heart of the distaff. Sing of the tennis skirts and thighs of Rolaine Rosen.

Rolaine of Synagogue Beth-El, its stained-glass windows endowed by her pop, Rolaine of the Elderberry Country Club, Rolaine, heiress to the Rosen Faucet fortune. Rolaine's mother too was a romantic, who read the Chanson in her own impressionable days and named her firstborn, a girl, Rolaine, the conqueress.

Her sire, Indomitable Rosen, red-cheeked Rosen, gin player, union buster, eyed Larry from the den that served as his throne room away from the faucet works. The paneling was teak, the floor a linoleum designed to simulate quarry. He had originally had real tile installed, but it was cold to midnight feet, so he ripped it up and put in the synthetic instead. "Bet you can't tell the difference," he taunted the supplicant who rocked heel to vulnerable heel upon the forgiving surface. Before the put-upon youth could answer, Lord Rosen swiveled in the direction of a laser projection television set hung from the ceiling. Three contestants jumping each other on a life-sized checkerboard vied for the prize of a laser-projection television set. "I hope the teacher gets it. How about you?"

Brave Larry addressed the lord with unaccustomed spunk. "I always hope the teacher gets it."

Rolaine giggled.

Finally, the sovereign of Wellcroft Avenue snapped off the television, shifted his adjustable throne into an ominously upright position and demanded to know the lad's intentions.

Brave Larry replied, "We're going to the movies."

Of course, Indomitable Rosen meant for the lad to track his lineage, and said so in plain English. "What's your father do?"

Larry's manner spoke for him. "I too am of noble ancestry. My father and his father of yore were the masters of Western Foundations, bra makers to the trade, gross sales in the eight figures."

Rolaine clasped hands about her own worthy bodice, rose-tipped bosoms gripped in the Western armature, while her father proclaimed her suitor worthy. "Have a beer, my boy."

It was a fine romance, a match made under a benevolent sky. All was well.

A QUIET DAY, a normal day, as every day in Mamaroneck. The slow approach of the school bus, yellow prow to the wind.

"Do you know how much one quadruple bypass goes for these days?" whispered Kenny Loposthenes, Larry Resnick's best friend, his spear carrier and would-be office mate.

"No."

"Ten grand."

"Awesome," Larry said.

They had been the smartest two kids since the third grade,

when Larry had moved to Mamaroneck from Brooklyn. Before then, Kenny had been lonely; since then, they were inseparable.

Larry stared out the bus's tinted windows at the low-slung ranches and lush Tudors whose market value equaled that of a factory in the Bronx, excluding cash flow. By the time they arrived at school, he had forgotten what they were talking about.

Undaunted, Kenny continued, "Listen, this is important. One of us has got to take a course in tax shelters, investment strategies, that sort of stuff." He opened a locker in the hallway, removed books for his first class, slammed the metal door and spun the wheel to seal the tumblers into place. "I mean, life's not all ventricles and auricles. . . . Tap, tap," Kenny knocked on Larry's cranial cavity. "Anyone there?"

"You were talking about oracles."

"Right."

"Sorry, I was just daydreaming."

"Sneak quiz in French today."

"How do you know?"

"I have my sources." Kenny tried to be mysterious, but everyone knew that he had snuck a peek at Madame La Farge's workbook. 'Twas not for his athletic prowess the lad was known as Brilliant Loposthenes, or, to those whose envy was tainted by malice, The Weasel.

"Does Rolaine know?"

"Why should she?"

"She's in the class too."

"So is everyone. I mean everyone who counts."

"You mean everyone who can count." Larry scoffed at the non-college-track kids whose lives theirs intersected only in gym and shop.

"Anyway, the whole point of inside information is that rarity maintains value. You spread it too thin, you lose the effect. It's like diamonds. Basic economics. You've got to know these things if you're going to invest the money from our practice, Resnick."

"Fine," Larry said, too tired to argue. Besides, Rolaine had entered the corridor, her dramatic upswept blond hair bearing down upon him, leading a flying wedge of be-Benettoned belles. There was Debbie Schwartz of the swim team, Shelley Roth, cheerleader and sipper of sloe gin fizzes, and then, the foil to their beauty, there was Estelle Oblomovitz, otherwise known as Oblomozits, Estelle of ungainly tread, Estelle of the drumstick, the gravy, the onion dips and drips and spots upon her garb and countenance.

Brilliant, but unkind, Loposthenes said, "Hers is the face that lunched a thousand chips."

Larry couldn't inform Rolaine of the quiz in company, but he was determined to do so later, despite Kenny's admonition. It ought not to have been difficult. Rolaine was in almost every class of Larry's, but so was chocolate-munching Estelle, lurching lockstep beside the young lovers on their path from English to History to Biology. Then came fourth period, when the sexes were segregated. The males marched to shop while the wearers of brassieres were shunted off to home economics where they were taught the different kinds of stitches to use for a hem, makeup, and basic recipes. Afterward the sexes reconvened for lunch, to be followed by Geometry and French.

Larry didn't have a chance to speak privately to Rolaine until midday, when she arrived in the cavernous dining room in a frenzy.

"I hate it. I hate it. I hate home eck with a passion."

Estelle left to stock up as if cafeteria food were caviar.

"What's the matter?" Larry asked.

Unfortunately, Rolaine had failed casseroles. But after a good sob, she lifted her head and said, "You know what I made?"

"What?"

"Reservations."

Loposthenes grudgingly admitted, "You can't say the girl isn't self-conscious."

The boys, meanwhile, alternated semesters between metal shop and wood shop. Larry disliked the former. He was afraid of the sharp sheets of tin that sounded like thunder when rattled. On the other hand, he found wood shop to be oddly satisfying, far more so than Loposthenes or the other future professionals resigned to the fate a smart adolescent must endure under the tyranny of a set curriculum.

Larry hated to admit it, but he also enjoyed the easing off of the pressure that he occasionally felt in Rolaine's presence. She was great, no question about it, her wit, her charm, her figure, but sometimes he was afraid that she was about to pull a hula hoop out from her under her skirt and say, "Lawrence, can you please jump through this for me? It will only take a minute, and I do wish to show my girlfriends what tricks you can perform." Every once in a while he needed the exclusively masculine calm of the long narrow workroom in the basement. There was a warmth in the material, a glow to the sawdust-saturated air.

Recently, he had been making a sign for his parents' front yard. He sanded and resanded so that the surface was smooth as paper that read: "14 Primrose Lane, The Resnicks." Its serrated edges came to a series of points that echoed the blade of the saw that created them. It was that sort of observation that made Larry's morning.

He tried to sing to Rolaine of the roar of the ripsaw, the hum of the jig, the deftness of the Phillips head, each tool sublimely fit for a specific task, each perfect in its place. "You understand what I mean?" he begged concord of his beloved.

"How proletarian," she replied with a fetching toss of the head.

After all, they were the scholars, the doctors, the investors of the morrow.

"I'm sorry," Larry said. "I'm tense. Get it, Rolaine, tense, as in *J'adore, tu adores, nous adorons.* Be prepared."

Kenny scowled, his vision of the curve reformulated to accommodate one more at the top.

"I get it," Rolaine said, but "it" did not help her an hour later come the terror of Miss Lafleur, a.k.a. La Farge.

Rolaine was having trouble conjugating the irregular verb *etre,* while Brave Larry was attempting to pass her the secret of the pluperfect, when the school's guidance counselor interrupted their ordeal. Nobody could remember the last time anyone had seen Miss Wolfe outside her cramped office. There she foraged through hundreds of catalogues, aiming to find the best spot to which to boot the graduates of Mamaroneck High for the following four years. Now she stood in the doorway of the college-track French class, her arm on the shoulder of a boy a good half head taller than she was, his black hair in ringlets that rode the collar of a deep blue blazer ornamented with gleaming brass buttons.

"Pierre," she called him, all but stroking the European cut of his cloth in front of the class.

Loposthenes whispered, "Since when does a guidance counselor hold the hand of a sixteen-year-old?"

"Since she likes his veins."

"Read my palm, oh wise one."

Rolaine looked at the hunky exchange student, who smiled in her direction and said, "*Ciao.*"

Loposthenes tried to stifle his laughter.

"Kenneth. Lawrence," La Farge barked. "Perhaps you will enlighten us as to what you find *très humeureuse.* Perhaps you will take Pierre into your confidence."

They looked daggers at the newcomer, ten seconds off the boat and teacher's pet.

"In fact, why don't the two of you show him the school after class? Why don't the two of you introduce him to American society?"

So they were obliged to drag the intruder around for the rest of the week. What made this particularly galling was that it gave Larry and Kenny a cachet with the local women that they might have enjoyed more if they were not so clearly middlemen. Less than twenty-four hours after she failed her French test, the luscious Rolaine made herself comfortable at the table occupied by Dour Larry, Sullen Loposthenes and their unwanted charge. "Hey, *bonjour*! What are you guys having for lunch?" she asked, lording her connection to Pierre over the other girls, Debbie and Shelley and moony-eyed, foul-faced Estelle.

Pierre never said a word, except in French class, in which, of course, he excelled. In fact, he once dared to correct Miss Lafleur, but did it with such savoir faire that he and the ogre ended up by comparing impressions of the Left Bank.

Rolaine was so smitten by Pierre's unctuous continental charm that she dared enter the male preserve of wood shop, oohing and aahing at all the heavy male machinery she had so recently disdained. For once Larry wanted to tell her to scram, when Pierre screeched from the far corner as the sweet little jigsaw at which he had been working on a replica of the Eiffel Tower sliced off the top of his pinky, which lay like an eraser nub on the dusty surface.

He hopped up and down, *très humeureuse,* and yowled, "Get me a doctor!"

Larry met Loposthenes' eye. They shared the same thought. "The guy knows English."

Despite the calculating nature this revealed, Rolaine ran to the wounded dreamboat, knelt beside him and repeated, "Do what he says!"

Then, before the arrogant order could be obeyed, Pierre and Rolaine left the room together, ostensibly headed for the school nurse. It was a ruse to escape from the watchful eye of Brave Larry, the fingertip a sacrifice on the altar of love. As soon as they left the wood shop, drops of his foreign blood clotting in the sawdust, Larry knew they would not return.

The Brave One raged, he ranted, he retreated to wood shop after school and cut six-foot boards into splinters. He cut them and hammered them, drove nails into them like spikes into a vampire's heart. An hour after school, he was wet with the sweat of the effort. Loposthenes stood in the door and said, "You wanna walk home?" but Larry just glared, his anger unsated.

Larry sank into depression. He could not concentrate. He could not remember all the bones of the inner ear.

"She's not serious," Kenny said, doing his best to alleviate his friend's distress. "He's a toy, an indulgence."

"Well . . ."

But the Brilliant One could not resist the impulse to wit. "Just think of him as a French tickler."

And he was right. Larry could feel the "we're just friends" talk coming on between him and Rolaine the next time they went to the movies. Even as she allowed him one last nuzzle of her aromatic nape, Larry could tell that he had lost her. The ship had sailed.

The brokenhearted swain desperately considered approaching Rolaine's father. But even the Indomitable One was helpless before his strong-willed daughter. "Well rein her in, guy," he would growl, precisely because he no longer could. There was something pitiful about the lord whose kingdom extended only so far as the signless boundary of his front lawn.

Finally, Larry decided to attack with the only weapon a girl who made reservations understood. He poured his allowance and accumulated savings into an extravagance from Moderne Jewelry at the county mall.

"Christ," Loposthenes expostulated. "That's enough for a down payment on an X-ray machine!"

Unfortunately, the bracelet Larry purchased spilled its charms as Rolaine's undoubtedly lay open to the intruder's nine good fingers. Brave Larry could hear the unclasping of his father's merchandise a municipality away.

In a way, he knew that he was better off without her, and Kenny subtly tried to affirm that wisdom, but Larry had his pride. If some second-rate Adonis could steal his girl, what sort of a man was he? He would recapture her, if only to punish her. The question was, how?

He was distracted throughout the week, sleepwalking from class to class. The triumphs he had once found in his studies were hollow without Rolaine to share them. The only place in which he could find any solace was wood shop. Only there, amid the amber glow of the sawdust, did he feel the kind of strength that might conceivably regain his stolen inamorata. But it was not merely the power of the hammer; it was the potential inherent in the wood itself that engaged him.

Most of the stock was pine or ply, but there was also a rack of exotic hardwoods used by the vocational-track boys who were going to grow up to be carpenters. There was walnut, mahogany, oak and ash. Larry stared at the different grains and textures and decided that he would make Rolaine something that brains could not earn nor dollars purchase. He didn't know what, but he tried to read the lines on the entrails of bird's-eye maple. And as he stared, he saw a shape emerge from the raw material. It was a horse.

All girls loved horses. Of course, Larry knew the Freudian interpretation. It was part of his premedical training, but he felt that the implications went deeper than sex.

He tried to explain how the appeal was not merely biological, but cultural, to his friend, who had joined him in the silence of the after-school shop.

"Oh, no," Loposthenes groaned. "Not a Jungian."

"Hold the bit," Larry commanded, and the Brilliant One obeyed while the creator drilled a hemispherical socket that was to contain the marbled eye of the nag.

It was not as easy as he thought. A sign for the front yard was one thing, a rectangle, the letters glued to the surface, the stain applied evenly with a soft-bristled brush, but something as creaturely as a horse demanded an epic intelligence.

He studied horses, from the angles of their heads to the structure of their hooves. He studied them at rest and in motion until he decided upon a stationary being, like a bronze statue on a pedestal in a park, only wood, because wood was a more convincing material, malleable and responsive. Wood was an emblem of the soul.

First he made a sketch on the surface of the board he had chosen from a private lumberyard. He did a rough cut with a hand saw and a fine cut with a coping saw. Then he used several hammers to join the sections, countersinking a dozen two-penny nails, covering their traces with dabs of wood filler. He supplemented the binding power of the nails with special glues and clamps. He even used the lathe to shape the delicate curves of the horse's four calves. He worked among the specialized tools with a sureness he had never felt before, experiencing a spiritual kinship to the world of carpentry.

After lesser craftsmen would have called their work finished, Larry was still adding details with passionate inspiration, carving out the line of the flank, knobbing the knee, stapling on a threaded mane light enough to fly back in a whisper of a breeze. He sanded the resulting beast, using first a rough grade, then medium, then fine, until ultrafine sandpaper caressed the wood to silklike smoothness.

He wrapped the paper about a block and rubbed and rubbed, like a man on a desert island rubbing the only bottle that's washed ashore in decades, praying against all legitimate expectation that it house the genie with the power to rescue him.

"Do you do back rubs too?"

Larry spun about, disconcerted by the female voice in the male domain. "Hello, Estelle," he said, trying to conceal the object of his labors.

Oblomovitz's eyes, however, were keen and her brain yet keener. She said, "She doesn't deserve it."

"Who? What?"

Estelle didn't dignify his evasion with a response. She picked at a pimple beside her nose.

The beastly girl's attitude bothered Larry more than he would have admitted. He felt that she was not only insulting Rolaine, but implying that his own actions were childish. "Are you saying that my feelings are . . ." he searched for the correct word, "minor?"

"I'm not saying anything of the sort."

"Just because I'm sixteen doesn't mean I don't know passion and . . . and . . . and wonder that is as deep and authentic as . . . as Hollywood. Just because we live in a mediocre age doesn't mean we can't accomplish great things. The grounds for inspiration are as fertile in Athens, Georgia, as Athens, Greece."

Estelle had been retreating during the course of Larry's tirade until she was pressed up against the wall beside the door, cheeks blotched and eyes teary with adoration and sorrow.

Oblivious to her distress, Larry slammed his point home. "Or Mamaroneck, for that matter."

"I sincerely hope so," Estelle replied, choking back as great an emotional range as even the orator could have aspired to support. Then she left.

Then, as he rubbed the awl inside the animal's crude nostrils, widening them, flaring them, something happened. He heard the intake of breath. Of course it was his imagination, and he knew that, but nonetheless it sounded like breath. That was when he realized that his horse was like a real horse, which is to say three-dimensional. Even if it couldn't breathe, it was still defined as much by what it contained as the surface that contained it.

Furthermore he realized what he had been aiming for since he first started playing with the individual pieces of raw wood, and he realized that he could accomplish his goal. Ecstatic, he sang the hymns of wood shop, sang along with the buzz of the circular saw, the whine of the blood-spattered jigsaw, the rasp of the rasp, sang and continued to sand with a wet emery cloth until the wood finally sang to him.

AFTER DINNER WITH the Westerners consisting of roasted chicken, mashed potatoes and a selection of regular or diet cola, Brave Lawrence descended the narrow staircase to the basement of the house on Primrose Lane. He tiptoed past the damp and shadowy laundry where heaps of clothes waited for the maid to iron, and toward the pegboard where Mr. Sheldon Resnick, the Master of Foundations, kept his own home shop.

There Larry took a large screwdriver, wedged it into the thin partition he had sealed several hours before, between the belly and the chest of the creature he had made, and pried off a single grainy rectangle of half-inch maple to reveal the hidden depths.

In a "real" horse there would be guts, the kind of organs and tissues a future doctor knew well: heart, lungs bred to unhealthy enormity in racing beasts, intestines, kidneys, liver, spleen, miles of blood vessels, tendons attached to ligaments attached to bones. In Larry's horse, however, there was air.

But the air within the horse was not the same as the air without. It was replete with a potential that would only be fulfilled when it was occupied. He wondered what to place within the sacred chamber, a love letter or a curse.

He sat with the horse in his lap, stroking its back and belly, allowing the individual fibers that made up its mane to drift out from between his fingers, looking about the basement at all of the discarded belongings that had gone to compose his life and shape his character. There was the stuffed leopard he had loved as a child, matted, rigid, stiff with a decade's solitude. There were puzzles with missing pieces and games he had outgrown: Life, Careers, Monopoly, Clue. A ship in a bottle that had been a souvenir of a family vacation to Miami caught his eye.

He peered at the spines of the books that were the heritage of his tribe, Hardy Boys, space explorers, and premedical textbooks. There was a much-loved biography of Louis Pasteur, and there were three toy soldiers that were the last remains of what had once been armies that had disappeared under couches, in sandboxes, behind hedges, one in a terrifying vortex down the toilet. They were marvelous replicas of primitive warriors, made of painted lead, with molded greaves, breastplates and plumed helmets. One was an archer, one a cadet, one a swordsman. The swordsman was the one that had always been Larry in the campaigns of his mind.

Before he knew precisely what he was doing, Larry inserted the three soldiers into the horse and jammed the belly shut again. He shook the animal to make sure the section held in place, examined it in the dim glow of the hall light and determined that no one besides a veterinary surgeon could tell the horse had been tampered with.

Waving to the parents who sat transfixed by their own large screen, he ran outdoors, across the many yards of the township, past the legendary fields where generations of heroes had fallen in their combat with girls. There was the drive-in movie, the water tower, the ledge near the Sound of Long Island. Cars were parked in each one of these locations, and even now grapplings were ensuing between boys and every possible Western Foundations undergarment. He cut across the arc of light from the Amoco gas station and Pete's Pizza, to Rolaine's front yard in a cul de sac off the Larchmont Road. He arrived, panting.

There was the Rosen castle, Cadillac parked in the U-shaped drive. Larry dared not make a frontal assault. A sticker in the sidelight next to the thick oaken door warned intruders of the services of mercenaries employed by the Home Protection Agency, whose logo was the profile of a viciously barking dog.

Somewhere in the farthest reaches of the castle, the beauteous Rolaine played footsie with the loathsome Pierre, even if only in her imagination. The failure to consummate, however, was no justification for the desire. The Brave One placed his devious offering on the doormat, an ironic "Welcome" scripted upon its nubby surface. He rang the bell and ran for the pachysandra.

The door opened, and a skewed rectangle of light spilled onto the lawn. Rolaine, a halo illuminating the endearing shape of her head, was a delight to behold.

"Hello . . ." she called into the darkness. "Oooh!" She reached down and lifted the horse with both hands, turning it in the light from within, appreciating the perfections of its contours, ignorant of its secret.

Larry watched, tempted to return the call, to step forward, to be lauded for his skill, but he remained hidden in the bushes, the shadows created by the moon on the boughs overhead speckling his hair, invisible to the object of his mystical assault.

Rolaine peered once more into the night, and then, as if suddenly aware that she was being watched, she brushed her hair backward, turned and shut the door. The raised panels seemed to vibrate with the impact.

Larry remained in place for hours, long enough to see every last light of Rosendom flicker and die. He returned home, humming.

SING, SOLDIERS, to life eternal. The same warriors who toppled the walls of Troy were released into an entirely new world. Although the territory was unfamiliar, their strength lay in their ability to adjust to the conditions of any given contest. In the Middle Ages, they would joust. Later, they would use the saber, blunderbuss, carbine or cannon. They would dig trenches if need be, strafe, maneuver helicopters, drop atom bombs. Here, surrounded by the customs of Mamaroneck, they would fight in the Mamaroneck manner, to the death.

The swordsman leader, a plan already forming in his leaden brain, signaled to his men to follow him down the hinge of the horse's belly onto a flat white countertop that ended in a fearsome drop to the distant floor. There was the scent of food, leftover noodles as long as anacondas dripping from a cleverly folded white cardboard carton. He directed the beardless cadet to blaze a path, the archer to scout for guards.

The cadet investigated a shiny metallic pool overhung by an enormous curved spout from which droplets of water the size of his head fell with absolute regularity. Perhaps it was a municipal timepiece. He looked about further and found a stiffened dish towel that hung to the base of the cabinet. He also discovered something far stranger to his Attic sensibility than anything he had yet encountered. "Hark," he called and pointed with trembling finger to a huge cylinder marked "Ajax."

They tapped at it, sniffed the powder, exhilarated by its potency. They slid down the dish towel.

Next, they crossed the living room, stopping in front of the television. " 'Tis a beast set to guard the fair maiden, but fortunately for us, it sleeps. Methinks it ought to sleep forever." The leader took a nail he had extracted from the horse's rough hide and gave it to the archer, who sent the missile flying with uncanny accuracy into the center of the mechanical Cyclops. They were all thrown back in a violent explosion; luckily none of them were hurt. The commander brushed shards of glass from his lead shoulders.

They were ready to proceed up a series of immense plateaus that reminded the world travelers of the steps of the pyramids. At the summit, they paused to contemplate the four doors opening off the hallway. One led to the sumptuous bedroom of Indomitable Rosen and his wife, the bestower of the name "Rolaine," a second to their beautiful child, a third to a linen closet, and a fourth to a bath of pink and lavender tile that would make a Roman emperor blush. It was a faucet maker's bath.

The soldiers ignored the temptation to explore the exotic terrain and diligently concentrated on their goal. The intrepid band entered the girl's bedroom, its thick carpet brushing their knees.

"Forge on, men," the commander said, parting the strands like cattails in a swamp.

Rolaine turned over and whimpered.

The invaders climbed up onto the sheets and marched past the dimpled knees and tennis thighs. They passed the cups restraining Rolaine's ample breasts, fearfully aware of the way the Spartan king Leonidas was able to defend against the Persians at the pass of Thermopylae. Nonetheless, they were compelled to tiptoe beneath the dangerous glands whose ominous weight was prettified by the lace adorning Western Foundations' top-of-the-line lingerie. At last, they arrived beside the head of the girl, whose exquisite features they could discern by the strange glowing dial by the bedside.

She was dreaming of Pierre.

These men, the dream slayers, knew that the soul of the princess belonged to Pierre, but the whimsies of romance were of no concern to them. They cared only for the will of their master, the heir to Western Foundations. Rolaine's offense to Brave Larry was an offense to them, as well as to his friend Loposthenes and to the entire eleventh grade of Mamaroneck High and to all the proud men of Westchester.

She had conveniently established the image of the class in her mind. They were lined up in rows, as if a formal photograph were being taken. They all had the same rigid smiles except for the traducer. They were stiff, but he danced. His teeth reflected the unseen photographer's lights. His brass buttons shone.

Suddenly, the shell that resembled Brave Larry clapped his hands. The shadow of a horse loomed over the peaceful tableau.

Rolaine twitched in her sleep. She had expected Pierre to lead her away to a land by the sea where they could pluck olives and dates from silver platters, someplace like Cancún, where the Rosens had spent the previous winter vacation. Betrayed, however, the moment she took the reins of the hollow mare, she watched helplessly as its supernatural progeny swarmed over the ramparts and violated the sanctuary of Rosendom. There were soldiers everywhere. At Larry's next signal, the dream archer pulled a bow back as far as he could. He let fly an arrow with a poisoned tip.

Pierre, fancy pants French dandy, was no wimp. He was, in his own fashion, deserving of the prize he had won. He dodged the arrow, which broke downward, its evil trajectory in thrall to an even more transcendental divinity than the minions of Larry could summon.

At home, Larry squirmed abed. He too tried to outdance the arrow, twisting his body, exposing the heel. The missile hit its unintended mark.

Rolaine had not given the rest of the class leave to move. Only their eyes darted to the Brave One, limping, collapsing, his blood a wine dark pool on the floor.

Loposthenes was the first to break ranks and run to Larry. He held his friend's head, cursing the girl who led the hero to his doom.

The soldiers crashed through the gates and grabbed the beauteous one out from the front row.

Pierre did his best to defend her. He tilted a brazier, coals spilling, catching at tapestries. Then he slew the cadet.

Loposthenes, however, turned his own sword upon the Lothario. Pierre parried the blow, but Loposthenes was relentless in his thirst for revenge. He hacked the rest of Pierre's fingertipless hand off at the wrist.

"Alas, Rolaine," her beau cried. "I too am killed in your name!"

"No!" she wailed, and thrashed about in her bed, flinging the archer from the parapet, but too weak to shake the swordsman's grip. He hung on to the strap of the brassiere that crossed her bare shoulder, and just before she woke Indomitable Rosen, who rushed to comfort the child he knew had no honor, Larry's last agent swept her up like so much baggage and escaped the burning citadel of love.

"HERE."

Back on Primrose Lane, the swordsman presented his captive to the wounded chieftain who lay half assassinated upon the blood-soaked mattress designed to enhance his posture.

Rolaine was curled at the base of the oak bedboard. She was terrified of the wrath of her captor, yet no less spoiled than ever, still regal in her humiliation. "If this is the way you treat a girl, Larry Resnick, I don't care if you're the hottest brain surgeon in Scarsdale."

"Shut up!" A voice like rattling sheet metal filled the room. It was Estelle Oblomovitz, larger than life under the best of circumstances, blown up to horrifying proportions in the dream world beneath Larry Resnick's cozy puppy-dog quilt.

Rolaine hushed.

Estelle reached down and pulled the lethal shaft out from Larry's heel, stanching the flow of blood with a hand-knit scarf, and then, putting her mouth to the wound, she drew out the poison and recalled the dying youth to life.

"I mean," Rolaine whined, "I really don't care if you're the last boy in Westchester."

"And I really mean, 'Shut up!' "

The swordsman thought Estelle had insulted Larry, and stepped forward, but the scar-faced goddess of Home Economics smacked the puny toy man off his feet. He fell to the floor in an insensate clatter.

Estelle turned to the cowering temptress. She knew what she wanted. She wanted to cut Rolaine's throat and feed her carcass to the dogs. If not, she wanted to set the vile, cute one adrift.

In any case, she knew that the momentous decision had to be made by he who had initiated the fierce contest. Only by scorning his trophy could the Brave One truly overcome her baleful influence. Wise Estelle turned to Larry and hissed her final contemptuous imperative, "Let her shop."

Larry turned to faithful Loposthenes to approve his submission to a greater power than either of them had ever beheld.

Alas, the Brilliant One knew when he was beaten. He had already left the wreckage of the battlefield, and had already commenced his arduous voyage home across the treacherous inlets of the Sound of Long Island (viz. *The Loposthony*).

Humbled, Larry asked, "Is this the end?"

"No," Estelle said. "It's the beginning. Sing, Larry. Your voice is sweet to me."

The pale hero nodded acquiescence.

Sing, Larry did, of the triumphs of the past and those yet to come.

Sing, Larry, of Rolaine disdained, Pierre dismembered, of the dead soldiers in funeral pyres flickering upon the bedspread to the horizon. Sing of Medical School. Sing of the sale of Western Foundations to a large conglomerate. Sing of marriage to Estelle, of children of Mamaroneck and grandchildren of Mamaroneck.

Sing of memory and valor.

Love dies. Art lingers. Sing to the scalpel that severs the quadrants of the human heart.

The Swap

———

B EFORE THE SPEECHES, DR. NELSON GREGORY PUSHED his wire-rim bifocals onto the bridge of his fat, flat and reddened nose and peered woozily down the dais. The honorees were sitting in alphabetical order of their field of expertise, so Dr. Gregory—M for Molecular Biology—found himself fairly close to the center. Maybe it was the champagne or maybe the tightness of the cummerbund he wore acted as a sartorial torture device, the masculine equivalent of an iron maiden, to coerce comment from the good and reputed doctor's constricted and beribboned gut. "Well deserved, well deserved," he murmured into his bristly white beard as if he were Santa Claus distributing goodies to a pack of orphans. Then he reached for the nearly empty bottle which bore the silver embossment of a medal attesting to the beverage's stature in the realm of the vine—as a similar medal bouncing on its drinker's belly corresponded to his own stature in the realm of the mind.

About half a dozen identical bottles stood at two place setting intervals down the rest of the table which led to the king, whose only testament to his own position was a tiny golden pin on the lapel of his tuxedo. For a moment, Dr. Gregory felt cheated by His Highness's lack of ermine, a crown and jewel-encrusted regalia. He imagined what might have happened if he had wished to be a king rather than a scientist; if that dream had been fulfilled, he'd have made sure to look the part.

Few of Dr. Gregory's fellow laureates looked at ease beneath the chandeliers in front of a tempest of maroon velvet curtains that would have suited the Loews Orpheum in the Bronx where Dr. Gregory grew up to a daily taunting familiar to any sensitive boy among hoodlums and the uniquely awful nickname "Nelly." There they sat, like the doctor, drinking less excessively and sweating less effusively, but drinking and sweating nonetheless, though surely not from the perfectly calibrated temperature of the banquet hall, but rather from the giddy and terrifying knowledge that this evening was the pinnacle of their various lives. Indeed, as the king was saying, never had such a concatenation of intelligence and diligence been gathered in his humble domain, at least not since the year before when Gregory's nemesis, Dr. Ivan Ivanovitch—how the hypocrite loved the redundant patronymic—Nickolaev walked away with their mutual profession's ultimate reward.

At the thought of Nickolaev's sallow face, which Gregory had last seen laughing—the only time in memory Nickolaev had been known to laugh—at the then-youthful Gregory's early studies on hormonal norms, Dr. Gregory stabbed at one of the perfectly round meatballs on his gilded plate and stuffed it into his mouth, which already contained a fluteful of Moet '64. Unable to determine whether to chew or swallow, Gregory wedged a thick, gouty finger between his bulging neck and starched collar, as if trying to make room in his throat for both processes. Unfortunately, the moment his bow tie was loosened, a chunk of meat slipped down whole, as the champagne sluiced out. Dr. Gregory's nose and pendulous cheeks turned redder than ever.

The only one to notice Molecular Biology's distress was his

neighbor, Literature. Hardly in great physical shape himself, the reedy novelist gently tapped Gregory on the back, but he would have done better if he had used a copy of the twelve-hundred-page opus that had earned him a seat at the table. He continued to tap with the modesty of a penitent at a confessional, until Dr. Gregory lumbered to his feet and toppled the bottle of champagne.

Casting about fearfully for help that was not forthcoming, the novelist had no choice. He too rose, and extended his arms as far as he could around the doctor's enormous paunch. Then, unpleasant as it was necessary, he jerked his fists violently inward and upward, causing the Swedish meatball lodged somewhere between his peer's lower chin and stomach to shoot forward into the puddle of expensive bubbly.

"Hmph," said Gregory. "Nice Heimlich. And you're not even a doctor."

"*Honorus causa*," the novelist corrected the scientist, and sat down.

"Thanks. Wouldn't do to expire just yet, eh?"

The novelist ran over plots in his mind. "Put a severe crimp in the king's evening. Make all the papers, though."

"Been there. Done that."

So had they all, the chemists, physicists and mathematicians, even the wizened Inuit shaman who won the Peace Prize that year for chaining himself to a polar bear in protest of the Bering Strait Bridge. Some had been rewarded continuously through the decades, while others only came to acclaim with last month's announcement of this award, but one way or the other—or a third—all of them had experienced the frenzy of renown, and now all of them were brought together to bask in their success in this strange land of frigid blond royalty.

"Anyway, thanks," Dr. Gregory said, blotting some of the

spilled champagne from his chest with the edge of the linen tablecloth.

The novelist shrugged. "Ancient remedies."

"For ancient curses."

The novelist thought that Dr. Gregory was awfully poetic for a molecular biologist.

Dr. Gregory took the remarks he had prepared—each one of the winners had eight minutes to explicate his or her life's work, but traditionally only Literature and Peace used their allotted span—out of his inner breast pocket to peruse them. Despite his "Been there. Done that" bravado, Gregory was nervous, because, unlike most of his colleagues on the dais who had long since learned how to deliver a speech, his ascendance to speech-giving prominence had been unusually rapid, without the more common, less exalted plateaus on the climb to immortality. Oh, there were a few prodigies who had built intergalactic telescopes out of toilet paper tubes and rubber bands when they were barely out of dia-pers, but most of the now-venerable ones' careers started slowly with presentations to department chairs, which, when they received their own chairs, led to polite chitchat with deans and provosts and, later yet, international conferences and congres-sional hearings.

In this way, even the woolliest of mathematicians became quite worldly. Reputations within esoteric disciplines spread and they learned their market value, although the economists had long since been aware of that. In fact, Economy at the other end of the dais had won his seat by developing an elaborate formula that factored levels of fame as financial instruments. Ultimately, he posited an attention bank to which deposits could be credited by appearances on television talk shows and other media and withdrawals subsequently debited. For example, a quote in the *New York Times* might be exchangeable for a used Volvo with low mileage, whereas a national magazine profile was worth considerably more, a two-bedroom condo, say, and a lifetime health club membership.

Gregory was, however, an exception. His only apprenticeship had been under the unappreciative Nickolaev, and then—it seemed like overnight—his theories were published, lauded, rewarded. And what rewards! Due to the investment wisdom of the trust that administered the requitals, this evening alone was worth a cool seven figures to the current crop of honorees, but that paled in comparison to the value of the patents Gregory held—a man from Merck practically camped out on his doorstep while the guy from Pfizer proffered stock options like jelly beans—and the money paled in comparison to the ultimate prerogatives of fame. Graduate students looked at him with awe when he rolled across campus, and though the rest of the professoriate cringed in fear of PC constraints, Gregory made off-color jokes while deans pretended not to hear, so hungry were they for the sheer glamour of his presence. And as for that other contemporary academic taboo . . . well, consider Blythe.

She of the hazel eyes and chestnut hair, she who wouldn't have given him a second glance in his previous incarnation. She whose hazel eyes now batted flirtatiously, she whose chestnut hair thrashed wildly across the professor's pillow subject to the professor's inclination. Presidents might be accountable for their behavior; laureates were beyond accountability to any force but mortality. That was the trade-off, pure and simple.

The first lines of his speech were, "Genius always looks easy." So much for modesty, so much for thanking others "without whom none of this would be possible blah blah blah." Dr. Nelson Gregory looked at the novelist who had arguably saved his life. He felt no need to offer gratitude, but, on a whim, he said, "Hey, scribbler."

"Are you talking to me?"

"Unless His Majesty wrote anything I should know about."

"Yes?"

"I've got a story for you."

The novelist recoiled. How many times throughout his career, from his first tentative attempts at the page to his final universally acknowledged accomplishment, had he met someone, a relative, a neighbor, an elevator operator, who thought it was easy? They always said, "I've got a great idea. I'll tell you; you'll write it; we'll make a fortune," but they were always idiots, and besides, like Molecular Biology, he too had his million-dollar prize. Copyrights weren't patents, but you can't have everything. He too had the power of renown. Like Gregory, he too needed nothing, except perhaps the guarantee neither of them would ever have, that they could live for another few years to enjoy the fruits of their distinction.

"You want to hear it? I guarantee you've never heard anything like it before."

Fat chance. The more Gregory suggested, the less the novelist wanted to hear, but there was no way, short of changing places with Economy, that he could avoid some tedious revelation even here, among the geniuses. Politely, suspiciously, he repeated, "Yes?"

And Gregory was off, in the expanse of time. "One week ago," he started . . . "At least it seems like that . . ."

"YOUR IDEAS ARE ATROCIOUS, but your handwriting is worse," Nickolaev said to one of the two students cowering behind him while he peered down at the campus through the oculus window in his laboratory atop the Calhoun Science Center like a hawk inspecting a meadow for field mice.

Blythe snickered and pretended to examine her notebook.

Aware of everything that occurred in his private aerie, Nickolaev said, "Even Miss Carter knows better."

Both students winced at the double-edged comment that cut the two of them down with one swipe. Miss Carter was the princess with the pea-sized brain. So what if she too was a graduate student at the institute which rejected eighty qualified applicants for each one accepted. There was still a chasm between the few truly gifted young scientists and the rest. Keenly aware of her failings, she was doing work-study to make up for several semesters' worth of inability to grasp what the other student, he of the atrocious ideas and worse handwriting, would-be Dr. Nelson Gregory, considered to be most basic scientific axioms. The deal was that if she could type, she would pass. Also, Nickolaev had a roving eye.

"Blythe." He snapped her to attention. "Have you gotten the sixty-fourth-generation insemination figures yet? I swear, if those flies don't start fucking, we're going to rape them."

Under Nickolaev's leadership, his "team" at the lab had been mating and cross-breeding flies with the intention of charting learning curves among the invertebrates, which, as Nickolaev loved to repeat, "does not necessarily mean that we can apply such principles to lower life-forms such as doctoral students."

Nickolaev mocked their intelligence, their character, their looks and other traits over which they had no control. They lived in terror of his random assaults, which culminated when he turned on the second figure in his office. "And why do you have two first names, Missssster"—he hissed the appellation—"Nelson Gregory? Is it because you haven't the maturity for a last name?"

This comment was particularly ironic since Ivan Ivanovitch Nickolaev arguably maintained three first names, or variations thereof. But he was a Slavic aristocrat who, nearly a century after his grandparents fled St. Petersburg, still believed in autocracy. Students, as far as he was concerned, were less than serfs: to be used, abused and have their degrees refused as the spirit moved him. "Here's what I want you both to do; I'll try to keep it simple," he sneered. "Miss Carter, you start typing, and Mr. Gregory, you stop thinking."

"But sir, I've been working on these theories for the last six—"

"Look . . ." Nickolaev pivoted and glared at the young man who held forth a trembling sheaf of paper. "When you have been to Sweden you may play with theories. In the meanwhile, I suggest that you consider facts. Is that comprehensible . . . Nelly?"

It was the use of his childhood nickname that made Nelson Gregory understand that Nickolaev's disdain for him was not merely part of the great man's loathing for the world outside his head, but personal. When Gregory had been chosen for the institute, he thought he had gone to heaven, but now it turned out that the god he worshiped, the giant in his chosen field, a man who ought to have been above such petty mundanity, genuinely hated him. Nickolaev snarled at all of them, but reserved his most vicious invective for Gregory, the brightest of the bunch, Westinghouse scholar, Phi Beta, et cetera. But why? Gregory was the high priest's most promising acolyte, the one most likely to carry on his tradition. He approached Nickolaev with humility and adoration—and also the burning desire to supplant him— fully acknowledging that he had not yet attained the wisdom of the émigré eminence; he was there to learn.

"One more thing, Gregory."

"Yes, sir."

"Shave."

"Shave, sir?" Gregory fingered the faint wisps on his chin that had just begun to curl together into a coherent body of hair.

"Shave!" Nickolaev screamed. "If you're so damn interested in aging, then look in the damn mirror and shave!"

Later, in the library carrel, Gregory examined the papers that the great man had shunned. Admittedly inspired by Nickolaev's intellectual example if not his evil temper, Gregory posited a radical theory that, through the manipulation of the enzymes that determined growth and decay, the tide of time could be slowed down, turned on an axis and reversed. According to his speculations, one could theoretically grow younger. Of course, he required much further proof that only extended and expensive laboratory procedures could achieve. But such a notion went against the standard notion of time as linear. It was ontologically heretical, not to mention incomprehensible, to anyone less than a relativistic Einstein, and he couldn't get anybody to so much as look at—let alone fund—his proposals.

Once, when he had coaxed Blythe out for a post-lab cup of coffee, she had shaken her lovely head dubiously and administered the coup de grâce by naively asking, "What does Nickolaev think?"

"All he does when I try to explain is scream at me and tell me to shave."

"Shave?"

"Shave!" He thought he was funny when he imitated Nickolaev, but instead of humoring Blythe he seemed to frighten her.

"That poor man is so unhappy," she said with unfathomable sympathy for their tormentor, and then said she had to leave.

Where was Einstein when you needed him? Gregory thought miserably as he decided to seek solace in cheesecake and soda at the Snack Shack, a local institution with as many flies as the lab.

"Makes sense to me."

Gregory was jolted from his reverie by a middle-aged man in

a checkered cabbie's hat that made him look like an extra from *My Fair Lady*. He hadn't noticed the man sitting next to him at the Formica counter of the Snack Shack, and wasn't eager to enter into discussion.

But the man was leaning in his direction and pointing at the documents. "What do you want with those x's and y's?"

"If you really must know," Nelson said, and tried to speak in laymen's terms, but the second he used the most modestly technical word, *control*, the man interrupted him.

"No, no, that's just the science. I mean what do *you* want to get out of this. Personally."

"The truth."

"Ridiculous," the man scoffed. "Nobody wants the truth for the truth's sake."

"Scientists do."

"Scientists least of all. Why else do they name everything in sight after themselves, mountains on the moon and species of butterflies, all with these idiotic Latinate versions of Hank? Do you want money?"

"Well . . ." Gregory thought of his rapidly mounting student loans. He was nearly thirty, still A.B.D., with no prospect of anything but years of further disrespected indentured servitude to Nickolaev leading to an adjunctcy at an inferior institution—if he was lucky—and endless dunning from the federal government. "Well, yes, of course I want money, but that's not all."

"No, no, of course it isn't. There's . . . science." The man crudely hawked a gob of phlegm on the floor between his and Nelson's stools. "So how do you hope to get this money that isn't all?"

"Through research."

"Oh, you mean hard work, for decades, until you're so weak you can't stand."

The man certainly had a way of making things look bleak.

"But the value of my work stands by itself."

"Oh, yes, if it's good, someone like Nickolaev will slap his own name on it and call you an assistant, isn't that the way it works?"

At the moment, it didn't occur to Gregory to wonder how the man knew Nickolaev's name, because that was indeed how the system worked. It wasn't fair.

"It isn't fair," the man said.

"Right."

"So what you really yearn for is justice." The man's eyes twinkled with this little joke.

"Not precisely," Gregory huffed.

"Of course not. Truth and justice are not coincident values. But nonetheless, if you were in Nickolaev's shoes, you could publish this tomorrow."

"Yeah."

"And if you were in his shoes, you could do all sorts of other things, like . . ."

"Like what?" Gregory asked, and blushed as he thought of Blythe.

Again, the man's eyes glittered with a humor he declined to share as he spoke deadpan. "Well, mostly you could just be yourself, with the respect you deserve." He took a ring with a dozen keys out of his pocket and started jangling them. "Right?"

"Right."

"So, how about it?"

"How about what?"

"How about we arrange this?"

"Just as easy as one two three."

"Or three two one," the man counted backward, and chuckled elusively. He saw Gregory's confusion and said. "Look, you can have anything you want. But you've got to pay for it."

"That's the problem. I don't have money."

"We already established that. But who mentioned money? You can pay in the only coin you have."

But all Nelson Gregory had was the pathetic willingness to work of the eternal graduate student, and that was spoken for. "I don't have the time."

Now the man smiled an engaging grin. "Wrong," he said. "Dead wrong. The only thing you do have, young man, is time. That's your asset, that's your stock in trade."

Gregory thought he was wasting time, and stood up. How easily he once stood!

"The only thing we need to find is someone who wants what you have, and then arrange a trade."

"Trade?"

"Barter, swap."

"Swap what?"

AS IF WAKING with dream dialogue on his lips, the novelist listening to Dr. Gregory's sad tale supplied the last line of the first part of the tale as originally delivered at the Snack Shack. "Why, lives, of course."

"How did you know?"

"I've heard this story before, with variations. Faust, for example. And Oscar Wilde did it quite beautifully."

"Who?"

The ignorance of scientists was appalling. It went hand in hand with a single-mindedness that could not perceive life beyond test tubes.

Gregory went on, though he probably couldn't tell whether he was speaking aloud or thinking to himself.

"Let's take a walk," the man in the cabbie's hat said, as he laid down a bill for both of them.

"Sure," Gregory agreed. He was a cheap date.

They walked across the street and onto the quad dominated by the Calhoun Science Center. The cabbie was talking strangely, muttering something about multiple routes to the same destination. "You see, you can take the back roads or you can take the highway, but sometimes the back roads are quicker when the highway's jammed. You've got to strategize in my business." Then he stopped abruptly and said, "How about him?" He gestured ahead to a cranelike senior faculty member loping across campus under the weight of a satchel of books.

"Who's that?"

"Him? That's Federman, philosophy, tenured, unhappily married, could be a good prospect."

"What would I want with—"

"Just kidding, kid. I know what you want. Science, pure science. Science and . . . there." He pointed to a low stone wall where Blythe sat, knees protruding from under a checkered skirt that matched the cabbie's cap. She was so fetching that Gregory almost didn't notice that Nickolaev stood beside her.

"That lecher. He's old enough to be her father. It's pathetic."

"Grandfather, actually, but of course it's pathetic. That's precisely why it may work. You see, he too has desires, and believe it or not they're as potent as your own. It wouldn't work otherwise. He may not admit them and that may make him testy, but he has them."

"What are you, a psychiatrist?"

"Let's say a facilitator."

"I still don't know what you mean by *it*," Literature interrupted.

"What? Who'd you say you were? Where was I? Well, neither did I. I felt as if I were sleepwalking. I tried to analyze the situation scientifically, and was about to leave when he said the only thing he could to keep me there."

"Which was?"

" 'Chronological inversion,' that's what he said, as if he had absorbed the entire theoretical construct of my dissertation during the ten-second glance he had at my papers in the Snack Shack and applied it to . . ." Suddenly, everything he was saying sounded so stupid and his drunken vulgarity seemed so obvious that Dr. Gregory hesitated.

"Go on," Literature requested. He might as well have said, "You tell me the story. I'll write it. We'll make a fortune."

"Well, he applied it to taxi driving in Calhoun, and showed me a map of the village streets, which everyone knows are impossibly complicated. They were laid out on cowpaths or something. People regularly get lost two blocks from home. But the second I saw the map, I froze. It was a spring day, but a chill came over me. The streets reproduced the neurological pathways of the brain. Not entirely, of course, but uncannily, like a transparent overlay with some of the detail missing. It was astonishing. He showed me several shortcuts that nobody knew, and then, he lost me here, he explained that the atmosphere inside a taxi echoed the pathways outside and that the transformation—"

"What transformation?"

"*The* transformation." Gregory spoke with the hauteur that came automatically these days.

"Sorry I asked."

"Never mind. He said that the transformation had to happen internally and externally simultaneously."

"Somewhat like the structure of a novel," Literature mused.

"Well, maybe, I wouldn't know. I've never read one."

"You've never read a novel?" Literature was shocked.

But Nelson Gregory was back inside his story, and recounted the cabbie's precise words. "He will naturally take the back seat. There will be room for you, but you will not take it. You will sit in the jumper seat instead. But what you've got to do is get him to change seats with you. How you make this happen is your business, but you must exchange seats, and then, this is important, you've got to pay the fare. You cannot let him pay the fare or the deal is void."

"I still don't understand what this deal is." Again, Literature echoed the words of the story before the storyteller, as if reading ahead.

Exasperated, the cabbie lost patience with his potential fare. "Just pay the driver, okay?"

Feeling drunk, though he had never been drunk before—though he would be many times in the future—A.B.D. Nelson Gregory surrendered to fate. "Okay."

"And one other thing, I hope you're mature enough to know. I hope I don't have to explain."

"Yes?"

"Tip well."

"DR. NICKOLAEV." Gregory interrupted the private moment on the stone wall that bordered Mt. Raymond Street, which bordered the campus.

The professor shuddered, as if caught en flagrante instead of in a genial chat with a student.

"I have class," Blythe said, stood, smoothed down the pleats of her skirt, and started away.

"What can I do for you?" Nickolaev asked sarcastically.

"I . . . um . . ." Gregory looked around, but his companion had disappeared. "I saw you here and . . ."

Suddenly, out from the anonymous stream of sleek modern cars zipping along Mt. Raymond, a clattering yellow Checker cab pulled over, its engine steaming, its window open, a hairy wrist hanging free.

"And I thought maybe I could give you a lift, Dr. N.?" Gregory asked with feigned nonchalance, his heart beating swiftly.

"No, thanks."

"Oh, come on. I'll drop you anywhere."

"Didn't I say no . . . Nelly?" The professor glared at Gregory and stepped into the street behind the taxi.

Humiliated, the student was about to give up and slink off, defeated, when he looked in the rearview mirror and saw the driver's face shaking his head with dismay.

Gregory shrugged. He could hardly kidnap the professor. He was a scientist at heart. It was science's surety he craved—that and the recognition of the particular scientist's surety. He needed help.

And then, as if it were his entire future receding, the taxi started away from the curb.

"Wait!" Gregory shrieked, and the vehicle responded. It shifted into reverse, slid back toward the curb and the rear wheel rolled smoothly over Dr. Nickolaev's elegantly shod foot.

"Yeeow!" Nickolaev started screaming, while the taxi, in perhaps the most incredible moment of the entire, incredible episode, did not vamoose, but simply remained, waiting calmly for its fare, lock popped up with an audible *ker-chunk*.

"Here, let me help you."

Gregory lifted the doctor, who seemed curiously light as he swatted his benefactor's shoulders and yelled so harshly he lost his Slavic accent, "You idiot. You moron. You dolt. Let me down. You're through here, Gregory."

"Yes, yes, let's get you home." He deposited the prizewinner horizontally and flipped up the jumper seat, a crudely made but elegantly functional mechanism that unfolded from the floor like metal origami, and the taxi was off.

Rolling now, Nickolaev begrudgingly revealed his home address.

"Maybe you'd be more comfortable here." Gregory stupidly patted the uncomfortable metal base of the jumper seat.

"Shut up."

"I—"

"I said, shut up. If I hear one more word from you, I will personally feed you to the flies."

Nickolaev continued to mutter and curse darkly as the taxi passed the Snack Shack and looped around the colonial square in the center of the town. It cut curbs and rounded corners in the tangle of streets that composed Calhoun, seeming to pick up speed with every turn, traveling faster and faster until the scenery blurred. Losing track of all time and location, Nelson was terrified. He couldn't concentrate on his mission, and gripped the bottom of his little folding seat to keep from spinning into space.

"Slow down. Hey, slow down, you." Nickolaev leaned forward and pounded at the glass partition that separated the passengers from the driver, who paid them no heed. Sometimes he took the highway, and sometimes the back roads, but whatever route he took, he continued to veer and careen with increasing madness.

"Stop, I say, I order you to stop!"

The taxi jolted to a halt, and Nickolaev flew forward and

landed on Gregory's lap. "I'm getting out," he declared, and reached for the door.

"Wait," Gregory cried again. Vaguely, he remembered that he had to do something, but could hardly recall what it was. Then he slipped out from underneath the man he hoped would be his mentor, who, to keep his balance, clutched at the jumper seat like a child the seat was designed for. Gregory plopped into the broken-springed back seat.

And suddenly, things were . . . different. Sitting in the back seat that was still warm from the professor's body, Gregory felt a surge of energy pass through him. If he had been a physicist, he might have compared it to lightning, a natural or unnatural force starting in at the cranium and flashing through his neck, torso and groin to ground on the last digit on his right foot, but he was a molecular biologist and merely felt that his entire chemical structure had changed. And changed for the better. Though he couldn't define the difference, Gregory liked it. He felt secure for the first time since he entered college, like he was holding on to a winning lottery ticket. Still, the change was tentative, revocable, and he felt one last needling fear that the ticket might be a forgery.

Most bizarrely, the professor who had hated Nelson Gregory, and was bound to ruin the remains of his career, was smiling too. Instead of castigating Gregory for his behavior, Nickolaev tipped an imaginary cap in the air and left the cab with a spring in his step.

Immediately, the charge revving through Gregory's body subsided. It didn't disappear, but shifted into a low and perpetual hum.

"That wasn't so difficult, was it?" the cabbie said delightedly. "He didn't even offer to pay, the cheapskate. Usually, they insist.

Second thoughts, I guess. But you, I can tell, you're lucky. You'll get what you want, boyo. Now, where was it that you wanted to go?"

GREGORY KNEW THE slanting wooden stairs to the top of the three-decker at 14 Isabel Street well, but there seemed to be more of them than he recalled. Or maybe the wild ride had taken the vigor out of him in unexpected ways. Still, he was reluctant to pause for rest for fear of his landlady, a widow he referred to as "The Mite" who inherited the building from her late husband and lived on the second floor. He had been avoiding The Mite for the last rent-past-due month, but was so exhausted by the climb that he had to stop on her landing. Unfortunately, the steps were creaky, and The Mite's door swung wide as if she had been waiting in ambush with a wrinkle-circled eye pressed to the fish-eye lens.

He half expected her to cry, "Ah-ha!" but instead of lashing into him as if she were the long lost sister of Dr. Nickolaev, she whispered so quietly he had to strain to hear her, "Good afternoon, Dr. Gregory. And how are you doing today?"

If this was a sinister joke, it wasn't funny, but if the harridan could pretend to flirtatious deference, her victim could pretend to stern authority. "Hmph!" he growled, and climbed the last flight.

Upstairs at last, the familiarity of the premises comforted him. There was the hooked rug he had purchased at the Salvation Army and his books set on planks supported by bricks stolen from a local construction site. In the kitchen, a poster of Louis Pasteur was thumbtacked to the wall along with an array of Calhoun's finest take-out Chinese menus. Home, sweet home. He collapsed in his broken armchair, so spent that, when the doorbell rang an hour later, he almost didn't wake. But the bell rang more insistently, so he stood and limped—why was he limping?—to the door.

Blythe stood awkwardly on the dimly lit threshold, eyes cast shyly downward, clutching several textbooks to her chest like a child hugging a favorite teddy bear. "Hi," she stammered. "I was in the neighborhood and thought I'd drop in."

An hour later and tired, tired but happy, he escorted her to the door, and noticed an envelope that must have been slipped underneath during their encounter.

The envelope was made of the heaviest paper stock Gregory had ever seen and bore some sort of ornate seal and a foreign stamp canceled by wavy lines. His name was written in fine blue calligraphy. Feeling both anxiety and surety, he slipped a finger under the seal and broke it into waxy halves. Inside, the letter read, "On behalf of His Majesty, Olaf XIV . . . we are delighted to inform you . . ."

LITERATURE EXAMINED Molecular Biology as cautiously as an epidemiologist looking at a new strain of smallpox under a microscope. Scientists were generic to him, yet here they were categorized into multiple species: Chemistry, Biology, Physics, Physiology. Why wasn't Literature equivalently divided into Fiction, Poetry and Drama? Maybe that boosted his own grandeur as the only man of letters invited to Stockholm, but he liked company.

Also, he felt obscurely disappointed in the simple end to the dubious Dr. Nelson Gregory's story. He had hoped that it would be different. "What do you think this means?"

"I don't know," Gregory admitted. "I just don't know. Is it possible that I forgot something? Or everything." Surely he must have spent time in a laboratory, developed some formulas, issued some paper, even if it was with the idiot savant nature of the artist. He must have said something to the journalists who besieged him besides, "Genius always looks easy." Instead, all he recalled of the decades that must have passed since his cab ride was the burning which preceded the cab ride, which must have incinerated the intervening years until all that was left was a flame of the wrong color. "Is this some form of Alzheimer's? Maybe while I'm here I should ask the other doctors."

"Work is life." Literature tried to comfort the increasingly incoherent and hysterical Molecular Biology. "I spend years on a book and don't see my children. Then the book is finished and the children are grown."

"You don't understand," Gregory practically wailed, drawing sidelong glances from as far down the table as the three-member team of Chemists and the solo practitioner of Physics although the Peaceful shaman refused to be distracted from a ceremony he was conducting over the soul of the fish he was about to devour as waiters served the laureates one by one in reverse alphabetical order. "I'm one of the children, and I'm grown, but I don't remember a thing. Where did the years go?"

"That's the real secret of aging," Literature sighed sagaciously. "Everyone remains twenty in their heart."

"I'm not talking about my heart, which, incidentally, my physician tells me is like a balloon about to pop. I'm talking about my body. Did I get married? Divorced? Did I ever move out of that dump on Isabel Street? Did I have a life?"

Gesticulating more and more frantically so that even the king peered inquisitively down the dais, Nelson Gregory's arm smacked into a young waiter about to serve him his own plateful of trout almondine. The fish's yellow sauce and a few seared slivers of almond slopped over the edge of the gilded china and landed on his shoulder.

"You idiot!"

"I'm terribly sorry, sir."

Something about the waiter's pale complexion and high forehead was familiar. And his tone of voice: though the words were deferential, his eyes shone with mockery.

"Haven't we met? Someplace else. A long time ago."

"I don't see how, sir."

"Don't 'sir' me, you . . . you . . ."

"What, sir?"

"You . . ." Gregory's lungs were congested and his breath came faster and faster, as fast as an out-of-control taxicab, and with a whiff of rank regret that Physiology, commonly known as Medicine, recognized as mortality. Molecular Biology needed more than a Heimlich, but he couldn't focus on his condition or even his surroundings. Instead, all he noticed amid the glittering surfaces of the banquet hall was a faint shadow blueing the smooth-cheeked waiter's chin. "You . . . youth," he blurted the worst word he knew.

"Yes, sir." The waiter smiled, because he was planning to attend a real bash after this old folks' shindig adjourned. He'd be the life of the party, regaling his friends with tales of the outrageous behavior of the intelligentsia. He scanned the room and winked at a waitress dressed in a low-cut Scandinavian peasant blouse. Indeed, the waitress came as if a summons had been sent, but she brushed right past the callow waiter and patted the elderly laureate's wheezing chest.

Gregory felt dizzy and disoriented, yet the waitress's bosom leaning against him was a delight, and, goddamn it, it was his, because he had given up everything else to obtain it, and deserved it. Youth was miserable; youth was poor. The only real aphrodisiacs were power and money and renown. He had no dreams left; they were all fulfilled. He felt a numbness ascend his own chest and constrict his throat. Nelson Gregory's days might be numbered; his hours might be numbered, but they were good. His minutes.

The waitress turned on the waiter and said, "You thug, Nicky."

"Nicky?" Dr. Gregory gasped.

"Yes, sir?"

"Shave, you little fucker!"

"As you request, sir," the waiter replied, smiling because he had no intention of obeying the elderly scientist's ludicrous, last command.

"And you, you, scribbler."

"Yes," Literature answered, without the "sir." Even if Molecular Biology was dying, he too had a keen sense of stature. He would treat his peer with respect, but not servility.

"Do you know what I think?"

Without missing a beat, Literature meaningfully repeated his initial reply. "Yes."

"No," Gregory gasped as he blinked in and out of consciousness, heart athrob, arteries ready to explode. The waiter had youth and vigor and years of youth and vigor ahead of him, but Gregory finally understood that aspiration was easy; genius was hard, and he had won it the only way he could, at the greatest possible expense—and wouldn't have it any other way.

Unrepentant to the end, he said, "You couldn't possibly know what I think, what I really think. What I really think is that I'm the luckiest man in the world. It was worth it."

"Yes," Literature sighed.

"How would you know?"

In response to the strange truth or the stranger lie that denigrated all of them, Literature pushed his chair back from the table, as if to flee from the shabby spectacle beside him or to summon Economy and Peace and Physics and Physiology and the Chemistry triumvirate to join him in evicting the fraud from their august assembly.

Eyes fluttering, Molecular Biology looked down, under the dais, where beneath the fringe of tablecloth he saw Literature's foot encased in a white plaster cast, and, extending from there to the podium where the king congratulated them all as the banquet hall broke into hearty applause, a long row of broken feet.

The King hobbled off the platform on his crutches.

Filophilia

——

YOU DO WHAT YOU HAVE TO DO TO FEEL WHAT YOU MUST. Sometimes a man will go to a hardware store and buy a tool, a router, say, which he'll unpack and never use, but just enjoy, because it's there in his basement, because the molding of wood is an idea that gives him a deep, enduring pleasure. Even if he never accomplishes a perfect ogee, the concept of the curvature of pine satisfies him. That's harmless and we can smile at the indulgence with . . . indulgence. But sometimes the indulgence is more provocative.

Sometimes it's a midnight phone call to an old friend or an old lover, and the meaningfulness of the call to the caller will frighten the one who's been called, because he may think he's safe in his new life, the most vital characteristic of which is that it proceeds without you. You evoke a past better left untouched when you finger a number that by all rights you should not have, preferably on a dial that glows in the dark. You do not even know what state the area code represents or what time it is there. It's a number that a judge in a court has told you that you had better not dial.

Though criminal, obsession is, nonetheless, comprehensi-ble, within the range of normal human behavior, because everyone's felt such need—even if almost everyone has wisely refrained from acting upon it. But what about the needs that few feel and fewer still fulfill? Now we cross an interesting boundary, enter a different territory, where there's no area code.

Now we must consider an act that everyone—judges, lawyers, neighbors—considers vile, taboo, a trespass of basic moral posture. Sometimes it's killing teenagers and eating their hearts. That's bad. I know that. I agree. I have incorporated the values of my civilization, some of them, to some extent. I have no craving to devour anyone's heart. I have more rarefied tastes.

What if the loathsome pursuit—and capture—hurts no one? Why then is it so universally condemned? Rationally, irrationally, I don't know. Something is encoded in the genes for the benefit of the species, something which only I—is it possible?—only I— are there others?—can say has served its day—to keep humanity from devolving into brutes with curly tails and no brains— because now there's birth control.

What a nice term. I've used pills, spermicidal sprays and unguentined plastic devices. Tiny copper coils were inserted inside my body by doctors who would have rather inserted . . . no, that's speculation. That's suburbia.

No, it probably happens in the city too, with judges and lawyers.

The fact is that now we can indulge.

Indeed, some of us must.

Some of us do.

Some of us say, "Wallace, come here."

FATHERLESS, FRIENDLESS, weak-chinned, eleven years old and hardly able to read, Wallace comes when his mother calls him. He gallops across the low-ceilinged room, blocking the television, which is always on, casts a swift shadow. He leaves his notebooks: Colonial Jamestown, Elementary Mathematics, Earth Science. His class is gathering and categorizing leaves, discovering observation and method for themselves. He is "slow," but he knows what wisdom is. He does not look past the undusted Venetian blinds to see if the neighbors are watching. This house, the neighbors are always watching.

"Wallace, come here."

"Coming, Mother."

THE VERY WORD is an accomplishment. "What have you done in this world?" they may ask in court mundane or celestial, and my instantaneous reply, assured as a duchess, will be: "Him. I made him. Whatever he is."

And I will do anything to make him happy—even if it makes me happy too.

THE DAY THAT BOY beat up my Wallace, I felt no hesitation. I did not sob and fret. I went out and beat him, not Wallace, though a different mother might thrash her own son from misdirected humiliation. I beat the other boy, the neighbor boy, with a garbage can lid. It rang on his five-year-old skull like a heavenly cymbal. Then I drove him into the basement with my shoulder, frail and brassiered. His ear swelled up, and I hit him again as he cringed and pled mercy.

"Please, did you say?" I taunted him. "Wallace said 'please' and begged you not to bloody his lip. It's fat now and tender," and I hit him with objects from deep storage, things that had once served a domestic function, first a broom and then a router.

I picked up a brick left over from when the patio with the built-in barbecue was constructed, and I would have hit him again if his yelps had not summoned his parents, both of them, a man with a moustache and a woman with a hat, who swore at me and dragged him away. What was she doing wearing a hat in the middle of the day anyway? I followed them to the perimeter of my property and stood with the brick, and then I heaved it through my own living room window, and left the splintered glass to remind them forever of their own son's tendencies.

THE POLICE COME here frequently. They know the address, the area code. Wallace and I seem to have problems with the community. But our taxes are paid. The lawyer takes care of that as long as I promise to cease making awkward phone calls. I never see accounts. I receive checks. I pay bills, occasionally on time.

Their blue lights illuminate the crumbling driveway and barbecue, and they voice the same suspicious inquiries as always. But I say, "No warrant, no entry." I know my rights.

After they leave, I say, "Come here, Wallace."

HIS LIP WAS BLUE and thick as an earthworm. I dabbed antiseptic cream on it, but he winced. I knew of only one more sure cure, but for a moment I hesitated. For whom?

For them? To satisfy their notion of who I should be?

I have an obligation, because no tie is tighter, no bond stronger, no glue stickier. I clamped my own lips down upon his wound to draw the poison from his flesh.

Wallace murmured and his eyes rolled up inside his head as I drank of his fluids as he had once mine. I might as well have inserted a syringe into my pulse, strung a clear plastic tube from wrist to mouth. Circulation of the blood. The taste was delicious. We were one.

I HAD GIVEN HIM my breast half a decade ago, when another man who played stupid games with tools shared the twin cones that grew from my rib cage, items of flagrant, mysterious appeal. If I saw them in the freezer at the supermarket, I would pass them by for the veal that I find more seductive. But there's no accounting for tastes; the cones served their purpose when they were not so large, but more refined in angle and texture, when their tips pointed north, like soft magnetic needles.

No man has seen those breasts since Wallace's first teeth, nibs barely protruding from his pink gums, created a cavity of blood beneath their dimpled surfaces. In those days, I lay back against the tasseled brown velvet couch in the living room and cried for pleasure. The hunger he felt—that slight, uncharmed child.

My shoulder was bruised where it had jammed the neighbor child's chin. The strap of brassiere was burning my skin, as if a film of gasoline were brushed down the blades and across my back and over my shoulders to form twin bull's-eyes on my bosoms, and set aflame. I quenched the flame. The air was cool. I offered Wallace the only comfort I could. Just like I had five, or was it five hundred, years ago. Or five million? I always thought I could have become an archaeologist.

WALLACE DID NOT wish to return to school the next day. The guidance counselor reported to me. Wallace was afraid, so I had to give him strength.

So I did. The guidance counselor called again, because he thought something was "wrong." We don't shy away from words in this age, There is none of the between-the-lines delicacy that gave *Five Smooth Stones* its scandalous flavor in my youth. I know how to read, even if Wallace cannot distinguish *here* from *hear* or even *to* from *too* from *two*. We don't need two; we are one.

The counselor thinks I'm an idiot, but I have a degree. I studied algebra. I knew what I had to do.

Every day. On the same couch, now threadbare, untasseled and stained.

ALONE WE LIVED, and the neighbors peeked through the slats of the dirty Venetian blinds in order to witness my nudity while I held him, that no longer tiny, incandescent creature.

He was so hungry. I was a fertile field. There was no scarecrow to chase him.

NEIGHBOR MEN, all but the father with the moustache, offered their tools when they saw me, dressed in Bermuda shorts and a halter top, attempting to maintain the premises. For more than a year I mowed the lawn, cleaned the barbecue. There I was, crawling across the shingles, dredging gutters, tossing handfuls of rotted sycamore leaves from the holes they had plugged, causing overflows and leaks.

I spurned their offers, but I couldn't stop the leaks. Tears of rusty brown water streaked the wallboards. Floorboards buckled, mildew spread.

Wallace and I moved into the basement, searching out the depths to escape from the encroaching damp. It has a stall shower like a vertical coffin and a miniature stove and sink, so that I felt like I was living in one of the dollhouses my own father—a thin, brown goatee—once purchased for me when I was Wallace's age.

A parabolic volume of snow drifted through the living room window, but the basement was insulated right down to China, except for one air well with one window. The light at night must have been like the glow on a telephone.

Our new subterranean dwelling bothered the neighbors, but they are easily bothered by many things—more every day—like the quarter acre of grass, knee-high, spread with wildflowers come the spring, which come summer began to spread creepers up the brick wall of the untended barbecue where steaks ought to be dripping fat onto hot coals. Instead, the blind plant growth probes at the mortar with tentacles with tiny puckers like octopuses. The mortar seeps out and accumulates in tiny drifts like snow, which returns come winter.

"Appalachia," they whisper disdainfully, and in the supermarket when I shop for veal—for even a mother must eat—their women—no different, no different, no different no matter what they think—shun me.

But I don't care. I enter the house, ignore the loosened and scattered strips of parquet, the befungused couch, as I skip down the stairs to the basement. It has one bed.

HE HAD TO GO to school or else yet another authority, a man or a woman who wears a hat and walks like a man with a clipboard tucked under her arm, would appear unwanted in our lives. Every morning I gave him strength and every day they made fun of him, all of them except for the boy who beat up my Wallace. He fled whenever I stepped outside to examine my property.

Wallace didn't mind, but kept the same sweet, baffled expression and displayed the same intractable inability to read and to count.

Six, seven, eight—Wallace grew and struggled, and I read primers to him. "Go, dog, go."

Together we tried to memorize multiplication tables with flash cards dealt across a converted shop bench under a pegboard. "Three times three equals nine. Three times four equals twelve. Three time five equals fifteen." I tried to teach him about the world beyond the basement, because I believed that was how I was supposed behave.

But when he'd stare at the numbers as if they were ancient hieroglyphics, I was the one who learned that none of those numbers mattered. Add, subtract, divide or multiply, whichever process you choose, all digits always reduce to one, the only truly prime number.

Wallace was sated by his daily dose of sacramental fluid, but I wasn't. The more he taught me, the more I understood my ignorance. The more I fed him, the hungrier I grew.

THE MAN WITH the moustache offered to feed me during one of my less frequent fits of responsibility. I was examining my property when he shocked me by speaking from the opposite side of the shrubs he had planted between his yard and mine. His moustache through the foliage reminded me of a centipede.

Then he was gone and then he reappeared by my side—no clipboard—safe.

He had circled, and strode calmly forward to investigate the remains of the barbecue, collapsed in on itself.

"Can't fix that," he said.

"Can't fix anything," I replied.

"Can fix some things," he said, and moved hands forward.

He was offering me relief, though I knew it was wrong. I ought to have scorned him, but once again I felt the boiling deep inside me, like the broth of the guts of a witch at the stake.

Flat, shielded by shrubs, vines and the ruined barbecue, I obliged, in hopes of cooling the heat. Hairs bristled, a wild boar, snuffling and grunting.

I was on fire, but he was consumed; I was unconsumable— at least by his light. And unlike a witch, I was not lashed down by hemp. I was tied only by thin, insignificant strands of propriety. I watched the invisible strands fray then fly apart. My hand spidered across the ground. I took a brick.

WALLACE TURNED TEN—one plus zero.

He attended a "special" class with children who gibbered and wet their pants.

A recording informed me that the phone number I dialed had been changed, and that the new number was not listed. I knew then that the checks wouldn't come anymore and the bills would come due, but I didn't care.

The house next door was for sale.

In the supermarket, I learned to slide plastic-wrapped packages of veal under my skirt. Still I was hungry. Doesn't that count?

Letters with official seals piled high. The telephone ceased to work, but the dial still glowed, until the electricity was shut off.

Only water remained, the damp from the living room coming down, puddling at the feet of our bed with no place to drain, and the shower springing on the inexorable power of its flow from the main from the reservoir from the sky from the ocean in an eternal go-around.

AND WHAT IF I ATE? Finally. After years of yearning. It took as long from the day Wallace's lip was bruised until the day of dominion as it had from the day that smiling, squirming beast appeared out of my belly until the day his lip was bruised.

Eleven. One plus one. The logic was impeccable.

A night when nothing out of the ordinary happened, when none of the neighbor boys made faces at our solitary window and none of the fathers next door spied upon that window with his binoculars.

I looked at the moon and became an enemy to all that's defined as sane in the world. "Wallace, come here," I said.

Although the hour was late, he thought this was merely a variation on our daily ritual, and he drank deeply. For the first time, Wallace was wrong. This was no midnight snack, no indulgence. It was time for a meal more nourishing than the raw veal we had been eating for weeks. I felt his head, hair thinning, scalp smooth. It was wonderful, as always, but . . . my fingers felt something new as they roamed over his pate, traced his ear, cupped his chin and discovered—hair. Not a bristle, but a wisp.

Invisible in the light of day. A glowing filament in the dark.

For the first time, the well did not slake our thirst.

JEANS ON THE FLOOR—whose?—Colonial Jamestown by the bed—his. The traditional preliminaries weren't enough. So easy and so vital to continue. When everything is dark and there is one light, that is the direction you travel—without asking why.

"I'll show you what to do," I said.

Living with me, Wallace had not imbibed all of society's values or science's truths, but somehow he knew that what I contemplated went beyond. He hesitated. Eden grew faint.

"Come here, Wallace."

He backed off and bumped into the pegboard. Tools clattered to the floor.

"What's fair is fair, Wallace," I said.

He danced about the basement, retreated into the shower, but that was a trap. I turned on the water in order to teach him without distraction. This, Wallace could learn. Knowledge brings its own reward. Hair on the chin and a trembling from the source deep in the earth, from where all liquid flows. My reluctant scholar. Now he was brilliant.

And why is that wrong? Is there something cosmically untuned about taking the body that emerged from your own and returning it to the home it came from? On the contrary, Judge. That doesn't seem wrong to me. Together, we rectify all wrongs. Together, we straighten the curly tail. Together, we take everything that is broken and make it whole. We do it so you will have a reason to hate us. Because you have never known ecstasy.

But, Microsoft!
What Byte Through
Yonder Windows Breaks?

———

Sick of the face, which was, after all, just a face,
even if it was—granted!—an extremely well put together one,
Henry Wheelwright stared at the pages his friend Ernest Wilson
had thrust into his hands, and raged, "What? Is it now illegal to
produce a magazine without it? Does everyone know some law
that I haven't been informed of?"

He slammed the magazine face side down to avoid those
lips, that chin, those eyes, that forehead, but there, on the back
cover, she shone up at him, Absolut Monella, a ghostly image in
the distinctively shaped bottle of vodka. Those lips, those eyes
glowed between the widow's peak—like an inverted Vesuvius,
spilling a thin stream of jet-black lava a quarter of an inch down
from Monella's brow—and her cleft chin, which managed to
connote a masculine strength while maintaining the essence of
femininity necessary to represent every product from vodka to
haute couture to hip hop. It was a cleft to go spelunking in, and
Henry imagined disappearing into that fissure and popping
through somewhere under her lower palate, to tap three times
on her teeth until they opened. He'd peek around like a ground-
hog and then dive back under.

Henry jerked away and inadvertently caught a glimpse of the

rack of magazines on the wall of Hey, Joe, the coffee shop he and Ernest preferred among the score of such establishments in Pioneer Square, because it was least contaminated by the yuppie—or was it muppie, since some of them weren't so young? or yummie, since you could only charitably call them professional? or maybe myppie, because most of them shunned the city for the clean, safe suburban campus?—arriviste. But there, against the honestly exposed brick—hiding a Medusa's tangle of wires that snaked out to connect the consoles of the geeks in the room with the consoles of similar geeks in similar rooms across the planet so that they could happily communicate with their virtual partners while eschewing real people sitting in the actual flesh across from them—it stared at him in gaudy, abundant array, splashed across the fashion pages, but also beaming in pixels from a screen on the cover of *Computer World*, and gazing spiritually skyward on *Millennium Today*, and adorned with a—rest assured, false—tattoo on *Skinned Alive*, and—full body shot here—fiercely concentrated on Colorado white-water rafting, attired in a carefully art-directed, achingly, semi-sopped T-shirt, in *Mondo Sports*, and there, worst of all, in another copy of the magazine whose duplicate lay on the table. Wearing a cozy, mini, flannel nightie, legs coyly tucked under her immaculate thighs, Monella sat, ostensibly reading a tome heavier than her heavenly head, in a wing chair on the front cover of *Antipathy: A Journal of the Subversive Arts*. Henry spilled his coffee, and fled.

But there was no escaping Her. Everywhere he turned he saw The Face: on bus shelters, billboards, rippling and fluttering in seasonal poses from calendars in shop windows. Every other woman on the street appeared to have a widow's peak and a cleft chin, as hair transplanters and plastic surgeons did land-office business fulfilling a mad universal craving for the Monella look. Also, more literal replication was being considered. Henry knew this immediately when he spotted an intern eating a salami—no bread—for lunch on a bench in front of Seattle General, flipping through a copy of *Clone Digest*, in which a renowned geneticist speculated about the glories of an army of Monellas making all other terrestrial females superfluous.

She surrounded Henry like the air, except with a lower oxygen content, which made it difficult to breathe in her unavoidable presence. Hyperventilating, Henry climbed up the Rialto Street hill to seek refuge in his shabby studio apartment, apparently the only Monella-free zone on the West Coast.

There, he tried to concentrate on the article on the modernization of the Seattle postal system he was supposed to have delivered three days earlier to *Street*, the alternative newspaper he wrote for, "alternative" meaning that the writers for *Street* had no other alternative. But he was terrified to make even one tentative research call lest he discover that the postal authorities were just thrilled to announce their new Monella stamp to take the place of the flag in day-to-day exchange. Besides, he hated the mail, almost as much as he hated Her and Her ubiquitous face, and yet he could no more resist plucking the rubber-banded daily delivery out of the battered steel case in the lobby than he could breathing.

There was a flyer for a new pizza parlor (@www.vesuvius .com.), two bills, both for computer repairs, and a familiar manila envelope, his own, self-addressed, containing a copy of the latest excerpt from his endlessly growing and increasingly unpublishable novel that he had sent in to *Antipathy* only eight months earlier, returned at last with a form letter regretting that "the editors" (a.k.a. Mike and Ike, who hung out at Hey, Joe) would not be able to use his submission because of the "many fine works" submitted to their damn five-hundred-circulation 'zine, most of the copies of which were probably on the racks and round marble tables of that one dinky coffee shop, and an offer to subscribe by returning half of the handily enclosed post-card, notched down the center along a picture of—yikes!—The Chin.

Thus, an hour of crashing around the apartment later, Henry found himself penning the words that would, under his byline, break onto the cover of—who knew? he dreamed!—*Time, Newsweek, Le Monde, Der Spiegel, Pravda*—there were no limits. He sat back and stared at the two world-shaking words he didn't know he had in him: Monella Speaks.

"SHE CAME OUT of nowhere," Henry typed on his newly refur-bished, memory-expanded and glottalized PC, "and suddenly she was everywhere, as if the very constellations of the firma-ment decided to form their own super-constellation composing the star among stars. And yet beneath that celestial image known to all lies the soul of a little girl."

He loved the secret double meaning of that last verb. Who said he couldn't write? Who besides virtually, actually, every book and magazine editor in the country?—except for the geniuses at *Street.* He continued, "We met secretly at Monella's mountain hideaway that I can only reveal is equidistant from Las Vegas and Saskatoon. A contemporary log cabin, a modest twelve thou-sand square feet with all the amenities one might expect, hot tub, fireplace in the bathroom—just think about that toilet for a second [too explicit?]—private ski lift to its own slope, but lack-ing one small domestic object commonly found in every other house in the world: there are no mirrors."

Nice touch.

He paused to appreciate his work so far and resumed typing. "And, of course, where other, less self-assured stars frame their

movie posters and magazine covers up on their living and bedroom walls, there are no images of herself on the rough-hewed,
wooden surfaces Monella has chosen for her retreat when the
hurly-burly of hype and hucksterdom"—he did love alliteration—"grows too great."

Henry drummed his fingers to the beat of a radio set to the
local oldies station, hummed, "Come on, baby, light my fire,"
and continued. "Instead, her walls are decorated with reproductions of some of history's greatest works from . . ." he thought of
paintings he admired, "Vermeer to Van Gogh." But it was time
to move into the interview.

*"I've had enough," were the first words she said as she greeted me
chastely [effusively? chastely effusive? effusively chaste?] at the door.
"And I'm so grateful to you for helping me to break the silence."*

H.W. "Hey, chill, girl, and tell us how Monella-mania began."

M. "Ach du lieber, it was so long ago." (she sighed)

H.W. (sympathetically) "Six months can seem like forever."

M. "I'm tired."

H.W. "Let's take a rest."

*Imagine being alone with Monella in a lushly appointed cabin
miles from anywhere. She lays back against the cushions on the ox-
blood leather sofa with antique brass rivets, stretches [is leoninely
clichéd? gendered? hegemonic? what does that mean?] and gazes
across the meadow.*

*H.W. "But you know, for all the pictures, we know nothing about
you."*

*M. "Maybe you know everything. Maybe I am what you perceive.
Or maybe they all want me to be something I am not. Because they're
not interested in what I really am. The real me."*

*She fixed her eyes upon this interviewer and grew vehement. Yes,
the real Her.*

M. "I hate the hypocrisy, the lying. But, you know, sometimes, I

think [that's why she am, hah hah] and you know what I think sepa-
rates people from animals?"

H. W. *"What?"*

M. *"I'll give you a hint. It's not caring for the young—someday I*
too wish to bear and breed my own second-generation Monella, tem-
pus fugit—*many species do that. Not an opposable thumb either.*
With the new K-model ergonomic keyboard you don't need one any-
more. No, what makes us different from the beasts of the field is that
we lie. But you know what a lie is?"

H.W. *"What?"*

M. *"All a lie is is a desire for things to be better. Think about it:*
nobody lies and says they're older than they are, or weighs more than
they do. Anybody who says the job will be finished tomorrow or the
check is in the mail probably hopes that the job will be finished or the
check really is in the mail. A lie is the creation of an alternative . . ."

Henry winced.

M. *"Are you okay?" She is so considerate.*

H.W. *"Yes, go on, you were saying . . ."*

M. *"Alternative reality. It's the use of the imagination to create*
the image of a more perfect world. But you know what?"

H.W. *(grasping for rather than fully grasping the philosophy)*
"What?"

M. *"I don't lie. I don't know how. I'm really no better than an*
animal. That's my terrible secret. It is terrible, c'est oui?*"*

H.W. *"No."*

M. *" 'No' is not a part of my program."*

H.W. *"You seem to use a lot of computer language."*

M. *"I always wanted to be a programmer, but I wasn't smart*
enough."

Refreshingly modest, unexpectedly contemplative, urgently
physical, the divine Monella continued with this first ground-
breaking—even if totally hypothetical—interview. Henry gloated

as he typed passage after passage, answer after question, reflecting candidly on The Face and her fame.

Disdaining no camera, Monella had made herself available to any photographer, from the guy who hung her shadowed nude in the Museum of Modern Art to the one who slapped her profile on a can of beans, but this was the first time she had submitted to words in print, and the result was galvanizing. So what if the interview was whole cloth; therein lay Henry's genius. Or, if Monella could be believed, his humanity. Unlike her, Henry could lie. Yet the one truth he had caught was that Monella, wherever she was, did accede to the demands of any image-maker on earth. And the world's desire for Monella data was so insatiable that it would surely, deliberately, ignore any doubts about Henry's veracity. People *needed* this interview and Monella herself would not dare deny her public once it was out. Besides lie, the one thing she didn't do was disappoint. Monella was the goddess who never failed.

Finally, exhausted, about to collapse upon his PC, Henry returned to an earlier point.

H.W. *"You really don't know how to say 'No'?"*

M. "Nyet."

Hey, you, reader, stop thinking what you're thinking right now! This was all on the up-and-up. Anything that happened afterward was strictly off the record. Let's just say that she was extremely user-friendly.

SPENT BY HIS LABORS as he had been unlucky enough to spend himself upon any flesh-and-blood female in Seattle for the last year (or more), Henry typed in his full name and bio ("author of the forthcoming *The Real Romeo*") and scrolled through the interview, chuckling. It was sheer dynamite. He tinkered with the phrasing, coyly adjusted his own position vis-à-vis the celestial one and, with more satisfaction than he had felt writing the first sixty-two chapters of his novel-in-progress combined, set the email merge connecting his computer to every modem in the country from the editorial desk of the *New York Times* to the Monella Chat Room and punched: "Enter."

BUT SOMETHING WAS WRONG. Henry's own internal search engine cruised along the corridors of his mind to the RAM point where his fervid imagination intersected with his personal, historical memory. The strange fact was that he had known Monella. Way back when. That, more than her ubiquity, was the source of his torment. How long ago? When she had a last name, though he couldn't recall it at the moment. But if the name was vague, the sensation he felt the moment she walked through the varnished maple door into Mr. Zelasnik's algebra class in Teaneck, New Jersey, remained vivid.

Zelasnik, a wattle-chinned, chicken-shaped man with stick-thin arms and legs extending from his potbelly, stood at the blackboard expounding on the mysteries of quadratic equations while the jaws of Henry and every other student in Room 114 dropped. The brood of boys as well as their female counterparts had long taken comfort in the legend of the ugly duckling and continually awaited their own transformations. Only then, a blink after the intolerable excrescences of adolescence reached their white-headed peak, their bepimpled selves would pop, revealing the pure complexions beneath. At that moment, fat would coalesce into muscle, gawkiness blossom into elegance, horniness smooth into sexuality. But that glorious moment of metamorphosis had not yet arrived when in walked—no, floated—the swan.

Fifteen years and four months old, five feet six inches tall in socks, her skin as clear as a country lake while theirs was as pocked as that same lake during a July shower, Monella was already as prematurely, preternaturally perfect as the would-be doners of later years could imagine.

Zelasnik, thirty years chronologically but not ten seconds emotionally more mature than his students, choked out a welcome. "You are the new student, Miss . . . ?"

"Monella," she replied, and took a seat, extending legs as fine as Ionian columns out from under the cramped one-piece chair/desk-set across the aisle toward Henry, and raised her hand.

"Yes?"

"Shouldn't the functional sine/cosine valuation of x minus $3y$ squared over $2x$ cubed minus 7 equal 2?"

Still murmuring, "Yes, yes," until snickers in the class alerted him to the fact that he wasn't reading *Ulysses,* Zelasnik finally replied, "I mean, well, it's a complicated problem and I don't think you understand that . . ." He stared at the numbers on the dust-gray chalkboard, x's and y's whirring through his two-bit mind at the speed of fourth-class mail until they arrived at precisely the conclusion she had. "Yes!" He hurried to erase the wrong answer.

But Henry didn't notice. Monella's toe had touched his, and his head smacked onto the hard wooden desk.

WASN'T SMART ENOUGH? Is that what he had her say? Henry's head, slumped against the simulated wood-grain surface of his writing module, ached after the exhaustion of his imaginary interview, and he recalled the all-too-real humiliations of the rest of that year.

Foremost, physically, emotionally and even visually, Henry maintained what his friend Jordan referred to as a "flagpole that's never at half mast."

Henry cringed and said, "Anyone ever tell you that you give sophomores a bad name, Jordan?" But his friend refused to let up.

Responding to Henry's embarrassment in the gym locker room, Jordan crowed, "Man, are you lucky! If word gets out about this phenomenon, people are going to travel for miles to see those inches."

"Thanks for the help, Jordan," Henry moaned, and bent lower into the permanent crouch that would, years later, require the efforts of Seattle's finest chiropractors to straighten. And that was a consequence of merely thinking of Monella. In class, her presence was nothing less than agony. Besides the posture problems Henry developed from hunching to cover his shame, his left eye twitched so relentlessly sideward that it continued to do so even when Monella herself no longer occupied the seat a mere three feet to port. Maybe if Henry had been courageous enough to stare directly at the object of his desire and sit straight with a proud bulge on display, his eyes wouldn't have gone spastic and his spine wouldn't have curved into a question mark. But then he wouldn't have been Henry Wheelwright.

Yet Henry's sorrows were minor compared to Zelasnik's. Monella sat in the chicken's roost, endless legs demurely crossed at the ankle, while equations rippled off her perfect pink tongue as fast as other students could recite the alphabet. Only a C+ in English II, the girl was a mathematical genius who so dominated algebra that Zelasnik might have been a ventriloquist's dummy.

This triumph was insufficient to sate Monella. After school, she insisted to Henry and Jordan at the bus stop, "Trigonometry is infantile. There's no reason why we ought to have to do it. A machine can process numbers swifter and more accurately than a mind, so why should we bother? And, hey, there's no reason why letters should not be transposable into code, and documents and files. Why, the right kind of machine could do an entire semester's work in a day."

Jordan pointed out, "There are such things as computers." He referred to secret government installations, lead-lined, air-conditioned rooms with gigantic machines whirring and humming, shuffling punch cards like a riverboat gambler.

"I know that," she pouted, ignoring Jordan's sarcasm and Henry's contorted body. "But I believe they can be smaller, swifter and used by every man, woman and child. I believe there can be computers in every house, in every room, even kitchens . . ." And only here did she lose her classmates with the fervency of her idealism. This was 1973, and Monella was years ahead of her time.

Exuding sexual energy yet as ignorant of her power as a female sun, Monella was, at heart, a nerd. Had she had to wear Coke-bottle glasses, had she a plastic pocket protector upon her chest instead of a Maidenform Cross-My-Heart bra, had she been a boy child with a cowlick or a crewcut, had she had to endure not the adoration but the detestation of the Teaneck football team, she might have survived in her natural form. But as the years went on and she skipped fetchingly from Teaneck to the state math team championship, one dark cloud remained on her horizon. Nobody took her seriously.

Nor did Monella take them seriously after a certain point. She already knew everything any teacher in Teaneck could teach her, and she spent time in her family's garage tinkering.

Henry looked around his studio. Twenty by twelve, all it contained was a bed, a dresser and a ratty desk warped from the Seattle fog, with an old computer and printer and separate modem. He didn't think of himself as especially computer-savvy—especially not compared to the rest of the population on the Rialto hill in southwest Seattle not ten miles from the epicenter of the cyberage—but it struck him that his room and millions of others now resembled the garage behind Monella's parents' house. That was where, jet-black hair pigtailed behind the nape, brow so wrinkled with concentration that her widow's peak seemed but an extension of the mental crevice that overleaped her nose and lips to alight and carve its indentation into her chin, she worked. Jammed into a corner behind the family's '70 Dodge Dart was a tiny wooden bench with a few of her father's garden tools pushed to one side to make room for a clunky old oscilloscope she had stolen from the Teaneck Senior High School laboratory. "How'd you get this?"

"Never mind. *Ich kann nicht anders*," she said, and showed him that she could make the green dots on the oscilloscope screen into numbers that formed a girl who did a silly little dance and curtsied. He nearly died of cuteness, because it was just a game—wasn't it?—yet when he turned to congratulate her, Monella was crying.

H.W. "Hey, what's the matter?"

M. "They won't take me seriously."

H.W. "Who?"

M. "Sperry-Rand, Hewlett-Packard, Big Blue."

H.W. "Huh?"

While other students were mailing transcripts and letters of recommendation to colleges, she was sending off her 800 SAT math score to IBM. One led to an interview, but the second the personnel officer got a gander at her other numbers, 36, etc., he started drooling and said the engineering position wasn't available, pretty lady. Now thanks for the nice ideas and thanks for the peek below the neckline, but marry a boy.

———

ERNEST REFUSED TO BELIEVE that Henry had gone to school with the most striking creature on the planet. He sat in his arm-chair, phone held to his ear with his shoulder, clipping his fingernails, watching MTV with the sound off and scoffing.

"So don't," Henry said.

"Man, do you know how much time has passed?"

"Hey, some things never change."

"Faces do."

"Maybe she's the exception that proves the rule. Maybe it's the magic of photography. Maybe it's even her kid, but I'm telling you that it's the same face. That's why I can't stand it."

"Earth to Wheelwright. That must have been like twenty years ago."

"Twenty-three."

"And do we have any knowledge of what she did or where she was for those few short decades?"

"No, because she disappeared before the end of her junior year."

"But . . ."

"Let me tell you about the final exam in Zelasnik's class. It was five questions, not true or false, not multiple choice, but five long problems. Everyone in the class sweats it out, some get two of them right, yours truly included, some get partial credit on the third, a couple, maybe Abnormal Norma Sachs and Kenny 'Born to Go to Harvard' Van Dern got four, but like nobody, almost nobody, comes close to the fifth. Zelasnik doesn't really expect anyone to answer it; he can't answer it himself, but just puts it on the test to torture us. Monella comes into class in a hurry. She sits down, skips the first four questions, bored, looks at the fifth, a flicker of interest. Does some calculations in her head, scribbles at the bottom of the page and raises her hand. Goes to the bathroom—"

"Monella in the bathroom," Ernest sighed.

"My *pensées*, precisely, I can hardly breathe, but ten, twenty, thirty minutes go by, and she doesn't return. Nailed that fifth question on the forehead, but in fact . . ." Henry, who did know a good story when he told it, paused. "She was never seen again . . . by anyone except . . ."

"The whole world."

"Starting a few months ago. But back in '73, later that night, it was me."

Henry stirred at the sound of a strange rattle he couldn't place. Another pebble at the window. A third, and he was awake and standing beside his oak-trimmed single bed, rubbing his eyes and looking down past the azaleas and assorted shrubbery to the suburban lawn where Monella stood in moonlight. Even from on high, he could tell that she had been crying.

Half a minute later, pants hastily zipped, shirt buttoned wrongly, the barefoot boy tiptoed past his sleeping parents, and practically ran into the yard. Up close, Monella's tears formed two sad rivers on her luscious cheeks. "What's up?"

"I told you. They don't understand."

It took a lot of sobbing before Henry figured out that "they" was Hewlett-Packard, with whom she had had another failed interview after she skipped out on the final exam. "They can't see through . . . this." She gestured from neck downward, inviting Henry to look and share her suffering.

Another girl might have gotten angry and embraced the early feminism of those days, but Monella didn't have time to change the world, at least not politically. After one too many rejections, she made a momentous decision. She didn't tell her parents and certainly not her teachers or the psychiatrists they surely would have referred her to, but she did tell Henry. "Henry," she said, "this is the last you will see of me in this program."

He didn't understand what she meant, but later that night she stole the Dodge Dart with the Slant-6 engine, seat-belted the oscilloscope into the passenger seat and vanished entirely off the face of the earth.

"That was the last I saw of her until . . ."

"Until?"

"Until this." He waved the postcard of a chin from *Antipathy* in the air, forgetting that he was on the phone.

"Did you tell anybody else?"

"That's the weird thing. I tried to get in touch with one of the old gang, somebody who might remember. Wait a minute, I want to make myself a screwdriver." Henry padded over to the refrigerator, where a single bottle of nameless-brand vodka met last week's instant orange juice, and returned to the phone. "Where was I?"

"The weird thing."

"Yeah, Kenny Van Dern died of a freak heart attack in Cambridge the week before his graduation. Norma Sachs was in an automobile accident twelve years ago and has been in a coma ever since. Laura Westland and Steven Gilbert got married and went to Mexico, where they were both killed in a peasant uprising. My old friend Jordan . . . it's too horrible to tell. You want to know the rest?"

"I don't get it."

"Every single member of Zelasnik's class is dead—well, Norma's effectively dead—besides me and . . . her."

"Spooky."

"No shit."

"What about Zelasnik?"

"That's even weirder. I couldn't get in touch with him, but I found out where he is."

"Yeah?"

"Here."

"Here?"

"Stop repeating what I say. Well, almost here. He's up there." Henry pointed to the Seattle hills, and realized that Ernest couldn't see through the telephone lines. "In Redmond."

"In Redmond?"

"I want an echo, I'll go to Mount Washington. Yep, he's a guru for, well, you know who." A chill ran down Henry's spine. "Prognosticates for the highest of the high. Old chicken-legs did okay for himself, but I sure can't get through to him."

"Not with all your journalistic savvy?" Ernest pressed the remote to change channels.

"What's that?" Henry jumped.

"What's what?"

"I heard something."

"Not here, bubby."

"It sounded like a pebble. I've got to . . ." Henry walked across his studio to the window just as another small object came flying through the glass and exploded.

THE LIVING ROOM STRETCHED a Pacific city block that ended at an expanse of glass more appropriate for a department store. Outside, a familiar yellow meadow rolled toward a distant mountain range. Inside, the decor was half Stickley, half Sony, and Henry felt a warped version of that apriorily warped perception, déjà vu. He hadn't actually been here before, but he had written about it. To make sure, he slid his hand down beside his thigh and felt the seat beneath him. Leather, riveted. He didn't look, but he knew the color: ox-blood.

Henry blinked at a painting in the cavernous depths of the room and it was suddenly illuminated by a hidden spotlight. He was still groggy from the gas that had enveloped his studio an hour, two hours, how long? ago, but he knew a Vermeer when he saw one. Henry always had a soft spot for Vermeers, those golden glows, those dense fabrics and mysterious maps. Nice.

"Git you sumpin?"

Henry blinked again to see a young woman wearing red tights that abruptly terminated at a broad swath of mahogany thigh beneath a frilly white skirt. He wasn't sure if he was dreaming or not, but it was nice.

"How bout some oh-range juice and vodka." She offered his favorite drink.

"Hold the orange juice," he croaked.

The girl in the painting still leaned over a tapestry-covered desk, but suddenly she wasn't wearing any clothes, and suddenly she was black.

"Them pitchers supposed t'be changin cordin to what you wants, so doan let them spook you." The maid poured the vodka and stepped up to the semi-Vermeer. "Uh-huh. Not a bad like-ness, but you certainly am one bad boy." Then she left the room.

Henry stood to shake the wooziness out of his head. He walked to the kitchen—knew precisely where it was—which he had already imagined down to the teapots except for a newsprint magazine on the marble counter: *Street.* It was the only place that picked up his bogus interview. The headline read: "Monella Speaks."

"Guess that's how the Ma'am found you, honey," the maid said.

"How did I get here?"

"Boy, she been in one holy funk since that thang come."

"I'm sorry."

"Doan haf to pologize to me. You done nothin wrong to yours truly, cept maybe strip off my fine garments."

"I didn't intend to."

She put a hand on her hip. "No?"

"Well, maybe in my head, but not in real life."

"Zif anybody round here know what that is."

"I'm sorry." He was getting redundant.

"Hmph," she snorted and turned to the sink, but Henry thought he heard her murmur, "Too bad."

Henry wandered back to the familiar living room, thinking. If *Street* had taken his piece from the modem and Monella had read it, there was still no way she could have built an entire house to the specifications of the article in a day. But why did he assume it was a day? Frantic, he ran for the nearest bathroom— knew exactly where it was—to check a mirror to make sure he hadn't been kidnapped and put in a coma or on cryogenic ice for several years, but as soon as he opened the door of the facility that was as large as his entire apartment, he knew before the light went on—which occurred before he could touch the switch—what he would see: nothing. There were no mirrors in Monella's house.

Backing out of the bathroom, he confronted more creepy black squares that kept turning into illuminated canvases as he padded the hallways. None were too esoteric, each one immediately recognizable, but not because Henry's frame of reference was so vast. Rather it seemed as if the gallery were strictly a function of his own personal knowledge, summoning forth images from Teaneck High art appreciation class. The *Mona Lisa, Starry*

Night, American Gothic burst into display as he passed as if the black squares were ransacking his memory, just as music emerged from hidden speakers to play Henry's own personal favorites—was that The Doors in the background?

Somehow the house embodied visually, aurally, even tactilely all of the references that shuttled around inside his head. Surrounded by the stuff of himself, he felt alternately lulled and uneasy, because there was no longer any boundary between his imagination and the world. For a second he wondered if this was what it was like to be dead, and immediately the painting before him, something by Hieronymus Bosch, came to life and the skeletal figures started dancing. Instead of being pleased by this immediate response to his unspoken reverie, Henry fled back to the living room, where he closed his eyes and thought, "Let the mountains disappear. I want to see whatever is really, really there." And the windows that once overlooked a meadow midway between Las Vegas and Saskatoon turned into a lake that lapped gently at the footings beyond a paving-stone patio to which the doors slid open obligingly as he approached.

"Nother?" The maid waited on the terrace with a pitcher on a silver salver.

But all Henry wanted was to know where his hostess was and how she could do all this. He looked around at the dark eaves of the enormous house and said, "The modeling business must be good."

"Not this good, honey."

"What's your name?"

"Whatever you wants it to be."

"I want it to be whatever it is." In this strange place where every dream came true, he yearned for nothing more than truth itself. A modest request.

"Miranda."

"Well, then, why don't you tell me what is going on, Miranda?"

"I tol you all that I kin."

"Does this happen for everyone here?"

"I doan know. We ain't never had nobody else."

"Nobody?"

"You is one red-letter day, child."

"How long was I unconscious?"

"Bout fifteen minutes."

He looked at her, and believed her. "So, um . . ."

"You wants to know what the story be?"

"Yes," he sighed gratefully.

"You here. You the story. You got the run of the place. You go where you want, do what you like. I kin give you the menu."

"Menu?" Henry perked up.

"I useta work shoat oder. Got any complaints?"

"No."

"Like I said, you gots the run of the place, cept for Miss M.'s private chambers."

"And where might they be?"

"Uh-uh." She shook her head so that long corkscrews of black hair bounced cheerfully. "This gig be too good for me to be givin it up on account of your sweet cheeks. Nobody goes in theah."

"Not you, Miranda?"

"Nobody."

Henry shrugged and knew that wherever "theah" was was the only place worth going. Suddenly he worried that as the paintings and the music seemed to read his mind, his intentions were obvious, but Miranda showed no further interest. All she said was, "You need anythin but that, and I do mean anythin and I do mean but that, doan you hesitate to aks."

"How?"

"Just call my name and I'll be theah."

EXCEPT FOR HENRY and Miranda, the house did seem to be empty as Henry, reportorial and other instincts aroused, trotted down hall after hall like a miner in an underground labyrinth. Intuitively, he knew the entire ground-floor layout, but unfortunately he had only written about Monella's public rooms and left it up to the reader to figure out where her bedroom was, so he had to figure it out as well. At first, disconcerted by the music and images—and was that the smell of berries?—that created a moving sensorium, darkness ahead, darkness behind, he walked forward in a span of light that traveled with him, undoubtedly signaling to some higher control his position and his desire at any moment in any position. Then he stopped.

Now, where would he put a bug if he had to? He slipped a finger under the lapel of his jacket, found a tiny speck of metal with tiny claws embedded in his tweed, retracted it, deposited it in a lily-filled vase in a niche and walked off down the dark hall while the obliging mechanical programmer behind him shifted into:

Ah, honey, sugar sugar.

Okay, he still liked The Archies, so sue him, but where to now? Heat rises. A wide, simply banistered staircase curving as delicately as a flank of calf rose onto a landing large enough for soccer practice. Off to the left, he found a dozen suites, clearly untouched, for the guests that Miranda said were nonexistent.

To the right, a series of framed pages from some book of manuscripts led down another hall. Henry paid no attention to the pinched ancient gray-brown text interspersed with strange scratchy diagrams as he peeked into room after room, each designated for a specific purpose, an exercise room more like a gymnasium, a media room complete with, well, everything, all the better to secretly review her *Sports Illustrated* TV special or the episode of *60 Minutes* on the making of an icon. Did vanity rear its ugly head here, or was she just keeping in touch?

He continued and passed more rooms, scientifically laid out as if they served, and served to define and compartmentalize, each individual part of the mind. Yet the mind so utterly clear about itself also knew that it contained a body. After all, Monella had to keep the instrument of her renown in good shape. Beside the gymnasium was a solarium with climate-controlled environment that could be set to everything from "mist" to "monsoon." Henry felt he was closing in as the rooms became increasingly intimate, as if he had broken through her widow's peak into the crevices of her brain. He came upon a series of "closets" for clothes, forget it, think Bloomingdale's, with a row of display counters for her jewelry: a collection of Patek Philippe watches, an emerald bracelet, a sapphire brooch, a ruby tiara, and, sitting on a black velvet cloth, a diamond as big as a disk.

And then, at the end of the corridor, past one coy turn, he confronted a single door. He opened it. A field of white carpet led to a bed, oddly small though certainly customized beyond king-sized. It occurred to him to wonder briefly how the place stayed so immaculate if "nobody" ever entered these premises. Even the divine one's shoes must lift a speck of dirt occasionally. But such thoughts fluttered away like a flock of disturbed pigeons, because there She was, in the bed, the widow's peak visible above the pitch and wave of a white satin sheet. The sheet lowered, past her chin, and lowered again, past . . .

She blinked and said, "Long time, no see."

"THAT WAS LOVELY, Henry," she purred from the white chaise lounge under a long horizontal window.

"I . . . suppose so," Henry mumbled, more disoriented than ever because he couldn't remember a thing. A second earlier, he had been standing and she was in bed, but now she was in the lounge and he was in the bed and he wasn't wearing any clothes and, perhaps for the first time in twenty-three years, his erection was gone. If he had indeed scaled the peaks of ecstasy only dreamed of by most every male on the continent, the experience had been so intense as to obliterate any trace of itself, leaving only the same grogginess he felt when he woke in the living room. He looked at Monella's features, the ones he remembered from so long ago, the ones he had seen a thousand times over the last few months.

"My *cheri amour*," she whispered.

It was her voice and it was her body, but something was wrong. She wasn't . . . smart. He thought back to Miranda's statement. Nobody goes in the private chamber. *Nobody* goes in the private chamber.

There she lay cooling, and her eyes, those eyes, as if they read his mind as keenly as her house and walls read his mind, flickered out the window for just a second. Immediately, Henry followed in that direction where he saw . . . cars.

Parked outside a small ramshackle structure that jogged his memory, a whole fleet of vehicles bore a royally engraved M. He was certain he had seen some of those cars outside the renovated and regilded Seattle Opera House, outside the spanking-new Seattle Museum, outside the impossible-to-get-a-ticket-to Seattle basketball arena, outside every sign and symbol of Seattle resurgent that he had not been allowed entry to, but if Monella really lived here it surely would have provided extravagant fodder for the local media, which, prideful as Henry was of his own abilities, would not have waited for the scoop from *Street* to avail themselves of opportunity. He stood.

Monella patted the lounge.

Naked, Henry stepped to the window, where he saw his own transparent body and, through it, that badly asphalted garage about a dozen times too small for the wheeled armada. The layering of images made it appear as if the garage were sitting on top of the rumpled bed behind him. He stared at the garage until he realized: it was an exact re-creation of the garage outside the semidetached house in Teaneck, and he recalled the words of Miranda: "Nobody goes in theah."

He spun around and looked at Monella and then spun around again and looked at the only inadvertently reflective surface in the house, and again at . . . her . . . in the lounge, again at the window/mirror. He was there; the bed was there; the garage was there; she wasn't.

IF MIRANDA WAS the only other sentient presence in the huge house, itself sentient with video, audio and olfactory capacities, the grounds outside were crawling with guards. They circled the house at regular intervals and returned to at least two large towers from which they maintained 24-hour vigilance, but even they kept a distance from the single garage.

Barefoot, Henry timed the regular rotations of the guard and then slipped between them and peeked through a tiny square of window in the garage door. The first thing he saw was a thirty-year-old Dodge Dart that took up most of the space in the garage, but beyond it he saw an oscilloscope, the same one he had seen in 1973, with the same cute little girl from 1973 still dancing and curtsying in an arrangement of green dots, and in front of it, back to the interloper, a short, stubby figure bent over the console.

Henry's eyes roamed around the garage, precisely as he remembered it in every detail, from mud-crusted rakes and garden shears hanging on a pegboard to a row of half-filled paint cans and cardboard boxes marked "Christmas Lights" on a shelf that jutted over the oscilloscope and its fervent manipulator.

Yet something was different, and he couldn't put his finger on it until he realized he couldn't see through the Dart's windshield, because it wasn't a windshield at all, but a gigantic computer screen. Indeed, instead of a steering wheel, the car had a keyboard. The entire inside of the vehicle, from seats to glove compartment to AM radio, had been gutted and transformed into a computer center replete with, he knew, just knew, as many bits and as much cache as any technology on earth.

Henry also knew that this—not a mere bedroom—was the forbidden space that Miranda referred to. "Nobody goes in theah," echoed in his head as, unable to stop himself, he opened the door to the private chamber where Monella's own true self lived, and the figure in front of the oscilloscope turned and their eyes met.

Glasses, she never wore glasses. Thick-lensed, heavy-framed, plastic glasses. Short tousled brownish hair the length of a matchstick. Wearing chino pants, an Oxford shirt and Weejun loafers, with a single, gleaming copper penny stuck in each slot. And worse, much worse. Those goggly eyes; those enormous teeth. In a gigasecond Henry knew . . . the horror.

Here, by the green glow of the machine, the distinctly male figure grinned and, in a squeaky sort of voice, said, "Long time, no see."

"But you're . . ."

"Monella."

"Monella?" he repeated stupidly.

"The one and only." Slowly Henry heard the whole miserable story. After Monella stole the family car, she drove north to Boston, where she cut her hair, but that wasn't nearly sufficient to fool them at MIT. She had extraordinary surgery in a clinic off the Combat Zone to remove her breasts, but neither did that work. She replaced her vocal cords, changed her voice, underwent more dramatic surgery. "Of course I paid for it with the only medium for exchange I had. Those filthy doctors. But I had to do it until I was . . . this."

"No!" Henry blurted out. She had utterly destroyed herself. Yet something remained of the girl he loved. Under the skin grafts and hair transplants and hormonal implants.

"Yes, I'm a prisoner of . . . him." Thick, stubby fingers with violently chewed nails stroked the revolting countenance. "But, hey, it's a man's world. Only this way would they allow me to accomplish what I knew I could. But maybe you're right. Maybe that's why I had to bring her back. You see, your interview was wrong in one respect. I can lie. My whole life is a lie."

Henry jerked his head back toward the house. "Who, what, is that . . . that thing upstairs?" Somehow he had known that it wasn't Her all along.

"Pure imagery. Computer-generated. It's really very easy." He/she/whoever inhabited that hideous corpus fiddled with the dials on the oscilloscope, clearly a sentimental shell for another, infinitely more powerful machine, and the green-dotted happy face grew denser and more complex. It formed into a mesh, which morphed in front of him into the Monella he had once known, the Monella he had seen everywhere for months. "I placed them in the media as I wished; it's amazing what you can do with money," the figure said as image after image from *Antipathy* to *Zoetrope* flashed onto the screen with the speed of REM, all designed with an aim to remaking her as real in the world as she had once been, when all that was left of her was the totally ersatz Monella doll that had drained Henry upstairs—that and M.

"Of course"—the voice turned strangely mechanical— "there was one risk to bringing myself back, even if it was only through imagery."

Henry knew the answer, but he had to ask the question: "Which was?"

"You. That is, you and anyone else who knew me in my previous incarnation. You see, if the truth came out, the effects would be ruinous. Think of the stock."

Forget the stock, Henry suddenly thought about his classmates. "You killed them."

"They knew me."

"But . . ."

"All except for two. Zelasnik's in chains, golden chains, of course. You wouldn't have thought it, but he really was rather bright—it was that last question on the final exam that clued me in, let me know he had potential. He helped immeasurably with some recent products."

Henry didn't have to ask who the second was.

The ogre focused on Henry as (s)he took off the heavy glasses to dab a handkerchief at large wet eyes. "Yes, I always had you, Henry. Here." (S)he touched the Oxford-clad box that contained whatever within it passed for a heart. "I've watched you carefully for a long time. That's how I know everything about you. The images in your head, the soundtrack of your mind." (S)he hummed, "And you got me wanting you," and turned to him. "I even created a personal Henry program to keep me company through these lonely years. Would you like to see it?"

"No." He shuddered.

"And, of course, you knew me too. How else could you have written that uncanny article? We're really soulmates, deep under the skin where the operating program is." (S)he gazed at Henry with a terrible, yearning hunger. "Kiss me."

For a second, Henry was tempted. Yes, he was aware of the rewards for acquiescence, but more so he remembered the girl of his youth. It was that, finally, the way the fiend had obliterated the best parts of herself, that appalled him. Nonetheless, he took pity and sought an excuse to avoid this contact, no matter how feeble. "But I . . . I thought you were married."

"Oh, Melinda is made of the same stuff as Monella. I was saving myself for you. And when you wrote that lovely piece, I knew you were ready too. Now we can be together." (S)he stood up from the console and came toward him, eyes gleaming with twenty-three years' worth of thwarted desire and several times twenty-three billion dollars', more or less, depending on where the stock closed that afternoon, worth of industrial power.

"I . . . I think I have to leave."

"Oh, no, Henry. That's the one thing you can't do. Anything else, and I do mean anything." (S)he started to unbutton the Oxford shirt. "But now that you know the truth you can never leave." (S)he opened the car's passenger door. "Come, Henry, ride with me . . . into the future."

Henry backed against the garage door so sharply that the glass cracked.

"Into the car, Henry. Now take me," a steely timbre came into the voice. Monella's smooth coo was gone, in its place the undeniable command of a tyrant used to absolute obedience. Wherever inside that awful facade Monella had once been had long since been erased.

Into the car Henry jumped, but not the passenger side. He

took the driver's seat, reached across and, in one swift motion, slammed the passenger door and punched down the lock.

"Henry, what are you doing?" (S)he yanked at the locked door. "Henry, let me in." The voice combined passion and rage.

Henry looked down: the key was in the ignition. He turned the key, and the computer that was still a vehicle roared to life.

"Out. Out, Henry. Henry, you don't understand. You are mine," Monella ranted, pounding now on the safety glass and then turning toward a single red button on the wall. "You'll never escape," (s)he shrieked, and pressed the button.

Alarms, sirens, the entire sky illuminated with searchlights. Through the rearview mirror, Henry could see a squadron of armed guards rushing out of their tower and fanning across the expanse of lawn, and one other figure standing at the edge of the terrace, one real-life, flesh-and-blood female.

Left hand on the mouse, right hand on the stick shift, he had seconds to act. If he went backward, out the garage door, he'd be surrounded by guards immediately. Ahead lay the oscilloscope.

The eyes of the creature that had once been Monella flashed toward the machine with the same involuntary twinge that the eyes of the duplicate Monella made to salvage the last remnants of a prior self had when she looked toward the garage from the bedroom. Surely, that simple box controlled the Dart as it controlled everything else in cyberspace. The creature jumped toward the panel as Henry pulled the stick to drive, jammed the pedal to the floor and plowed over the man who had it all and into the machine that may have looked like a toy but was the nerve center of M.'s entire universe. The oscilloscope toppled, sparks flew and the green girl on the screen curtsied one last time and died.

Suddenly the Dart's internal screen, signaled by the demise of its motherboard, asked, "Save?"

Henry pressed the *N* key, then shifted to reverse and shattered the garage door behind him into splinters. Bullets pinged through the car door and a guard leapt out of its way as the car lurched violently backward across the lawn and up onto the terrace.

Above, the house, also controlled by the oscilloscope, was starting to tremble. Inside, paintings flickered madly, a cacophony of a hundred different songs poured from a hundred hidden speakers and smells from berries to brimstone poured from a hundred secret ducts. Windows popped out of their casements, stones bulged out from mortar and a heavy belch of black fire shot from the chimney.

Only two forms weren't running wildly as more bullets flared into the misty Seattle night. The first stood calmly in the bedroom window, idly turning her head this way and that, trying to make out her reflection in the broken glass, while the other stood on the terrace, one hand insouciantly on her hip, the other held outward, thumb extended in the direction of the highway. Henry rolled down the window. "Need a lift?"

Miranda looked behind her as the mansion, programed to self-destruct along with its master, shook into a million, a billion, many billions of pieces, before it blasted itself into a Vesuvius by the water, and said, "You sho do create a ruckus, young man."

The whole lake was shimmering now with chunks of burning debris, and snakes of flame rushed after them, the guards fleeing pell-mell for their lives. Right now it was imperative to get out of this hell forever. In the light of Monella's strange genius, Henry Wheelwright understood how inadequate to the new world he was, and he was glad. To himself, he swore that when he got home he'd buy a typewriter, or a ballpoint, or a pencil, or a quill and a roll of papyrus, or a cuneiform tablet and wedge-shaped press, anything at all besides another modern tool that killed as it served. Besides, Henry didn't want to be rich; he didn't want to be beautiful. For one glorious moment, he knew exactly what he wanted. He looked at Miranda.

"Guess I kin always go back to shoat oder."

"Besides which," Henry said, "I've got a perfectly lovely studio," and opened the door.

Tongue of the Jews

———

CORN-HIGH, WHEAT-THIN EDWARD HAWKINS III SURVEYED the room. Besides himself and the tuxedoed black waiters, not a man was taller than five-six, and besides his wife, Jane, and the cooks preparing canapés in the kitchen, not a woman smaller than size twelve. Silver platters of smoked salmon and enough caviar to serve generations of etiolated Hawkinses disappeared as if they were crusts of moldy bread devoured by starving peasants, which, in a way, they were.

The scene was a cocktail party, the setting an apartment overlooking the United Nations. Half a dozen spacious rooms with fabric on the walls gave through to a terrace filled with marble statuary that the hostess, who had purchased them in bulk lots at Sotheby's, blithely referred to as "my chachkas." Everywhere about the suite there was the glottal undertow of Yiddish and the unique scent of cash. Every one of the short squat men's suits was Barney's custom, while their rotund spouses' dresses came from Martha of Park Avenue, who might have sewn them out of the remnants of the wallpaper, for all they knew. But this was the costume of the society to which they had striven to become accustomed and, despite their outlay, failed. Sure, they were able to purchase everything their Beekman Place predecessors did—including Beekman Place—but although their money was welcome, they were not.

No matter. They formed their own society. They sent their children to their own schools, favored their own vacation spots and supported their own charitable institutions, hospitals and museums, for one of which this gathering was raising funds. Edward Hawkins III briefly wondered if his grandmother had lived in this building and what she would think of the new people.

"Mr. Hawkins. I have heard so much about you. And vhat vonderful hair."

It was the hostess. The object of her address thought she was complimenting his wife, whose natural ash pixie cut crested above her exposed and projecting shoulder blades, but it was his own lank gray that impressed the woman who came bulling out of the crowd of bald heads. Hawkins said, "I've heard about you too, Mrs. Moscowitz."

"Call me Chanka."

"I read your book."

"And I have yours," she replied.

"It's a very moving story," he said.

"I'm sorry, but I haven't read it yet."

His pale features turned pink with embarrassment. "I meant *your* book. Your autobiography, ma'am."

"So do I. It's too bad the writer isn't here, but he wasn't invited. A nice young man, he wants to tell the world about dead people, who am I to stop him? But I don't have as much time to read as I would prefer. Besides, I lived it, so vhy should I read it?"

"Well, then, a remarkable life."

"Pssh," she waved a multiringed hand in front of her pleased crinkly features and gazed around the room at the other guests. "Oh, there's Simon. You must meet him."

"You mean Simon Keeper?" he asked, but Chanka had already ventured off and didn't return, leaving the Hawkinses momentarily alone.

"Were you flirting with her?"

"The woman is a heroine, Jane."

"I can tell you what else she is."

"You promised."

"I keep my promises." She stopped one of the circulating waiters for her second glass of champagne and stood back while a cluster of the bald men surrounded her husband. His head stuck up among them like the lighthouse in Newport harbor.

"Ned's Jews," she called them, this one group within the wider community of the chosen. They were not the doctors of West End Avenue, not the tailors of Grand Street, not the rabbis of Borough Park nor the assimilated Jews of Great Neck, but the so-called survivors of Europe. More particularly, they were a tiny subset of that cohort, those who had arrived with the address of some second cousin in the Bronx sewn into their jacket linings yet conquered the New World according to its own rules. One owned the world's largest brassiere company, another a chain of suburban radio stations. Several were in retail and a slew in real estate, their holdings measured in millions of square feet and multiple millions of dollars. Hawkins was endlessly fascinated with their drive and chronicled it in his book *From Depth to Pinnacle*. But whatever made these people distinct to Hawkins and their bankers was lost on Jane. She said, "I don't blame the Germans for putting numbers on their arms. Otherwise it's impossible to tell them apart. The clothes. I mean . . . really. There is a difference between money and taste."

"Yes," he said, knowing that it was easier to agree with Jane than not, and less likely to create a scene, as she reached for a third fluted glass of bubbly. She felt the need for liquid sustenance to counterbalance his own mood. Whenever he was near these people he grew impossibly somber.

"Mr. Hawkins, yoo-hoo!"

"Call me Ned."

"Simon Keeper. Ned Hawkins." Chanka performed her duties, saying, "Ned's going to speak to us later."

"I look forward to that."

"I . . . I . . . didn't expect you to be here."

"I have to be somewhere. One can't write *all* the time," he sighed, as if burdened by the world's expectations.

Mildly rebuked, Ned stuttered and tried not to stare at his companion. Of all the Jews in the room, Simon was the only one who had nearly the hair of Edward Hawkins. Perhaps that was the foundation of their bond. As Samson's hair gave him a brute muscular strength, so their locks gave them intellectual might.

"Aren't you going to introduce me?" a voice slithered into the conversation from the ether by his side.

"Mr. Keeper, my wife, Jane."

Simon took her hand with a courtly, continental half bow.

"Even I have heard of the great Simon Keeper," she replied.

"Sometimes I am not certain that I know who that is," he said humbly, but the grammatical implication of his well-formed English was that sometimes he knew very well who the figure from the White House dinners and the Op-Ed pages was. Whenever there was a trial of some octogenarian murderer or a stupid movie misrepresenting the war, he was called upon to pontificate. He was the voice of atrocity, the witness to history, the tongue of the Jews.

If Edward Hawkins III felt more comfortable in this room with the crowds of self-described "greener" than he did anywhere else, he was awkward in the presence of this man with whom he had that trait in common. Simon Keeper also enjoyed this company more than he did that of the statesmen and movie stars he hobnobbed with. Presidents were intimidated by his moral stature, but his best friend, the brassiere manufacturer, felt free to tousle his abundant hair and mockingly call him "Schreiber," so they were able to play gin without the score representing History.

As for Hawkins, if Keeper was the voice of these people, he was the voice of Keeper, or yearned to be. After *Pinnacle* described the worldly progress of the Chanka Moscowitzes of the world, he moved to a more spiritual, philosophical plain. He had commenced research on a biography of Simon Keeper and was already steeped in the legend of the man. He was planning to request an interview when he was ready, but he was by no means ready. Meeting the man whose works he aspired to explicate was as close as the good Episcopalian could imagine to meeting God. He felt diminished, his natural elegance stifled.

But Jane was at ease. Lubricated by Moët, her laughter floated over the crowd. So Edward slunk off to the corner of the vast living room to discuss the mine at Mathausen with one of the builders. "Resilience" was the theme which he was to speak on later, after Chanka's introduction. That was why Hawkins had been invited, as the token righteous gentile to kick off the campaign du jour. By recording these people's success, he implied a moral obligation to which they concurred. The supermarket magnate paid his stock boys minimum wage; the builder bought cheap steel in Korea; and the media czar knew how to manipulate politicians to maintain his franchise, but each sent a substantial portion of his profits to the Holocaust Museum in Washington in the marble lobby of which their donations were engraved for all time, or until the building was abandoned and turned into a warehouse for government archives. Their social lives together always involved the opening of a pocket, in this case for a Center for Jewish Culture in Berlin.

"Excuse me, everyone. Our special guest this evening . . ." Chanka tapped a crystal glass with the edge of a spoon.

And so Edward Hawkins spoke, and they sat as properly as schoolchildren, all except for his wife and Simon Keeper, who stood together in the entry to the terrace and, as he brought the stock speech to a conclusion with a resounding, "Rebirth does not come easily. It involves the same pains as birth itself and the same responsibilities. Never again," he noticed that both of them had disappeared behind the fabric wall.

Chanka commenced with a $50,000 pledge, which was matched by one of the men and then another. They did good; they recalled history. They would not let the world forget.

Yet they also laughed. That was how the evening ended, with someone teasing Simon about losing at cards, and someone else telling a humorous anecdote about a grandchild.

"That's the amazing thing, Jane," Ned said later that night, peeling his faintly sweaty socks off and dropping them into the wicker hamper in their closet. "For all they've been through, you go into a room with them and the room is full of life. Not like—"

"I know. I've heard this before. How pathetic, how valueless, how Cheeverly our lives. I like John Cheever. Not like your bug-eyed hero with the big prize."

"I thought you got along quite well with him."

"Yes, we were the only ones in the room who didn't pledge. We were the paupers."

"He—"

"I know what he is and know what 'He' does. I've heard it before, so please save the lecture for your grad students."

Edward sighed, let air into his boxer shorts and lay in bed. He felt Jane's bony wrist encircle his belly and the throaty whisper she adopted at times like this. "Cuddle?"

"Not tonight," he said.

———

JANE HAWKINS, NÉE HODGES, from a line as venerable as her husband's—railroads—had once been proud of Ned. She remembered him on the basketball court, All-Ivy, pre-law, senatorial timber. Their first home was a smart one-bedroom in a brownstone off Park, but she should have known then that something was wrong, because all of her friends were already on the avenue. She should have confessed her misgivings to his senior partners at Dobbs and Litmus; they would have understood. But when he made partner, she relaxed and they moved into a three-bedroom at an address with an awning, where the tenants were vetted as severely as partners. They had children, Edward IV and Jeanette. Ned's hair turned gray, though he kept his physique with regular squash. Then he took "the case"—pro bono, no less.

Edward's white-shoe hours had always been brutal; but he had never brought his work home with him, not even when it involved the restructuring of Jane's family's railroads, faint rusty tracks long since superseded by airlines. Yet suddenly their bedroom was covered with papers and books, including those by Simon Keeper. This was before The Prize, when the chronicler of the survivors' history was still a relatively obscure taste and, for Ned, a source.

The case was that of a survivor seeking reparations not from the German government but the French, for its collaboration during the war. But the attorney went beyond the requirements of the case, and when he took his family to France that summer he insisted on an outing to Drancy. He was hooked.

Even after the litigation was brought to a successful settlement, Edward found other reasons to remain involved in the world of his Jews. He, who had hardly ever known a Jew, immersed himself in Hebrew tragedy. He looked backward past the Holocaust toward the Crusades, and spent his infrequent free time investigating the Inquisition as if he were plotting to bring Torquemada to trial. Worst of all, Edward Hawkins, whose great-grandparents had emigrated from Germany in the middle of the previous century, burned with shame for his origins.

He set out to write an article for a law review suggesting genocide legislation. It was published and he decided to relinquish the perks and salary of Dobbs and Litmus to teach Holocaust Law, but academia was not the manner to which Hawkinses and Hodgeses were born. A tenured professor earned as much as a first-year associate. Nor could he and Jane afford the leisure of his inquiry. For all Edward's social aplomb, his grandfather had lost everything in the Crash, given up the apartment that Chanka Moscowitz moved into years later and retired to alcoholic solitude at the club that would never allow the late Mr. Moscowitz to join. Jane's parents had to help with the kids' tuition at Brearley and Browning.

And by then even law became too dry for Ned. It was stories he craved. Gradually his interests shifted from issues to narrative. *From Depth to Pinnacle* had a serious intellectual surface, but it was clear that the book was written for the sake of the dramatic stories it told. And if the message of resilience and redemption was there in his characters' lives and his pages, it was absent in his life.

He stopped sleeping, stopped screwing. He grew gaunt, as if attempting to simulate in his own body the survivors who had, ironically, grown fat.

All of this was a tragic loss, but Jane accepted the academic lifestyle with as much grace as she could summon. She attended his depressing symposia, performed the good wife routine at graduation ceremonies and made the most of the meagerly stocked bars at the huge, horribly kosher dinners at Midtown hotels he dragged her to in the name of research, but the sight of the domestic extravagance at Chanka Moscowitz's home put her over the edge. And so, what she had said about that home when she met Keeper that night was, "Not bad for a refugee."

"Cozy," he agreed, and she couldn't tell if he was sly. He explained, "Her husband was in trading stamps."

"Collected them?"

"Created them."

"Deceased, I presume."

"Heart attack in Aspen. Chanka is hard to keep up with. Someone once called her the doyenne of despair."

"Who was the somebody?" she asked, fairly certain that she knew the answer.

"Me," he replied. "Obviously."

"And you, Mr. Keeper, how do you live?"

"Recently, I must say, well." He never mentioned The Prize, as a king never mentions his crown.

"And not so recently?"

"My friends helped me when I required help, when I was writing my first books. Velvel"—he gestured to the brassiere maker—"bought me an apartment a few blocks from here. I still live there. You must see it sometime."

"I would be delighted."

"Say Wednesday?"

"Two o'clock."

AT FIRST, JANE WAS NOT impressed. Keeper's apartment was as bad as her husband's study, book-lined with many of the same titles. Jane recognized the jackets with swastikas emblazoned on their spines. Right away she felt uncomfortable, but her host offered her tea, in a glass, with a spoonful of strawberry preserves, and she sipped.

"It's not usual to find a gentile so interested in the Jewish experience," he said.

"Then I'm afraid that I'm quite usual." She smiled.

He thought for a moment and then said, "Good. I don't like to be abused of my preconceived notions."

"Do you prefer to be abused in other ways?"

He sipped his own tea and looked at her. "There's a book I'm thinking of," he said. "I know it's here somewhere." He glanced at the shelves.

She recalled the way her husband would sit in bed reading and say, "Listen to this. It's awful. Just awful," to which she would usually reply, "Your son's grades are awful. The Jews spend time with their children and you spend time with the Jews."

"Ah, here it is." Simon Keeper handed her a copy of *Madame Bovary*.

And then Jane Hawkins got a gleam in her eye, and she effected a terrible mockery of a Yiddish accent. "Vhy bother to read it vhen von lives it?"

He remained silent.

"I really must be leaving," she said.

"Really?"

"Yes," she said, but as she approached the door, something made her hesitate. He stood waiting. But she was the one who made the suggestion. He had never heard anything like it before. "Cuddle?"

MONTHS LATER, a new book started to come to Simon, sentence by sentence, chapter by chapter, and, since the writer inevitably recycled his experience, from ghetto to penthouse, she recognized every word. There was the Jewish hero, Elijah, full of angst and suffering, and there was the gentile heroine, Joan, her hair described to a follicle, unmistakable.

Sometimes, to tease Simon, Jane brushed her hair against his ears as she read what he wrote at a sleek portable computer. She giggled at the thinly disguised scene at "Malka Horowitz's" when the fictional couple first met. But then, as she watched, the writerly imagination took hold. He described Joan removing her silk shirt while Elijah wrote. Jane had never done that, but she did so now, as if defying him to make up something which she could not make real, thus turning his disguise of truth into a new truth, which he could then revise to disguise, which she would subsequently reenact. But then he started a scene that she could not possibly do anything about, when he brought in the figure of the heroine's husband.

"Oh, what will he say, Simon?"

"Read it when it's published."

"Simon, I can't wait."

He was busily writing when she lay down on the floor in front of his desk and kicked off her shoes and repeated, "Simon, I can't wait."

He typed, "Joan lay down in front of his desk and moaned, 'Elijah, I can't wait,' and he put down his work for the day," and he put down his work for the day.

SHE CONSIDERED THE SCENE he had written when she wasn't there to inspire him. Rather stolid, it read, "After coitus, the lithe young Wasp lay on the Oriental carpet beside the swarthy Jew who had just taken her. He intoned, 'You have just had sex with a dead man.' Thinking of her clean, righteous husband at home with the children, she replied, 'Never mind. I've been doing it with a dead man for years.' Yet Elijah Rose was alive and vigorous, and his energy poured into his writing as did everything—and everyone—he touched."

But this time the book was not in manuscript or galleys, but printed and bound with an early blurb, "A radical departure from his previous work, Keeper's new novel is like Elie Wiesel meets John Cheever," and it was on her coffee table. Edward had purchased it that afternoon.

Jane watched as he read down the page where Edwin Brody, "corn-high, wheat-thin," discovered his wife's infidelity.

She wandered into the kitchen and uncorked a bottle of Merlot, waiting for the explosion. Life had grown ever so much more interesting since Edward had introduced her to people of vitality. She returned to the living room and bent her knees into a wing chair. The clock ticked and the pages turned. She could say one thing about Ned: scholars were swift readers.

"Cuddle?" Edward read aloud.

"Uncanny," Jane replied, as he turned the page. That was the scene where the tongue of the Jews . . .

AND SO, AS DID EDWIN BRODY II on page 253 of *Heart of the Jews*, Edward Hawkins III knocked on his wife's lover's door.

"Edward," Simon Keeper greeted him. "I was expecting you. Please come in. Tea?"

"I thought you drink coffee."

"Ah, the book . . . Well, certain details are inevitably changed."

"Dramatic license?"

The novelist understood the pun. "License, at any rate."

"But not the final scenes. They are pure fantasy."

"Oh, you mean when the husband discovers the truth and barges in on the writer?"

"Yes, particularly when he grabs the knife. It's so out of character."

"But first they speak, soul to soul, about the inevitability of betrayal. That is faithful to life, don't you think?"

"And what is faith?"

"Faith is an illusion born of the human need for certainty in an uncertain world."

This was the kind of talk that had brought Simon renown, and Edward hated it. He looked down at the Oriental carpet that figured in the narrative. "I'm not talking abstractly."

"Neither am I."

"Oh, so you're saying that 'Elijah' lives for betrayal. It's his stock in trade. As he was betrayed by God, so he betrays and becomes God. Very nice."

"Not bad," Simon murmured. He loved hearing critics discuss his work almost as much as he loved . . . other things. In fact, Edward's thesis was so irresistible that he started taking notes.

"You remind me of the medieval maniacs who believed that the Messiah would come when the world was either all good or all evil and since there was no chance of its becoming all good, they engaged in evil, and fornicated toward salvation."

"Slower, please," Simon begged as he jotted down "forn . . . toward salv . . ." not even noticing when Edward sat on the edge of his desk and plucked a razor-sharp letter opener out of a ceramic mug.

THE KNIFE GAVE NED an idea. He turned it, saw the light glint on the flat of the blade and pressed the edge into the ball of his thumb and drew it slowly until a short crevice opened. The twin folds of skin cleaved like the Red Sea and filled with a linear suffusion of life's own fluid.

Nobody's fool, Simon Keeper had already outwitted the Germans. He had proved himself on the world's greatest stages and then again, in this same room, upon this very rug, with the woman he had glibly referred to on page 46 as "the shiksa from hell." He knew danger when he saw it, but no mere disgruntled spouse would put an end to his illustrious career. His fingers clutched a heavy cobalt blue ashtray. He had already broken most of the commandments, so breaking another would only ornament his biography, unless of course he killed his biographer. Then the foolish man with the repetitious name shocked him.

III turned the knife that served as a letter opener around and held it, handle outward. He said, "I'd like to convert to Judaism."

NED HAD ALREADY DONE all the studying traditionally required for conversion. The unordained rabbi asked to take charge of the ceremony was impressed at the extent of his supplicant's knowledge of Jewish history, language, laws, interpretations and rituals, many of which he already obeyed. Without telling Jane why, he always ordered fish when they went out, because he had been eating kosher for years. Likewise, he subtly tried to observe Sabbath.

Sure of Hawkins's learning, Simon turned to his motivation. Judaism is not a proselytizing faith—one of the many reasons besides genocide for its lack of demographic success—so it was the job of the rabbi to attempt to dissuade the would-be convert. "It is not so easy to be a Jew. One must be serious."

"Take my word for it," Ned said. "I'm serious."

"There is one more thing."

Ned unzipped his pants.

Simon nodded and said, "This may hurt."

In response, Ned quoted the Torah's commandment to circumcision: " 'It shall be a sign of the covenant.' Genesis 17:11."

"That was how the Germans knew us. It was easy. God gave them a sign."

Ned leaned back on Simon's notes and said, "Let's do it."

"Very good." First, Simon found a thick rubber band that he wound around the fleshy protuberance at the tip of Ned's penis until it bulged outward. Then he lifted the letter opener, adjusted his spectacles, leaned forward and cut.

FIVE MINUTES LATER, still bleeding, woozy with the pain, Ned, newly reborn as Nathan, stumbled out of the apartment. He walked slowly, agonizingly, forward, step by step until he couldn't stand anymore. Fortunately, he noticed a coffee shop on the corner of Lexington Avenue and Seventy-fourth Street. He pulled the door of the fluorescent-lit premises open and sat down at the Formica counter, wanting nothing but refuge.

But business was business and the elderly counterman handed him a menu and asked, "Vat'll it be?"

Nathan's blurry vision moved from the text of the menu to the gnarled hand that offered it to him to the wrinkled flesh of the forearm that bore a six-digit number tattooed in aniline blue ink.

And Nathan felt absolutely at home, more comfortable with himself and his world than he had ever felt before. Cuckold and Jew, he perused the menu that listed the familiar fatty favorites of the tribe, the gray brisket and red pastrami and, of course, thick pebbly tongue, and then his eyes alighted on the true sign of the chosen people in his time. He folded the menu with a satisfied smile and said, "I'll take a ham and cheese on rye."

The Two Franzes

———

"the four men I consider to be my true blood-relations
(without comparing myself to them either in power or in range),
Dostoevski, Kleist, Flaubert, and Grillparzer"

—letter from Franz Kafka to Felice Bauer
from *Kafka's Other Trial* by Elias Canetti

PILFERING THE RUNT OF THE LITTER OF PINK MARZIPAN
bunnies from an open display case in Stern's Bakery off Staromestske Nemesti Square, the boy with a sweet tooth and an
empty pocket didn't notice an elderly man purchasing a chocolate ganache. The boy's fingers trembled as he slipped the tiny
almond-flavored rodent into his short pants and sidled toward
the door as the man extracted a crisp new hundred-krone note
from his kidskin wallet.

The image of the emperor on the bill fluttered between the
prosperous chocolate lover and the proprietress of the bakery, a
heavyset woman whose waist and cleavage bore eloquent testi-
mony to her establishment's riches.

Girth she had in abundance, mirth none. She was torn

between conflicting impulses, greed for the white-whiskered image on the banknote and outrage at the boy whose hand reached for the knob.

Outrage triumphed. Besides, the thief would be gone in a second, the money would remain. She was around the counter in a flash, and grabbed the large ears of the young culprit.

"I've told you that I never want to see you again," she shrieked as tears started down his cheeks as if a spigot behind his dark eyes had been turned on full.

"May I . . ." The gentleman began to speak with calm disdain for the shabby affair that appeared to offend his delicate aesthetic sensibility.

"Every week he comes in," the proprietress explained to her refined customer. "Every week he steals," she continued. "Every week a charade," she cursed as she dragged the boy across the bakery's tiled floor, skinning his knees, leaving a thin red smear. "This time the police."

"No, please," the boy wailed. "If my father finds out, he'll kill me."

"I'll kill you myself."

"May I . . ." the gentleman repeated as he tapped his steel-tipped cane at a spot of the boy's blood, and rustled the bill.

Franz Joseph seemed to wink.

"Certainly, of course. Terribly sorry. You, sit," she ordered the sobbing boy in the corner, and reached for the bill. "That will be three kronen for the ganache."

"And how much," the gentleman added, almost as an afterthought, "is the marzipan for my friend?"

"What?" Frau Stern didn't understand.

"He's with me," the gentleman replied.

She looked at the boy suspiciously. "Are you?"

The boy looked at the man, who smiled to himself and nibbled off a corner of the lush brown pastry. Avoiding the proprietress's wrath and the gentleman's cool humor, the boy tried to effect a quick calculation between the trouble he was already in and the trouble he might be letting himself in for, gulped and lied. "Yes."

"B . . . b . . . but . . ." she stammered.

"But what?" The gentleman rapped his cane on the display case.

"But nothing, sir." She curtsied awkwardly. "Sorry for the misunderstanding."

Again he tapped the cane, more peremptorily. "The cost?"

Still suspicious and frustrated, but unable to do anything about her suspicion or her frustration, she returned to her post behind the glass case where the hand-lettered sign above the remaining rabbits read, "Two kronen a dozen." She smiled now, a twitching at the sinister corner of her thick lips, and said, "Fifty."

He dropped the hundred-krone bill to the counter and said, "Keep the change."

"Thank you, sir," she said, but he ignored her. He was already holding the door open for his newly purchased dependent.

"Dirty little Yid," Miss Stern muttered under her breath while tucking the bill into her blouse.

"I LIKE CHARADES," the gentleman said as he finished the chocolate and tossed its wax paper wrapper into the street.

"I like bunnies," the boy said, savoring the marzipan. "They make me so . . . so . . ." He was at a loss for words.

"Hungry?"

"Yes. I stare at the glass, and sometimes I think that I could starve to death right there."

"Really?" The gentleman looked at him with even greater curiosity. "Tell me about it."

As the boy explained his fantasy of wasting away on the bakery floor, he hardly noticed that a notebook had appeared, and that the gentleman wrote swiftly on its tiny bound pages as they walked together as if either of them knew where they were going. He kept writing until the narrow, twisting lanes opened into a plaza approaching a long low bridge. "My hotel is in Mala Strana," the man said, gesturing to the far side of the Vltava.

"I don't leave the Old City without telling my father."

"But there are other things you don't tell your father." The man dabbed his handkerchief at the boy's mouth to wipe away the last few crumbs of pink rabbit ears.

They started up the gentle ramp onto the pedestrian walkway that arched over the blue-gray river beside the ranks of clattering carriages. They left the dank air of the medieval quarter behind, and, as they strode, attained views of the enormous Castle that loomed in the distance to the north.

On the same shore as the Castle, but way beneath its position atop the Hradcany district, another cluster of somewhat newer but still ancient gray-stuccoed buildings once again enveloped the odd duo. Yet the alleys were a wee bit broader, and trees and water were visible between the buildings.

"It's very pretty here," the man said.

"Where do you come from?"

"Vien."

"The capital?" the boy gasped. So exotic was the notion that his companion and savior might as well have said London or Paris or the moon.

"Of course." He shrugged.

"What's it like?"

"Well, you see that building there?" He pointed up past a funicular that racheted skyward to the vast walled enclosure that had governed Prague for a thousand years.

"Of course."

"Well, in Vien the Emperor's stables are that large."

"No!"

"Yes," he said. "Your Castle is for minor aristocracy, dukes and countesses and the like." As if the thought of such rabble were too demeaning to contemplate, he turned away from the Castle into a building guarded by a moustachioed doorman. A polished brass sign to the left of the entry read "Pensione Opera." He said, "Come in. I always stay here when I'm in Prague."

Agog, the boy passed beneath the jaded eyes of the doorman into a small but elegant lobby set about with brocade sofas and marble-topped tea tables.

"Have a seat." The gentleman plopped into a wing chair and gestured to another one.

"Well, Okay."

Immediately, a waiter dressed like a major to the doorman's general hovered beside them. "Can I get you anything?" the waiter asked.

"Coffee for myself," the gentleman said, clearly accustomed to giving orders and being obeyed. "And . . . will another marzipan be acceptable?" he addressed his companion.

The boy smiled.

"You're certain it's not too much?"

"Not at all."

"Bunnies if you have them," he instructed the waiter.

"I'll do my best, sir."

The two of them sat, the gentleman flipping through his notebook while the boy pivoted restlessly in his seat, avid to take in every aspect of the extraordinary scene, beautifully dressed ladies and other gentlemen sipping tea, occasionally a trill of laughter rising above like a hummingbird, until the waiter returned and deposited their orders like offerings before tribal gods.

The man took a sip of his coffee and said, "Good, now we can get to business."

"Business?"

"Yes, I will require an assistant of ingenuity and integrity, someone I can trust absolutely to serve me while I am in town. Can you suggest anyone?"

The boy may have been naive, but he wasn't stupid. He leapt to the bait. "I would be delighted to be that assistant, sir."

"I thought so."

The boy nodded.

"I will pay generously."

The boy may not have been stupid, but he was naive. He piped, "Oh, you needn't."

"Yes, indeed, I need. Only then, when money passes hands, will our relationship be clear. I appreciate clarity."

The boy, son of merchants and grandson of merchants, had never met anyone so remarkable in his life. He felt as if he were dreaming. But a response was clearly required, and he knew that a wrong answer would be fatal. Less naively, he ventured, "I appreciate clarity too."

"Good. Then we think alike." The man took another sip of coffee.

The boy bit into his marzipan.

"What's your name, boy?"

"Franz."

For the first time, the man's mask of aplomb slipped. He said, "Well, this is auspicious. My name is also Franz."

"Glad to meet you," the boy spoke with the greatest sophistication he could muster. A decade and a quarter of drudgery—mathematics and Hebrew homework and unremunerated labor after school selling towels and sheets and pillowcases in his family's store—had not prepared him for this. Only his infrequent bouts of shoplifting pastries and, if the whole truth was known, magazines with bawdy lithographs and other sundries from the various shops of Prague might have developed in the child the resources to deal with the unexpected. Of course, it was these extracurricular activities that had led his benefactor to him. The gentleman required an aide of proven abilities, and what better way to determine ability than through criminal intent and criminal activity, though perhaps criminal success would have been an even better indication. So be it; concessions were made.

"Very well," the elder Franz went on. "Very well, indeed. One pauses for a pastry and ends up with a protégé. Life is full of odd twists, don't you think? In any case," he continued without giving the younger Franz an opportunity to voice his own worldview, "Now that we have a business relationship, here's what you must do." He explained the job he had in mind—it was simple—and then concluded, "And from now on you will address me as Herr Grillparzer."

WHEN F. JUNIOR arrived back home after his amazing interlude, his parents were in a tizzy. They had just obtained tickets to the hottest show in town. Hermann Kafka was so excited that he stacked a pile of beige towels together with whites.

Waving the slim tickets in front of her flushed face like a miniature fan, Madame K. gushed, "One of your father's customers just gave them to us. Imagine. The play is set to open in Vien in two months and they wish to try it out here. It's called *The Poor Minstrel* and it's playing at . . . at . . . oh, let me look . . . at . . ."

"The Luria Theater," Franz helped.

She squinted at the tickets. "Why, um, yes. How did you know?"

"I . . . I . . ." Now it was his turn to stumble over his words, not daring to admit that he was scheduled to meet the play-wright in back of the theater after the performance. "Everyone knows. It's in the newspaper."

"Of course," his mother said, though his father peered at Franz a bit inquisitively.

"I have to take a bath." Franz scurried out of the showroom and up the rear staircase to the family's quarters over the shop.

Neither upstairs nor down could he find any peace. Nearly caught by parents in the shop, he had to contend with siblings, sisters, above. The second he lowered himself into the pool of lukewarm water he had drawn, he heard a ferocious knocking at the door. He slipped down the ceramic incline until the water plugged his ears, but the knocking came through in a series of dull thuds punctuated by fifteen-year-old Elli's screechy complaint.

"In a minute," he called.

"Now," she demanded.

"Just a minute," he begged.

"I have a date and have to get ready. Now open the door this second, you little insect, or I'll smash it down."

Dripping, he stood up, looked regretfully at the welcoming pool and wrapped himself in one of the ragged seconds from H. Kafka Emporium that H. Kafka insisted the K. family make do with for their own domestic use, and undid the latch.

Before he could escape from the room, his sister had barged

in and started removing her clothes. "What are you looking at?" she hissed as she slipped a brassiere strap off her shoulder, and he fled.

STILL TWELVE, not yet a Bar Mitzvah, Franz owned one pair of long pants that he wore only on special occasions. He waited until the house was empty before removing the trousers from his closet and donning them along with a checkered waistcoat and his best blazer, a deep navy blend with silvery buttons. Alone in the flat, he tiptoed into the bathroom, which still smelled of his sister's toilette, and slicked back his dark hair with a dab of pomade from his father's medicine chest. Examining himself in the mirror, he approved of what he saw except for the windmill ears. Perhaps someday, when he was older, he could have them surgically altered.

He timed his arrival at the theater across the square by the astronomical clock on the facade of the Old Town Hall. The show was scheduled to end at ten minutes after ten, so he was able to watch as the skeletal figure of Death raised and inverted his ominous hourglass to signify the relentless passage of time. Though he saw it daily, he was mesmerized by the performance, and waited until the last gong faded to hasten into the alley by the theater just as the audience, including his parents, began to flood down the marble steps.

The alley was dark, and a single silhouetted figure stood underneath the lantern at the far end. Franz picked up his pace, but he was so eager to make his appointment, and his eyes were so riveted to the figure, that when the figure turned into the light, revealing not the playwright he had expected, but an unmistakably female countenance dressed in a man's long over-coat and homburg, that he tripped on an uneven paving stone and sprawled at the woman's feet. She wore men's shoes of a very small size.

"Hermes, I presume." She laughed and, when he didn't respond, explained, "Messenger of the gods. It's a joke."

"I'm sorry. I don't joke."

She examined the boy at her feet. "No, I guess you don't. It's a pity. Life is quite humorous."

She said this so dolefully that he felt like sobbing as she extended a delicate hand to help him up.

It was the second time that day that he found himself on the floor. He looked at the welcoming hand. It was slim and its painted fingers with blunt-cut nails smelled faintly of tobacco.

"Or do you prefer a position of humiliation?" she asked.

He scrambled to his feet, noting with horror a hole in the right knee of his precious long trousers.

"I am—" he started.

"Franz," she said. "Of course, you're Franz. I've been told you're Franz. I can't escape that name. I'm a prisoner of Franzes. Between yourself and the renowned Grillparzer and, actually, my husband's name is Franz too, but he is . . ." She paused and waved her fingers. "Irrelevant. Of course, I mean that in a humorous fashion."

He didn't know what to say.

"Here." She extracted a thin envelope from her sleeve like a magician revealing a hidden playing card. "Deliver this."

As soon as he touched the envelope, she let go and walked swiftly to the square at the entrance to the alley. He watched her with a feeling of inexplicable yearning, and his heart nearly exploded when she turned and pressed one of her carmine-tipped fingers to her pale lips.

———

TEN MINUTES that seemed like ten decades later, Franz was still standing alone under the flickering lantern when the stage door opened and Franz Senior appeared.

"Hello, Herr Grillparzer."

"You have something for me?"

"Here, sir." The messenger was a tiny bit reluctant to part with the message that still bore the imprint of the mysterious woman's scent. He tendered it hesitantly, only to have the playwright grab it out of his fist and rip off the top as heedlessly as if it were wax paper from a ganache.

Grillparzer squinted under the flickering light and snorted. "Humph, tell her that it is absolutely impossible."

"But . . ."

"But what?"

"But how shall I tell her, sir? I don't know where she is."

"The Castle, you fool. Here." He whipped a pad and pen of his own from his pocket, scribbled furiously, tucked it into his own envelope and pressed a dab of sealing wax to the flap. "Ask for Madame Elena."

"The Castle, sir?"

"Do I have to tell you where it is?"

"No, sir, but it's nearly eleven o'clock."

"Lesson number one, little Franz: love knows no curfew." He flung several banknotes at the boy. "Take a carriage. Hurry!"

WHETHER THE LINEN emporium was at sixes and sevens because the son of the house was missing, he didn't know. Whether his parents enjoyed the play or not, he didn't know. He only knew that he was at the mercy of implacable forces, bouncing from the enormous courtyard of the Castle, where he had stood waiting for what seemed an interminable length of time, back to the theater, and thence again to the Castle, and yet again to the theater. What the dialogue he conveyed was, who was importuning whom, he didn't know, but twice an hour for the succeeding two hours he was flung between the twin institutions like a shuttlecock.

After the first round trip, he learned to keep the carriage and driver, who must have been entertained by his pint-sized passenger who ran up a tab that would sustain the driver and his six children for a week. "Back to the Castle, yer 'ighness?" he laughed with a Hungarian cockney accent.

The man had thin, pointy ears that Franz envied and a wisp of a moustache. He reminded Franz of a mouse, a curious notion that the boy tucked away in the crevasses of his mind for later consideration. He often had ideas that he didn't know what to do with. He remembered Herr Grillparzer's notebook and thought about it while the carriage jolted up the switchback trail to the Castle. Only as the carriage crested the hill onto the plateau above the city did he realize, in a blaze of moonlit illumination, what he wanted to do with the rest of his life.

All of his schoolmates were bound to enter into their families' small businesses. One would sell another cheese; the cheesemonger would buy shoes from a third; the cobbler rent a room from a fourth; and, should Franz wish it, the landlord would come to him for linens, which he would buy from the sons of his father's suppliers in order to sell at a profit to enable him to buy cheese. It was such an endless, dreary cycle. Even the most ambitious of his peers saw only accounting and the law as grand opportunities for escape. Accounting and the law made Franz gag. He thought they sucked.

Now, inspired by the great man, he saw a different path open in front of him. He would write sophisticated drawing room comedies. He envied how diligently Grillparzer set his own blazing inspiration to paper. First thing tomorrow, young Franz would shoplift a notebook from Brodzki's Stationery. In the meantime, he had a mission to fulfill. "Continue," he told the coachman with the air of one to hired transport born.

He was almost disappointed when Madame Elena, whom he had already deemed the "Countess" in his head, said, "I'll be retiring now. You can relay that to your namesake as well as this," and gave him her last envelope of the night.

"BITCH!" GRILLPARZER GROWLED after he read the message.

Franz was shocked. "If that will be all, sir, I have to get home and do some mending."

"Mending? What are you, a seamstress?" The better Franz knew Franz, the harsher his remarks.

"No, I'm not . . . sir." The better Franz knew Franz, the more cautious his response. "But earlier, when I first met the Countess . . . I mean Madame Elena, my pants ripped. If my father finds out that I ruined them, he'll kill me."

"That's the second time you said that."

Young Franz shrugged and gazed at the light of the square.

Old Franz pursued his inquiry. "How would your father perform the execution?"

"Well, maybe he wouldn't really kill me. Just punish me horribly. He'd probably make me write down 'I will take care of my clothing' five hundred times. Or worse, he'd—"

"What?" Grillparzer's pen was poised and his mouth was salivating as if he were unwrapping a chocolate ganache.

"He'd write it on me himself," Franz laughed, noting that he was capable of making a joke. Not a very funny one, perhaps, but a start on the road to repartee and literary renown. "Take care of your clothing. Take care of your clothing. Take—"

"Care of your clothing," Grillparzer murmured as he wrote the line down in his notebook as carefully as young Franz imagined it being written on his body.

Young Franz felt something eerie that he couldn't quite grasp in the elderly playwright's repetition. It was as if the writer were siphoning the ideas from his head. He said, "I've got to go home."

"Yes," murmured the playwright. "Same time tomorrow." He was already so immersed in his writing that he hardly noticed his . . . his what? his gofer, errand boy, secretary, amanuensis . . . his muse.

FORTUNATELY ONE OF the windows in the storeroom behind. H. Kafka Emporium was permanently ajar, and Franz, for all his perhaps preternatural instincts, was still twelve enough to have frequent need of secret egress from—and subsequent ingress to—the household. He pulled up a garbage can and bellied through the window, knocking over a stack of feather pillows—all the better to leap onto from the ledge.

He tiptoed between the storeroom's linens-filled shelves and up the staircase, into the bathroom, where he swiftly removed his pants and set to work with a needle and thread that the store also stocked. There he was, sitting on the edge of the tub in his blazer and vest, thin legs exposed, frustrated with the thread that kept slipping from its eye—impossible to rethread in the moonlight—when the door swung wide, and a sarcastic voice asked, "Need help?"

"What? I . . ." He tried to hide the pants, but impaled his thumb on the needle. "Ouch!"

———

THE NEXT DAY, having stanched the flow of blood and paid his second sister, Valli, a week's allowance in return for the promise of silence and five minutes of sewing, Franz wore his normal short pants to his appointment at the theater. He wondered if either Madame Elena or Herr Grillparzer would notice, and was both relieved and disappointed when neither did, at least not until two very late nights later.

This time, the romantic game—more intricate than chess, more physical than wrestling—played itself out between different venues, and, more vitally, to entirely different effect than the night before. This time, when Madame cracked open the great riveted door of the Castle to read Monsieur's message, her mouth turned up in a wry smile, and her eyes glowed.

Franz furtively tried to read the text that had melted the Countess's minor aristocratic heart, but all he could discern through the parchment was a line that seemed to repeat itself over and over down the length of the page. What the line was, he couldn't tell, yet the obsessive repetition seemed familiar. He was trying to pin it down, figure out where he had come across such a deliberate pattern before, but just as he felt understanding tickle the edge of his brain, she spoke and eliminated all thought from his head.

"Yes," she sighed.

"Yes, ma'am?"

"Hmph, oh, you. Well, yes. Tell Herr Grillparzer that I will be at the U Tri Pstrosu at midnight. Or, better yet, let me write that down. Come." Suddenly, without warning, she swung back the thick door.

If the courtyard flanked by the three wings of the Castle felt like some natural wonder—a vast cobbled steppe, perhaps—it was, at least, outside where immensity was in order, but the inside was so vast that Franz didn't know what to compare it to. It was larger than the Jewish Quarter synagogue, larger than the Luria Street Theater. Salons that each appeared the size of Staromestske Nemesti Square sprawled to the left and right of a hallway that could have contained a dozen soldiers marching abreast. He saw pianos and harpsichords awaiting a ghostly orchestra in one room and a dining table that stretched into the distant recesses of another, and Oriental rugs and a life-sized mural of an ancient battle at the city gate that practically rang with the clash of bloody sabers.

Did she live here?

He hastened to follow her clicking heels through corridors under chandeliers, each lit with a hundred gleaming tapers, until she arrived at a comparatively intimate study rather like the main reading room of the Prague Library, where she sat at an inlaid desk, removed a sheaf of paper from a drawer, dipped a fountain pen into an inset inkwell and set to composing her own letter.

Did she live here alone?

As her brow furrowed, Franz felt the gaze of scores of painted lords and ladies on the walls between bookcases filled with thousands of leather volumes. They stared down at him as if scoffing at his intrusion into their realm. Yet he also felt the ghostly presence of an army of servants who must have lit the candles and dusted the books and mopped the marble floors to a supernatural gleam. He thought he heard the laugh of children at the top of an enormous, curving staircase.

"Drat," she said, and crumpled the paper into a ball. "Drat and drat again," she dropped another unsatisfactory effort into a garbage can made out of a hollowed elephant's foot. She turned to the boy and said, "How do you . . ."

"How do I what, madame?"

"How do you manage to live with this, this . . ." Her eyes

fixed on the letter from Grillparzer, which she suddenly grabbed and kissed. "This sorrow, this splendor, this . . ."

"Well, I don't really live with—"

"Shut up. Never mind. I meant to say, 'How do you do?'"

"Fine, madame."

"Fine, indeed. Fine it shall have to be. I cannot match His Worship's words, so I can only offer myself in return. Tell him I shall meet him at midnight at U Tri Pstrosu."

"U Tri Pstrosu," he repeated. "The Three Ostriches. At midnight."

GONG! GONG! GONG! Just as the astronomical clock chimed eleven, the lead in *The Poor Minstrel* tripped over a prop in his eagerness to depart the Luria Theater for his own tryst with an obliging Bohemian waitress. Actually, it was the prop he was supposed to trip over to uproarious laughter in the second act, but this time he really broke his foot. Immediately, the stage manager called a rehearsal with the understudy, and the playwright was compelled to stay because the main reviewer from the *Prazske Noviny* had reserved two on the aisle for the next day. Hermes arrived a moment later.

"Alas," Grillparzer wailed as he heard Franz's good news. "Lesson number two," he said. "Never trust the theater. It will always break your heart."

In a rush, he scribbled a note for Franz to deliver to the café in his stead. Surely the lady would understand the delay, a matter of minutes.

And so the boy who had assumed that his duties were concluded for the night set forth once again into the darkened city. He had heard of The Three Ostriches—it was notorious—but had never ventured inside the café located in the cellar of a sixteenth century townhouse. At a bar beneath the mottled fresco that gave name to the place, and in dimly lit banquettes, men dressed in formal evening jackets sat, laughed and publicly cuddled with women whose dresses glittered with metallic threads and sequins. The women freely drank from bottles of champagne that sat in ice-filled silver buckets by each table. As one large man spread his arms, like wings, to possess two women on either side of him, a gun was visible beneath his tuxedo.

Franz recalled the cramped, third-floor schoolroom he wasted forty hours a week in together with forty other little boys, and thought, "Now, this is an education."

As he was gaping at the scene, however, a tall, angular, storklike man interrupted his thoughts. "May I help you?"

"Oh, yes, sir. I have a message for Madame Elena."

The man bowed abruptly as if he were about to peck. "I will deliver it to her."

Franz felt the envelope in his pocket and was about to pass it along when he heard himself reply, "No. I must deliver it myself." This was not part of his instructions, but he said it with determination.

"Hmm." The man made a sound entirely devoid of pleasure. "Follow me." Striding with the same mechanical motion with which he had welcomed Franz, he led the boy between the tables of the sophisticated club, and similarly pulled back a curtain to an even more private alcove within this extremely private domain.

There, the Countess sat on a red leather settee, reading a book by the light from a bronze wall sconce. The title was French. "You?" she said.

"I am sorry, ma'am." Franz handed over the missive.

"Sorry for what?"

"Sorry that it's myself here rather than . . . him."

"And he is not coming?"

"I believe the letter will explain everything, ma'am."

"His letters do more than explain; they illuminate," she said as she slid a knife into the flap and sliced it open as delicately as a surgeon might sever human tissue.

And yet her response changed as soon as she read the first words. No, the lady did not understand the delay, at least not as Herr Grillparzer described it.

Franz was amazed by the immediate, palpable power of words. The Countess was transformed. She trembled with barely restrained fury and stood so abruptly that a vase of ostrich feathers on her table wobbled.

Had the playwright deliberately insulted her?

"Shall I . . . ?" Franz hesitated.

"Shall you what?" she snapped.

"Shall I tell Herr Grillparzer anything?"

"Yes. Tell him to take this trite claptrap back to the popular stage where it belongs." She tore the offending letter to shreds and dropped them in her wake.

Franz followed her out of the restaurant as the maître d' commented to the bartender, "Filthy Jew."

"THE WOMAN WILL drive me mad!" Grillparzer continued the tirade he had begun the moment young Kafka entered the theater. It was the following afternoon, and the two Franzes hadn't seen each other since the boy had left the disconsolate playwright chewing up the Luria stage.

Nor had Franz's been a night to cherish. He had walked home alone through Prague's twisty maze, as frightened of the shadows that burly brown rats scurried into as he was of the rats that scurried into the shadows. Finally, at last, he had climbed through the familiar storeroom window, where, he should have known, both of his evil sisters were waiting for him. There went his next two weeks' allowance to purchase their silence. Actually, it wasn't a bad deal. If only he had enough cash left to take care of his parents, he would have had a happier childhood.

Now he was back at the theater and Grillparzer picked up his soliloquy without missing a beat. "Mad, I tell you, mad!" the playwright boomed.

"I'm sorry, sir."

"You're sorry! I'm the one who suffers. Lesson three: never trust a woman." And the creator of parlor dramas that could not have been more convoluted than his own life muttered to himself, "What to do? What to do? She makes me feel like . . ." He pulled his beard in frustration and peered long and inquisitively at his assistant. "What was it you said your sister called you yesterday?"

"Me?"

"You, you little . . ."

"Insect?"

"Yes, precisely. Grotesque. That won't do at all. Absolutely impossible." He paced back and forth across the empty stage while Franz cowered in the wings. "What sort of insect?"

"I don't know. I suppose a fairly large one, sir."

And as Franz told Franz his awful fantasies, Grillparzer grew rapt, started writing and only occasionally said, "Slow down. What was that part about crawling on the ceiling, let's say the ceiling of her boudoir? Yes, that's a nice touch."

CLUTCHING THE LETTER he didn't know he had dictated, Franz returned to the Castle, where he cooled his heels for a hour in the now-familiar courtyard. Only after the sun began to set in pink and gold splendor across the Vltava did Madame Elena deign to make an appearance. "Oh, you again." She yawned with theatrical ennui.

"Yes, ma'am."

"Don't you get tired?"

"No, ma'am."

"Very well." She opened the new envelope, and yet again she changed before she finished reading the salutation. Her lips quivered, and she sought to calm herself by fumbling in a beaded bag for a cigarette. Clearly, the message Franz conveyed from Grillparzer was acceptable in the way that the previous was not.

Adults had always been mysterious to Franz. His Hebrew school teacher was a vicious martinet who occasionally read the students dreadful sentimental poetry he wrote about an imaginary city he must have picked off a map of America. "New Ark" he called it, after Noah. The man was nuts, and so were the customers at H. Kafka Emporium who returned a bath towel when it got wet. And Adela, the Kafka family maid, who slept half the day and then woke and turned into a frenzied cleaning machine, she too was driven by obscure compulsions. As for Franz's parents, the boy had no idea what made them tick. But the Countess and the playwright took the cake.

Talk about running hot and cold. If the Madame's response to Grillparzer's letters were to be taken seriously, one sentence was genius, the next rubbish. Fortunately for Franz's employer, this text was apparently the former. She said, "The Hotel Europa."

"At what hour, ma'am?"

"Immediately."

"But—"

"We shall take separate conveyances. Call it a nod to bourgeois convention. Your . . ." she sought the correct word, "master will appreciate that."

———

BACK AT THE LURIA, Grillparzer wasn't taking any chances that another theatrically unlucky broken leg might keep him from his assignation. He flagged down the carriage at the entrance to the alley beneath a newly installed electric marquee that made it seem as if the moon were merely one more light in the firmament of blinking bulbs spelling out its message against the empire sky: *The Poor Minstrel.*

Franz obligingly opened the lacquered door of the carriage and stepped down.

"Where are you going?"

"Why, home, sir." Franz expected another long, lonely walk.

"Oh, come on. Come with me, instead."

"What?"

"And wait."

"Wait?"

Grillparzer patted the seat. "Good things happen when you're in the picture. You're my talisman."

But perhaps he ought to have found a more portable charm, one he could wear around his wrinkled neck or tuck into his pocket like a gold watch, because minutes after they arrived amid the hurly-burly of Prague's finest, most ornate temporary residence for bankers and generals and miscellaneous foreign diplomats and dignitaries who had business in the provincial capital, and deposited his talisman in the shadow of an enormous potted fern, probably seconds after he opened his mouth, he blew it again.

Across the gilded lobby, Franz heard Madame Elena cursing like a fishwife among the ambassadors. "How dare you?" she screamed. "You fraud! You turd!"

A maître d' stood at attention beside the table. Franz recognized the type. He might have been bred for the occupation on some farm together with his cousin from The Three Ostriches. Young Kafka wondered what he himself was bred for besides bafflement and dismay.

The Countess extended her arm toward Grillparzer and commanded the maître d', "Remove him."

"Hmph." The object of her disdain stood his ground. "I am not an ottoman."

Franz wondered why she called the playwright a Turk, or if he was one, and why that mattered.

Nonetheless, the maître d' gripped the elbow of the obstreperous playwright, who suddenly seemed more frail and elderly than he would have preferred.

"I . . . I demand to see the manager," he sputtered.

"I'm afraid that will not do any good, sir."

"And why not?"

"Because the lady owns the hotel, sir."

Grillparzer gasped like a fish on the floor of a rowboat as he tried to maintain a trace of dignity in the midst of clear debacle.

"The door, sir."

ODDLY, THE ONLY individual who appeared mature in the elegant room full of badly acting grown-ups was a twelve-year-old wearing short pants. Little Franz sympathetically led Grillparzer to the carriage, and, because he knew no better remedy for heartbreak, directed the driver to Staromestske Nemesti Square, where Stern's Bakery was redolent with pastry baking for the next day. Fortunately, the witch who owned the place was not nocturnal, and a cheerful, plump waitress served them. Franz paid out of the money he had hidden from his sisters.

"Why does she treat me like this?" the playwright moaned.

"Me. Grillparzer, author of *Hero and Leander*, *The Jewess of Toledo* and *Life is a Dream*." The more credits he listed, the meagerer they sounded. "*The Poor Minstrel* is going to be huge."

"I'm sure it will, sir."

"Huge, I tell you."

"It must be a real trial, sir."

The author halted midwhine. Like the Countess, he knew when he heard something notable, and needed to pursue it. "Explain."

Young Franz improvised. "Well, it sort of sounds like you're accused of a crime, but you don't even know what the crime is."

"Yes, that's it precisely."

"And then you get to a judge, but he won't tell you anything either." The more the boy said, the more fervent the playwright grew, so the more the boy elaborated. His shaggy dog story didn't particularly go anywhere, but if it kept his mentor from dwelling on his own sorrows, the boy would oblige. He could do this with his eyes closed. His eyes closed. He was in a trance, and didn't notice when the famous author started scribbling on napkin after napkin from the chrome container on the table.

Every word out of young Franz's mouth since he had met old Franz had struck a note, and together the notes formed chords that had touched both Grillparzer and Madame Elena's heart, but this was grander than his earlier songs about insects and mice. Sitting with his bare knees crossed over each other, he conducted a symphony of misery, anxiety and regret.

Somewhere in the middle of the recital, the playwright began taking care of the waiter, purchasing more and more marzipan bunnies every time Franz paused, until the sugary hutch was empty and the tale had been told.

———

"MY LORD REQUESTS one last opportunity, ma'am."

"Why should I give it to him?" she scoffed.

"He said that if you do him the great honor to read this, he will promise to never open his mouth again if that is your decree. I will sit here and wait." Stiffly, since he hadn't gotten much sleep the previous night, Franz set himself on the ground. He looked at the enclosure that defined the Castle and the wall that gave way to the city beyond. He looked up at the Countess and didn't know how he had such presumption.

"Only to keep you from catching a cold," she laughed. After all, life was quite humorous.

Fine, he thought; let her think what she wished for now, but he could predict her next words, which came an hour after she began flipping the napkins, which dampened with the first of her teardrops, which ultimately coursed down her cheeks as if a spigot had been turned on behind her deep green eyes.

"At last. At last. He understands everything in my soul. How could such a vulgar, tawdry . . . Ach, I do not care if he is a bourgeois boor. If the man is capable of this poetry, then he is my soulmate." She dabbed at her eyes with the final napkin and smeared a mixture of ink and mascara across her face.

"Should I tell him the door will open, madame?"

"Yes"—she smiled— "all doors will open."

"Maybe, but sometimes a doorway can be open and you still can't enter."

Say what you will, Madame Elena was attuned to language and usage. She knew an image when she saw one, a metaphor when it hit her, a perception that could only come from a particular set of mind. She stopped like a clock with a jammed gear. "Come again?"

"And sometimes you don't even know what you're waiting for."

"How interesting."

"Really?"

"Yes, really. Do you have any other interesting ideas, young man?"

"What do you mean, ma'am?"

"Have you ever mentioned anything like this to Herr Grill-parzer?"

"Anything like what, ma'am?"

"Oh, any similarly curious little notion. What have your conversations been like?"

"What conversations, ma'am?"

He wasn't exactly avoiding her question, but the boy didn't have it in him to avow himself. She had to lead in their intimate verbal dance.

"The conversations you've had regarding . . . me."

"Rather like a dream, ma'am."

"A dream perhaps of insects?"

"How did you know?"

"Or hunger so fierce that you felt like dying in a cage?"

"Why, yes, that too."

"And what about a judicial proceeding?"

"You're reading my mind."

"Or you're reading mine," she sighed.

"Life is a dream," he quoted the title the playwright bor-rowed from Lope de Vega.

"But sometimes you wake up, and suddenly you see the truth that you could never have imagined. Come with me, Franz."

"But Herr Grillparzer is waiting."

"Let him wait. One Franz is as good as another. In fact, one Franz may be better than another."

She opened the door to the Castle and he entered. Together, they walked along the endless corridors and eventually up the carpeted staircase and through another long hall, until she opened one last door to a room painted blushing pink. Inside was a bed, bathed in the glow of a single candle.

Before she drew him down, the son of a shopkeeper noticed the quality of the linens.

Ten Years Later

YOUNG KAFKA NEVER SAW THE PLAYWRIGHT OR THE COUNTESS again. He grew up, and, though he briefly attempted to write drawing room comedies, he succumbed to his destiny and became a clerk.

He was hard at work on the fourth floor of the Workman's Accident Insurance Institute, wrestling with a thorny actuarial problem concerning tubercular diagnoses, when he received a certified letter. Sent by one Herr Martin Prager, attorney, it requested his presence at 1414 Na Prikope near Wenceslaus Square.

Terror overwhelmed the minor functionary. What could he have possibly done to draw the attention of an attorney? Authority of all sorts was unnerving to him, and none more so than the law. For the first time since he had joined the institute five years earlier, he left work before the end of the day, and, for the first time in ten years, he hailed one of the city's black carriages.

Dreading the moment, he reknotted his thin black tie and combed his hair behind his ludicrous ears in the attorney's waiting room before he gave the secretary his name. Instead of sneering at him, however, she said, "Right this way, sir," and ushered him straight into a wood-paneled suite that smelled of responsibility. Behind a sleek modern desk sat Herr Prager. He was a clean-shaven man with small ears and thin wire spectacles.

The attorney got directly to business. "Herr Kafka?"

"Yes?"

"I apologize, but I must ask, do you have any identification?"

More worried than ever, Kafka showed his passport as well as the letter he had received.

"Hm. Yes, indeed. This will do. Please have a seat." He gestured to one of the chairs in front of his desk. Kafka felt as if he were being called before a tribunal.

"As you may or may not know," Prager commenced, "the renowned playwright, Franz Grillparzer, died last Tuesday in Vien. Most of Herr Grillparzer's estate has been probated in the capital, but I have summoned you here as local executor for a fairly unusual bequest. I am empowered to convey to you the contents herein." He pushed a heavy cardboard box across the desk.

Franz reached forward. Inside the box were several reams of typed manuscript pages.

"But first," the attorney said, "I am to read you the following letter."

Franz sat back, remembering only faintly the one episode of his youth that was ever worth anything.

The attorney cleared his throat and began,

"Dear Franz,

I believe you will recognize the pages inside this box. Alas, I could never publish them under my own name, because my audience—fools—would never tolerate their likes from the author of *The Poor Minstrel* and other poor excuses for drama. Also, they are not really, or not entirely, mine, although I have worked on them to the full extent of my power and range for the last years of my life. Now I am dead, as all shall be, and I intend to make small recompense to the one who gave me the greatest gift of my life. You may do as you wish with these pages, but I strongly suggest that before you do anything so rash as publish them you seriously consider burning them instead. They are a weight that I could not bear. But you are stronger, and will do as you must.

Sincerely yours,
Franz

"Hmph." The lawyer cleared his throat. "Extraordinary. In all the years I have managed Herr Grillparzer's affairs in this province, I never once had the sense of a private life. That is outside various, shall we say, affairs of the heart. But this is not my business. The box is yours."

"Thank you," Kafka said.

"Oh, and one more thing."

"Yes?"

"I have also been instructed to give you one hundred kronen to be used for the exclusive purpose of purchasing . . ." He hesitated, so absurd was the very last wish of the greatest artist in the empire.

But Franz already knew what the money was for. As an adult, he had developed the sense of humor he had lacked as a child. He finished the sentence. "Marzipan bunnies."

"Um, yes, how did you know?"

"Lesson number one, Herr Prager. Sometimes you get cockroaches and sometimes you get bunnies. If you'd like to accompany me, I will treat you to the best bakery in Prague."

The War Lovers

———

"Say we lay two hundred thousand bodies end to end," Max said as he reclined on the one-armed sofa he had dragged in from East Seventh Street and set under the mottled ceiling of his studio apartment.

"Say we lay two bodies side by side," Catherine replied as she curled up in the crook of Max's arm.

"Later. What's the average height?"

"Ours?"

"Theirs."

"I don't know. Same as ours, I'd guess. Five-five."

"How'd you get that?"

"I'm five-three, you're five-seven."

"Five-eight."

"Five-seven."

"Five-eight."

"Should I get a tape measure?"

"Anyway, some are babies."

"I don't want any babies yet." She stroked his thigh.

"I once heard that every baby is twenty-one inches. They vary in weight, but not height. That's ridiculous, isn't it?"

"Ridiculous. Besides, some of the men are seven feet."

"Good point. So what number are we looking for? Average. Say four feet."

The arch of her left foot rubbed against his right.

Max continued, "I think that's conservative, but let's use it. Four times two hundred thousand, that's eight hundred thousand. How many feet in a mile?"

"Don't you know anything?"

"I'm just fact-checking."

"You're always fact-checking."

Max snapped his fingers twice.

"Five thousand two hundred and eighty."

"Smart girl. Let's say five thousand."

"Look, maybe you can estimate height, but you can't estimate a mile. It is what it is."

"We'll adjust later. Right now I'm just trying to get the big picture. Eight hundred thousand divided by five thousand is like eight hundred divided by five is one hundred and sixty. Just to be cautious, we'll take one hundred and fifty to offset the other two hundred and eighty feet in the mile. Okay?"

"Fine by me."

"So two hundred thousand bodies equals approximately one hundred and fifty miles in length, enough to circle Manhattan about five times." He sighed and imagined the corpses ringing the perimeter of the island from the slice of East River he could see if he thrust his head out his window, turned left and looked through the fire escape's rusty grating. They'd extend up past the hospitals and the UN and under River House and Beekman Street and the swells, then past a domino row of new high-rises and Harlem. They'd loop Spuyten Duyvil just past the bleachers of Baker Field, and roll down the West Side, under the George

Washington Bridge with the famous kid's book lighthouse. They'd tickle Grant's Tomb and float past the piers of Midtown, including that place where all the jocks trooped to skate and golf and play squash, basketball or any other sport you could name. Head to toe to head to toe, they'd reach past the Village all the way to the financial district and Battery Park, where an installment art piece kept solar time—and then go around again four more times.

"And what about stacked up?"

"That's what I was thinking."

"Yes." Catherine swirled her wine around the cardboard cup bearing a convex image of a blue and white Parthenon. It was a harsh, grainy red Max had purchased on sale from a neighbor who had boosted it from the large liquor store on the corner of Astor Place. Why, if Loco was stealing, he couldn't steal a better vintage, she never understood. Why, for that matter, couldn't he steal half a dozen decent wineglasses? The store sold glasses too, and cork removers and a hundred other accoutrements of the trade. While Max continued on his morbid fantasies, Catherine's mind wandered. She had heard him in this vein before. It was what had attracted her that evening six months earlier at the launch party for some Internet magazine at a gallery which featured a piece of installment art, a glass case containing a reconstructed record turntable that took dollar bill after dollar bill and swiveled them into a flame located where the old spindle once poked through the 33 rpms, then reached for the next. Everyone else at the party watched, but Max did the math.

"Forty-five seconds for each bill, eighty dollars an hour, the party's gonna last three hours. That's two hundred and forty dollars, less than the cheese."

"But more dramatic."

"I'm not impressed."

"What impresses you?" Catherine asked the guy who sulked at the sight of the art and did math out loud.

"Death," he said.

She was impressed.

BORN CATHERINE, CALLED KATY from the cradle, reborn as Catherine when a name that evoked skinned knees and apple trees seemed too, too bucolic, she had moved to the city a year ago. Almost immediately, she had gotten a job in the publicity department of a department store, which meant that she had spent the last six months working on the store's annual parade, arranging marching bands and vast molded Styrofoam floats figureheaded by former television stars who needed the publicity so badly they were willing to ride down Fifth Avenue in rain, sleet or hail as long as the store provided long underwear. She vaguely thought she wanted to "get into fashion," because it didn't seem to require any particular intelligence, and she had a keen sense of her limited abilities.

"You know," she had said to Max back at the gallery, "you remind me a little bit of Hiram Halliston."

"Who's that?"

"He's the host of *Bet a Batch—Win a Bundle.*"

Max turned away and she had to think swiftly, because she hadn't met a man in two months. "He's almost dead."

Max turned.

"But at least he's well preserved. I think it's the vodka. We had to strap him into the float so he wouldn't keel over and fall off. What a disaster that would have been. He'd have gotten trampled by the marching band from Teaneck."

Well, genocide was better, but any form of catastrophe piqued Max's interest, and Catherine was cute. They adjourned to a local bar, drank too much, wove toward Max's apartment through silent predawn streets and Catherine moved in within a month.

The decision was easy. She had nothing to give up besides an overpriced share with two other girls from upstate. They called it "the barnyard" because of the animals they sometimes found in their beds.

The first morning she woke up with the knowledge that her clothes were in Max's closet, her toothbrush in his bathroom, she toddled off to that bathroom—a grotty cavern where plaster stalactites descended from an ancient leak above the toilet—and was shocked to find a photograph of herself mounted on the mirror of the dented metal medicine cabinet. She could see half of her red-cheeked, green-eyed morning face beyond the edge of the photo, and the other half in black and white still life, eyes closed in the center of the mirror. It was a lovely photograph, its shades of gray impecccably mixed, well-composed too, yet too, well, composed.

At first she couldn't identify the place where the photograph was taken or the wavelike surface upon which she apparently rested. Nonetheless it was familiar. Of course: rather than the speckled canvas backdrop Max used for portraits of bands and performance artists he took in return for tickets to their shows and a bar tab, the surface was a pillow, Max's pillow, the waves the bunched-up casing. The photograph was obviously taken while she slept and developed secretly as a gift for her. Catherine was touched, but wondered why Max hadn't taken a waking portrait. Okay, it wouldn't be a secret, but her eyes were her best feature, round and deep and, she thought, soulful. Here they were closed. Then she realized: the photograph was a death mask.

She shifted metronomically left and right, from the photograph to the mirror, back and forth, to reaffirm the fact that she was alive.

———

MAX LIVED ON THE FOURTH floor of a once-abandoned, city-owned tenement that he and his fellow squatters had occupied for years and ultimately purchased from the city in return for so-called "sweat equity." Said equity never quite materialized since the roof still leaked, the windows were drafty and repointing was several decades overdue. Nonetheless, it was home for him for now, and more so, his equipment. Max's bed and clothing occupied a sliver of square footage near the solitary window onto the fire escape, while his cameras, darkroom and developing material lived in the rest of the space.

A carousel was set up to flash endless photographs on the walls from the moment one opened the door. Some were his; others were classic photographs by everyone from Mathew Brady to the Starn twins. He reveled in his visitors' inability to distinguish between the categories.

"Do you ever read?" Catherine asked him.

"Look, if one picture is worth a thousand words, and there's two hundred and fifty words per page, that's four pages per picture. Say the average book has three hundred pages, that's seventy-five pictures per book. Since I've got over a hundred thousand photographs, that means thirteen thousand books, so leave me alone."

"Actually, it's one thousand three hundred."

"Just fact-checking."

But the facts Max so relentlessly needed to check remained private, since most of the photographs he had sold until he met Catherine went to the *Gotham Gazette,* a giveaway publication that paid him $25 a shot to illustrate its articles on bars and restaurants, which sometimes slipped him drink tickets in return for a particularly fortuitous spread.

"I'm tired of this!" Max muttered as he and Catherine left Ilan's Pita and Burrito Shack with a bad taste in their mouths one night. He waved the last ticket good for a "Pita With the Works" and said, "I'd rather have a five-dollar bill in my pocket."

"Here." Catherine veered toward the bank on the corner of Avenue A. "I'll get you one." Not that there were so many fives in her own bank account, but the combination of fried chickpeas and cheap wine made her feel generous.

"No, thanks."

"I insist."

Two men were on the other side of the glass door inside the single room with half a dozen bank machines, but the first didn't notice the second, and the second didn't notice Max and Catherine.

The couple, arguing outside as she inserted her bank card into the slot, didn't notice the two men either. Then, just as a light blinked green to signal their permission to enter, they heard a popping noise. To Catherine it sounded like a champagne cork, to Max a book dropping. Neither paid much attention. Catherine opened the door, and the second man rushed past her. The first man was on the floor, blood spreading in all directions from his chest. Catherine screamed, and Max fumbled for the camera he wore as permanently as a wedding ring.

AFTER THE HYSTERIA and the police interviews—"I can't believe I didn't see anything, maybe a leather jacket," Catherine sobbed—they went home, but only she slept. The next morning, when she woke up and shuffled into the bathroom, a new pic-

ture was taped to the mirror. It wasn't one of Max's usual photographs of a living painter who merely looked dead, but was an
actually dead man, hand holding the envelope his killer missed
outstretched toward an ATM machine, like an ancient priest
offering a temple sacrifice. The photo re-created her precise
reaction to the moment of its recording; she screamed.

Max was behind her in a second, contemplating the image
with admiration. "Amazing, isn't it?"

"It's terrible."

"Terrible beauty," he said. "Where's that from?"

"Yeats."

"You know," he said, looking down past her neck, "you've
got your own terrible beauty."

After the initial excitement of Max and Catherine's initial
foray into cohabitation had worn off, they had rarely slept
together, but suddenly Max was interested. He lifted the hem of
her nightgown.

"Now?" she sighed.

"Now," he answered.

"I've got to get to work."

"Now," he repeated.

AND IT GOT BETTER after he sold the photograph to a real circulation tabloid, which put the image under its banner because a
clever copywriter penned in the immortal headline: "The Last
Deposit."

"Front page," he crowed.

Oddly, it was Catherine who was critical. "They cropped it
wrong and lost some of the contrast."

"So what? It's the image that counts."

"How much did you get?"

"More than five dollars." In fact, he had been paid four hundred dollars, twice the amount found in the dead man's envelope, but he was a little reluctant to admit the extent of his windfall. "Let's go out for dinner. I'll treat."

The treat diminished slightly when Max tried to calculate the per-sip cost of their celebratory *vin*—nearly $1.25—and more so when a chirping noise broke into the French-Malaysian boîte they had chosen to dine in, the kind of place that was ruining the neighborhood, an appropriate venue, since Max was now one of the successful people ruining the neighborhood. He put down his fork and whipped an oblong black box from his pocket.

"Since when do you have a cell phone?"

"Not a phone. A communications system. I got it today. Here." He pressed a button and received a staticky message, "Four-oh-two. Four-oh-two. Four-oh-two at 125 West Nineteenth Street."

Max jumped up from the table, spilled five dollars' worth of wine. "Police radio," he explained. "Set to interrupt whenever a four-oh-two comes across."

"What's a four-oh-two?" she called as he headed for the exit, as their waiter arrived with a blazing baked Alaska.

"Murder," he cried.

"What? Whose?"

"I don't know." He stopped for a moment at the door and called behind him over the heads of the other diners, "But I intend to find out."

FROM THEN ON, MAX was constantly running off to some gruesome alley or cadaverous penthouse. Once, he inadvertently tracked red footprints into the apartment the following morning. When Catherine complained, he took several dozen photographs of this cha-cha diagram for the dead, washed the floor and purchased a doormat. He could afford it; he was in demand. One paper offered to put him on payroll, but he made more money as a freelancer. The crime rate was down in New York, but there was always enough bloodshed for a headline. In fact, the crimes stood out in bolder relief, because the safer the public felt, the more shocking murder seemed, and the more newsworthy. Max's became a common byline.

He got to know the homicide detectives, the accidental death, or AD, specialists, the coroners. He and the police department's staff photographers traded tips on lighting in low places. They liked him, because he wasn't a Weegee who caught smiley-faced cops at the scene of the crime and made them look bad. It was the dead he was interested in, and they couldn't resist his intrusion into their last momentary perception of fear or bliss. Max's images became metropolitan icons. Grinning, grimacing or at rest, their variety seemed greater than that of the uniformly cheerful baseball players and movie stars who ornamented the features pages.

Like Max's professional life, his and Catherine's private life together was more successful than ever. They dined out and attended press openings and their bed rocked. Yet one evening she returned from the job she had begun calling "Holiday Atrocities" to find him sitting in an armchair, reading.

"What's that?" she said.

"What's what?"

"That thing on your lap."

"It's a book."

"Just fact-checking. A book, you said?"

"You've heard of them?"

"Yes, but I thought seventy-five pictures were better."

"Actually, this one has pictures, but also words. And not just captions either."

"What's it about?" she asked, though she regretted the question the moment it left her mouth.

"The Rape of Nanking," he replied. "An amazing historical episode. Look at this." He cracked the spine and spread wide the centerfold in her direction. She caught a glimpse of a row of beheaded corpses before twisting sideways.

But Max couldn't look away. He needed more than the temporary fix of an ODed junkie found riding the shuttle back and forth from Times Square to Grand Central for hours, more than a few teen suicides, more than a psycho who carved up three hookers in Queens who reminded him of his mother. He needed full-scale disruption, corruption and disaster.

Over the next few months, he discovered books like *Las Vegas Confidential*, a moldy yellow paperback with an insert of black and white photographs of neon signs and acres of blackjack tables and a blood-spattered Bugsy Siegel, and *Outlaws of the Wild West*, which contained myriad hangings, as did, in a different context, a chronicle of segregation in the South. He also read about the Holocaust and cannibals in New Guinea and, illustrated rather than photographed, the Inquisition, the Crusades and the Spanish conquest of Mexico.

After reading, he'd put his volume du jour down on the splintery floor by the side of the bed and turn to Catherine with a look.

Afterward, his postcoital conversation was likely to begin, "We don't really know how to to kill over here. It's all more or less accidental. Even the gangsters just seem to be in the wrong place at the wrong time."

"Maybe you're in the wrong place at the wrong time."

"No, no, you read this stuff and you realize that for a journalist there's never a wrong time—or, always a wrong time, same thing. Someone's getting killed at every moment of the day. The problem is that I'm in the wrong place at the right time." He checked his beeper and went to sleep, dreaming of carnage.

MAX HADN'T ALWAYS been morbid. The son of decent folks—his father owned several suburban dry-cleaning stores and his mother played bridge while she wasn't working on her tan—he was a motivated student and attended a good college, but instead of joining the family business, he found himself downtown at a moment when his family and the country were prosperous enough to fund a finding of one's postcollegiate self that hadn't occurred since the sixties.

His parents would have found it more comprehensible if he had put on a white button-down shirt freshly laundered by his father and gone to law school or donned a buttonless polo and become a tennis bum, but he was determined, and abetted in his determination by the fact that none of his friends knew exactly what they were doing either. A few waited tables, a few drove cabs, yet they all claimed to be working on a screenplay or a performance art spectacle in their spare time. Max couldn't write and couldn't imagine himself on a stage, but he needed an aesthetic rationale for his life that was otherwise, irregularly, justified by the receipts from spots and spatters and ring around the collar. He found it in photography.

Anyone could be a photographer; that was the great thing about the medium. All you needed was a Nikon LB and the strength to define yourself, or so he thought while year after year of his self-defined and unremunerative artistry passed.

Until his lucky night at the bank on Avenue A, Max had had to remain content calculating the length of hypothetical bodies around Manhattan. Only then, when he inadvertently came across an actual body, was he able to act on his impulses. How did he know that his moment had arrived? One might as well ask that about any of the great photographers. The origin of Steichen's interest in nudes was obvious, but who could say what led Ansel Adams to take his first photograph of a mountain? Why did Lee Friedlander set off across the country with a Kodak Instamatic? How did Cindy Sherman get the idea to set the timer and pose in front of her own lens? Timing was everything. Timing and circumstance. Circumstance and the native intuition that told you when to press the shutter. He had found his métier in the moment of death, and constructed a theory to surround it.

But suddenly he couldn't wait for the police radio to report the vagaries of urban dementia. "There's got to be more," he complained to Catherine on a slow night when the beeper failed to ring and the city was at peace.

"What?"

"I mean . . ."

"You mean that someone in the world has to be killing someone else."

She meant her comment sarcastically, but Max took it literally. "Of course!"

"Of course?"

"You're right. Do the math. Make a graph. Check the figures. X number of murders, y minutes in the day. I don't think one passes when something isn't happening. I'm so . . . so . . ."

"Parochial?"

"Right. Think of religion."

"I do nothing else," she said, having been recently promoted to chief of her department store's Easter display. Someone had to come up with something besides an egg hunt for toddlers.

"Right. In Israel, Arabs are killing Jews and Jews are killing

Arabs. In Ireland, Catholics are killing Protestants and Protestants are killing Catholics. In Tibet, someone's killing Buddhists and the Buddhists must be killing someone."

"Bloody Buddhists." Catherine slapped her knee.

"Damn straight."

"Come to bed."

But the days when a housewife's revenge or a drug dealer's turf war was enough to arouse Max for hours had passed. His daily fare in New York was no longer sufficient to fulfill his appetite. Even the occasional bloated body fished out of the river or charred incinerants after a nightclub fire were no longer sufficient. Even murder/suicide no longer floated his boat. "Where's a paper?" he demanded.

"You haven't had a picture in the paper in days."

"So I want to read a little. Is that a crime? I want to know what's going on in the world."

"No, you want to . . ."

"What?"

She didn't dare say, but she knew, and wasn't surprised when she woke up the next morning and found a note on the bathroom mirror. Actually, it wasn't a note, but a photograph of a note. For a second, she marveled that he had written the note, photographed it and discarded the original in favor of the image. Then she read: "Gone to Chechnya. Back next week, with a roll of film, or on one."

MAX HAD NEVER particularly concerned himself with the ongoing catastrophe in the former Russian republic as he scanned the papers for his photographs. Yet suddenly, that night in bed, the light of newfound global consciousness blinked on inside his head. Where there were terrorists, people were terrified;

where there were bombed buildings, there had to be bodies. Not so many as in Nanking or Warsaw, but this era's entry into the international bad news sweepstakes. Just what he wanted.

Aeroflot to Moscow, the only all-smoking flight across the Atlantic, was an experience, and more so the twin-engine plane that eked Max and three representatives of the United Nations over the Urals to Grozny. There, after what seemed like an infinite wait at passport control, he took a taxi—actually a battered old Luba sedan, the odometer of which had clearly circled back to zero several times—which roller-coastered its way along the bomb-broken road to the capital.

The driver tried to make conversation, but Max couldn't understand a word through the man's thick moustache and dense accent. He should have known, but he would learn, that it didn't make a difference what anyone in these parts of the world said. What they wanted to know was what they had to do to get ahold of any of the dollars in your pocket: women, drugs, name it. Ironically, they had exactly what Max wanted if only he could explain. Here, bodies were the commonest currency, but it seemed too absurd that the stranger had traveled from New York for such a mundane commodity. But finally, as they arrived at the hotel, the driver offered one last way to bridge the gap: "Translator."

"Yes," Max practically cried with relief.

"My brother speaks the English."

"Tomorrow. Nine A.M. Can your brother come here? With you? With the car?" Max mimed a steering wheel. "To the hotel, tomorrow, *mañana*. You know, numbers; seven, eight nine. *Einz, zvei, drei*. Oh, heck," he sighed, and pointed to his watch.

"*Da*. Yes."

If Max had been able to translate the driver's appreciative nod, he might have had second thoughts, since it meant that the man would gladly chop off Max's wrist with a meat cleaver to obtain his Timex bottom-of-the-line timepiece.

LIKE THE CRATERED CITY en route to the hotel, the Grozny Grand had seen better days. One of its wings was collapsed in upon itself, and the sandbagged front desk at the end of an ill-lit 1950s lobby was vacant. Chairs were stacked as if to clean the terrazzo floor, but no cleaning machines were in sight. Only the hum of a generator provided a hint of occupation. Then Max caught a murmur of conversation from an alcove. Three men were sprawled along a curved couch that surrounded a coffee table covered with tall glasses covered with coasters. "You guys journalists?"

"No," one said without looking up.

"Do we look like fecking journalists?" replied the second, dressed in dingy khakis and a stained vest.

"Nobody here but us chickens," said the third, a fat man with a bushy beard.

"As opposed to Chechans?" Max said.

The second man glanced at Max and smiled. " 'Ave a vodka?" he offered.

Max looked at the watch he had just shown to his driver. It was noon, but closer to dawn New York time. "I'll take a beer."

" 'Ave the vodka. Or if you don't like that, you can 'ave the vodka."

"He can always have the vodka," said the third.

"Luckily, we've got enough vodka," said the first.

Max knew a stale routine when he heard one. "How long have you guys been here?"

"I'm the current record holder," drinker number one answered. "Four months, three days."

"What about Wilson?" asked the third.

"Current living record holder," the first corrected himself.

"Anyone else here?"

"Who the fuck would want to crawl up the world's arshole?"

"As you can tell," the third one informed Max, "we must be journalists, because we use words so well. Who you with?"

"Freelance."

"Congratulations. You can have Wilson's room. Here." He uncapped a bottle of vodka and poured several fingers. "You can also have Wilson's glass."

Max didn't say that he would have preferred Wilson himself—on film—as he took the glass and the coaster and, unlike the others, placed the coaster underneath the glass. "So it looks like you guys pretty much have the place to yourself."

"Only white folks here are journalists, that and a few aid workers, but they don't drink."

"So, uh, can I ask your advice?"

"Incoming."

Before Max could figure out what this meant, a low thud shook the building and a thin cloud of dust settled onto his drink like pond scum.

"First piece of advice: use your coaster properly," the third man said, emptied Max's glass behind the couch, refilled it and placed the coaster on top.

Max described his arrangement with the driver.

"One more bit of advice . . ."

"Yes?"

"Don't go."

"Don't go?"

"Wilson went."

"Look, Mac—"

"Max."

"Look, Max. We're all in this cesspool together. Have some vodka. Don't leave the hotel. Write your story and get out as fast as you can."

"But I told you, I don't write. I take photographs."

"Feckin photogs are bonkers," the second man said with an English accent as he gulped down his drink. "It's not too safe to do reporting from the lobby; them feckers 'ave to be in eyesight, means in gunsight, from the other side. Every other place I've been they've got respect for the press. 'Ere they don't know jackshit. The group that saves you today is jest as likely to kill you tomorrow. Frankly, I'd rather wade two hundred kilometers up the damn Dneiper to Chernobyl, see if any mushrooms are growing yet and make an omelet."

Max leaned forward with puppy dog eagerness.

"Yer first war, kid?"

"Yeah."

"Good. Get out of here and it won't be your last. Chechnya's the worst. I received me undergraduate degree with the Tamil Tigers, did some graduate work in Burundi, but this is postdoc. I think it's because they're Euros they're so feckin' nuts. They get bigger numbers elsewhere. Killin' in the equatorial zone is a way of life, die like tsetse flies, but 'ere it's more . . . inventive."

"Comparative Atrocity 101."

But Max was immune to the reporters' braggadocio; he needed more than the macho satisfaction of drinking in a war zone. He didn't have the words to explain himself, but he sought encounter with the genuinely serious, the deadly serious. Death wasn't dry cleaning; it wasn't posturing on the Lower East Side. The moment his finger pressed the shutter on the recently deceased, he was like a Catholic with a communion wafer melting on his tongue, a Jew touching a Torah, a Buddhist at satori. In the next fragment of a second, the shutter clicked and he returned to the life that his subject would never again know. Then, if she was nearby, he'd look at Catherine and notice the outline of her thigh under her dress.

He left the journalists and checked in with a sallow man who had appeared behind the front desk. The next morning, as scheduled, he met the driver and his brother, Sergei. The "translator" carried a machine gun slung around his neck as casually as Max carried the Leica 400 he had graduated to from his old Nikon. Sergei fingered the camera.

Before Max could utter a word, the familiarly rattling taxi set off into the obliterated streets of Grozny. Buildings that had stood for three hundred years had not been able to withstand recent aerial bombings, so they frequently had to detour around and occasionally back down streets blocked by rubble. Whoever lived here made themselves scarce, and only shadows broke from structure to structure. Speaking not much more English than his brother, Sergei waved at the devastation and said, "Moscow."

"Grozny," Max said.

"Moscow," the translator insisted.

What he meant was that Moscow was responsible for Grozny.

But Max didn't understand large-scale politics. He merely yearned to behold its resulting trauma, say two hundred thousand bodies, one by one, each for one thirty-second of a second. He did the math: 200,000 divided by 32, reduced to 100,000 by 16, reduced again to 50,000 by 8, and again to 25,000 by 4, finally reduced to 12,500 by 2, ultimately equalled 6,250 seconds or 100-plus minutes or slightly more than an hour and a half to record the decimation of a population—unless lighting conditions required a longer exposure. "Stop!" he shouted. Time for an f-stop.

The car screeched to a halt, and Max jumped out. A stream of bullets smacked into a wall several feet above his head, not close, but close enough for him to think, "Holy shit, I'm being shot at," as he rounded a brick corner, from behind which extended a pair of boots with holes in the bottom. Unfortunately, the boots were worn by a drunk snoozing in an alley with an empty bottle of vodka by his side.

"Him no good," said the supposed translator.

"No good at all," Max muttered, and returned to the hotel just in time to see the three English journalists jamming into a waiting minivan.

"Room for one more, mate," the bearded one said.

"What?"

"Alert from Whitehall: all British nationals are ordered to exit the country by midnight. There's rumors that Moscow is planning to nuke the place. I'm sure your State Department says the same thing."

"I'm not leaving."

"Kid, one last bit of advice—"

"Save it," Max said bravely, scorning those who abandoned ship when the waters got rough.

"Take it from someone who's been 'ere for four months and four days. . . ."

"Yeah?"

"It's something me mum told me years ago, but . . ."

"But?" Suddenly Max wanted to know the folklore from Yorkshire.

"Ah, forget it, I don't have time. . . . The cab's leaving."

Max hesitated for about a second, thought of himself and the hotel clerk huddled behind the sandbags waiting for the big one to whistle on down and then, out of wisdom or cowardice, necessity or preference, he said, "Let me grab my luggage."

———

MAX WAS DEPRESSED from the moment he returned to East Seventh Street, bank account and self-image both depleted by the wasteful journey.

Oh, he saved face by spinning his foreign debacle into an exotic adventure. "Here's the secret to wartime documentary," he educated his friends in a bar. "Wait. Wait till the moment of optimum terror, wait until your bowels are loosening, and then press the shutter. That's the picture that goes on the front page."

"So where's the front page?"

"Well . . ."

"Did you get the shots or didn't you?"

"Not exactly. The feckers confiscated my camera, so I didn't get the shots I really wanted. Luckily, I have a Minox on my tie clip, but I don't like the quality it delivers, so I'm keeping those pictures for my private archives."

Such dissimulation ensured that Max could recoup his financial losses. In fact, post-Chechnya, he was hotter than ever, but cooler than ever to hotness's opportunities, which all involved studio shots of the latest outrage to public sensibilities. A glossy lifestyle magazine wanted him to shoot a rock star who used computer graphics to produce a video of himself having sex with the president's wife—yawn. If only the trendoid would OD in a hotel bathroom, leap out of a hotel window, slip and break his neck or slice his wrist in a hotel bathroom, but no.

"All you have to do," the photo editor said, "is—"

"I know, snap the shutter." Max snapped the shutter on the plum assignment and sat at home, reading his books and the papers, seeking a place that would let him accomplish his true job.

It was a busy week: a tornado ripped through a substandardly built retirement village in Texas and an earthquake killed thousands in the Philippines, yet Max wasn't even tempted to follow these leads. For the first time, he understood the difference between himself and the AD guys. It wasn't just death he sought, but murder, not merely tragedy, but atrocity. The difference lay in human agency.

And Catherine was too busy to listen to his complaints, because she had recently talked her bosses on Herald Square into mounting an Easter extravaganza bound to rival the Thanksgiving parade for sheer sentimental vulgarity. Besides variations on the holiday theme and an ecumenical nod to the city's Jewish population with a float that would continuously create and part a block-long silken Red Sea with the aid of a portable wind machine, she was hip-deep in construction diagrams for a forty-foot mechanical rabbit. Max couldn't begin to get through to her as she paced about the apartment, cell phone clamped between ear and shoulder, screaming to some fabricator on the other end of the line, "I said hare, not hair. Well, if you don't know the difference, I'll find someone who does."

So Max looked at her, not precisely with longing, but with longing for the longing he once felt. Death was his personal Viagra; without it, he had no interest in sex, and his girlfriend didn't seem to miss it. Wondering vaguely if she was sleeping with Geoffrey, the store's chief designer, who had outdone himself with his concept for the enormous rabbit, he plunged once again into the news with an aim to finding a more satisfying venue than Chechnya, which the papers informed him had not been obliterated after all, at least no more than it had already.

West Africa enticed him. It was bad and, relatively speaking, undiscovered, at least compared to Central Africa, which had been mined to exhaustion by reporters in the glory days of Rwanda nearly a decade ago. Nowadays, Liberia was where the action was. There, on the dark continent's bulge into the Atlantic

Ocean, where freed slaves from the United States created their own nation in 1847, rebels laid seige to cities, and refugee camps were filled with the wreckage. Self-defined revolutionaries converted the agrarian proletariat to their cause by hacking off their limbs and reintroducing them to slavery. At least some had to bleed to death.

Max was on a boat three days later, air connections "temporarily" canceled, a good sign. Indeed, the omens grew more auspicious when he arrived to all the misery he had dreamed of. He still sought mortalilty, but, having learned his lesson in Chechnya, he was not about to be left without anything but an imaginary tie-clip Minox, and took photos of beggars at the harbor. The portfolio of these images, which swiftly included those of starving babies and preteen prostitutes, weren't his ultimate aim, but if worse came to worse or, rather, better, they'd pay for the trip. This was national magazine photo essay material—with an Absolut ad on the back.

An old hand, shooting par for this particular course, he checked into the capital's single international hotel, drank and swapped stories with the usual crew of journalists in the lobby. Already he was deft enough to say, "This is elementary school. Any of you guys been in Chechnya? That's postdoc."

Despite his bluster, however, Max never quite received his degree. Yes, he stayed in Liberia despite the State Department warnings that he now realized were as pro forma as the weather report. He even managed to find a translator who actually spoke English and convinced the man to smuggle him into the bush, where one tribe was always killing another for some good reason. Things were looking up. At the end of a two-day drive through a cloud of mosquitoes, he met a local chieftain who had allegedly engineered a particularly brutal massacre. Unfortunately, the man wore plaid shorts and a Mickey Mouse T-shirt instead of a necklace of skulls.

"Yes, dead people," he said to Max through the translator, and invited them both to join him in the kickoff of his tribe's annual guava festival.

"This isn't what I wanted," Max complained. "I thought you said he said 'dead people.' "

The translator spoke at length with the chieftain, who eventually shrugged.

"Sorry, the headman says that dead people would send the wrong message."

"Message! What fucking message do guavas send?"

The translator shrugged. "Something about agricultural prosperity, I guess."

"Fucking Mickey Mouse!" Max griped.

The chieftain grinned and nodded.

Even here, five thousand geographical and a million psychic miles from Manhattan (how many feet in a psychic mile?), public image won out over authenticity. Max felt as if there were a conspiracy to withhold the truth from him, and demanded to be taken back to the capital, where, after another week hotel-bound with a guava-induced bout of diarrhea, he called Catherine in New York, but all she wanted to talk about was the latest problem with her mechanical rabbits. "What?" he shouted over the bad connection.

"We've decided to go high-reality."

"What?"

"High-reality."

"Meaning?"

"These aren't greeting-card bunnies; they're rabbits, with anatomically correct ears and teeth—no genitals, that's too much, but otherwise genuine. The store let me hire a zoologist as a consultant."

"Whatever turns you on."

"I can't hear you."

He shouted, "Whatever turns you on!"

"Don't shout. Rabbits only turn each other on. How about you? Are you turned on? Should I talk dirty? We've got a hutch here; I can describe the orgy."

But Max was too dispirited to engage in intercontinental phone sex. Wherever he went in metropolitan New York, he found bodies, but wherever he went in various national necropolises, he found the diseased but not the deceased, the disfigured but not the transfigured. If he had been a death magnet in New York, he was a death-repellent good-luck charm in Africa. No matter how damaged his presumed subjects, they refused to expire in front of his camera. Dejectedly, he made one more trip out from his hotel into the desert south of the city, where a drought had decimated the population, but the Grim Reaper was too tricky for him. If he ducked out and sneaked back, the heavenly hearkener would duck out first. Only Max's final departure would allow the angel's final arrival. So evident was the photographer's mystical power that, before he left, he received as many offers to visit AIDS-ridden children in the hospital and wounded commandants of the revolutionary corps as he received stupid offers to photograph rock stars in New York. It was obvious that none of these people had any intention of dying.

FRUSTRATED AGAIN, Max departed via antique steamer from Monrovia, and arrived back in New York to read about the coup that must have occurred the minute his boat chugged out the harbor, but he knew that by the time he yo-yoed across the

Atlantic again, a truce would be signed. The powers that be weren't cooperating, and neither was Catherine.

"Oh, hey," she said when she found him in bed as if he had gone out to the corner newsstand.

"I'm home."

"I noticed."

"Just fact-checking."

"I'm sick of fucking rabbits."

"Or rabbits fucking."

"That too. The VP of public relations is already talking about installing a petting zoo in the store. I'd be in charge. He considers it a promotion, but I think that they're typecasting me as the house farmer because I grew up on a farm."

"Ms. Greenjeans."

"Greenjeans!" she wailed. "My entire wardrobe is black."

"That's why I love you."

"You love me?"

Max thought of her black pants, her black silk shirt, the black stone necklace she wore, and reached outward.

"No." She pushed him away. "I'm too depressed."

CATHERINE SAID SHE WAS depressed, yet she dove into her work with childish relish, poring over a dozen slightly varying swatches of pink fuzz, checking the motors that would set a yard-long scut to thumping to the beat of a brass band, comparing three different computer-simulated nose-squinchings for relative cuteness factors. She said she was depressed, but it was Max who sank into sluggishness and torpor. In all his enthusiasm for death, he had always felt alive. Now he could barely respond to the four-oh-two beepings of his police radio that picked up with an unseasonably hot early spring. So what if some kid in Corona "accidentally" shot his grade-school principal? The only way you could get blood on the front page anymore was if it came from a media billionaire or a supermodel or, preferably, both.

Max left Catherine in the middle of one of her endless conversations with one of her junior coordinators and went around the corner to a bar done up in mock-Communist decor. There he met several women from a local performance troupe, for whom he performed.

"How do you get into such situations?" he rhetorically asked himself. "It's easy. First, you arrange an interview with the strongman du jour. They're always willing to meet the press. You've made their day. In return, you get a great dinner—the royal food tester will nibble anything suspicious. Of course, if it's a slow-acting poison, you and the food tester may have cramps later, but it's usually pretty good. Dictators tend toward French cuisine. I wonder why. Maybe they all see themselves as Sun Kings. Or maybe it's because they know that their ultimate home will be a villa on the Riviera. You think Papa Doc and Idi Amin get together and play cards on a terrace and reminisce about the good old days?"

Max was a liar and a voyeur, like any true artist, and, like any true artist, he fooled himself as much as his audience. Mostly he fooled himself into believing that he knew what he wanted, yet ever since he caught and made the most of the scene in the bank, he had felt a sense of loss along with that of satisfaction. Perhaps it wasn't death he sought, but an unobtainable glimmer of the afterlife. Unfortunately, the door to that mysterious ATM room in the sky was shut—and no embossed plastic card would open it.

Suddenly he got an idea. The ATM room wasn't the bank and it wasn't the street. It was an interim space analagous in its commercial domain to the ontological state he sought, the moment between stimulus—a bullet—and response—cessation of brain waves. That was it. He yearned to behold the precise moment of departure, the click of the shutter coinciding to a thirty-second of a second with the end of life. Even as he blathered on for shot after shot of Jack Daniel's, describing shot after nonexistent photo shot of shot after gunshot, he set his sights on the razor between this world and the next.

"E-Day" as Catherine called it, was still two weeks away when Max's attention was gripped by an article on page 8 of the *Times,* beneath the weather map. It mentioned an Indian insurrection on the border of Nicaragua and Honduras. He looked at the weather map. At least this time he wouldn't have to change time zones.

"Catherine," he said when she had a spare moment. "I'm—"

"Going somewhere."

"I've got to."

He vaguely hoped that she would argue with him, but instead all she replied was, "No problem. I was just fact-checking."

LIKE THE THIRD FORAY in an archetypal fairy tale, Max's third journey abroad in search of large-scale international demise was finally blessed with success. Within minutes after his plane landed on the potholed runway at Managua, he saw his first body, and compelled yet another foreign taxi driver to screech to a halt so he could photograph it, just a shirtless laborer expired by the side of the road with no discernible signs of the method by which he had met his demise. The rebellion Max had read about touched the outskirts of the capital, so there were dead rebels and dead soldiers and dead civilians within five minutes of his five-star hotel. A bus crashed into a train, and, though he declared that accidents were for amateurs, Max was there too, on his own busman's holiday, to see the victims carried off, a thirty-second of a second each. He took so many photographs, he had to wire to Catherine to FedEx him more film, color, because this was beyond newspapers. This was even better than a photo essay, better than an Absolut ad. This had the potential for an oversized hardcover with an introduction by a laureate preceding images of stark ivory bones against a lush green jungle backdrop. He could see the title on the coffee table of his mind: *Tamarinds and Body Parts.*

He shot and he shot until, seeking further, more gruesome scenes, he hired another guide to take him to Xualtapec, a village forty miles up the unpacific Pacific coast, where not even the Pulitzer-starved dared go. Rumor had it that there were mass burials nearby, though each faction, rebels and rebel-squashers, claimed that the other was responsible. With a little luck, this could be major.

"You sure you want to go there?" the guide said.

"Sure." Max waved his roll of dollars.

And so they went, into the jungle, where the peasants, armed with the machetes they had previously used to slash at the thick trunks of plantain trees, had taken after anyone in uniform, and where nervous soldiers, abandoned by their generals, summarily executed anyone they thought looked suspicious.

Arriving among a hodepodge of mud-brick dwellings set along a single street like a rough stone necklace along a brittle chain, the driver said, "I'll wait in the car."

The street was silent except for two boys who bounced a pink rubber ball against a crumbling stone facade and called out, "Single. Double. Two runs, two outs."

A sign on the building read "El Posto" and a limp flag hung

in the damp air. Max stepped toward the door, slowed by the heat.

"You sure you want to go there?" one of the boys called, tossing the ball up and down.

These were the same words the driver had used and Max wondered if everyone in this country spoke the same Yankee vernacular. "Sure," he said, and offered the boys a few coins from his pocket.

Inside, the post office was as still as the street, with a smell that Max knew from his previous life in New York. Four-oh-two.

It was the smell of dried blood that Max immediately perceived between the postmaster and a unrolled spool of stamps bearing colorful images of mountains and waterfalls. Actually, he had to unroll the spool to make the picture more vivid. So what, the man was dead anyway.

Leaving the post office, he couldn't believe his good fortune; the two little boys both lay where they had last stood, bellies open, exposed intestines gathering flies; the whole town was dead. He looked for the rubber ball, because props always added to a scene, but he couldn't find it and wondered if the boys had been killed for the plaything. Max ran through the roll of film in the camera, flipped the finished canister into his pocket and reloaded. "Hey, Ramon." He gestured to the taxi parked down the street. "Juan, Pedro. Hey, you," he kept calling as he approached his car. "Esteban, Felipe, whatever your name is." He opened the driver's door. "Ooop."

The driver's body tumbled into the dust. Max snapped a shot.

"Try Maria," said a voice from the passenger seat.

"Um, hi."

"Drive, you toad."

She had dark skin and straight black hair and wore military

fatigues except for a necklace of green and blue feathers and a silver-handled gun aimed at his head.

"Fine," he said, sure that he was en route to the magic two hundred thousand he had once imagined.

Out from Xualtapec, the roads made Chechan back streets look like the Autobahn. About the only directions Maria gave were "Take a right at the big tree" or "Follow this stream," as they shifted from lesser to lesser byways, from crumbling macadam to planks of wood laid end to end, to rutted, washed-out dirt, until the fronds of trees swished at the windows like the bristles in a car wash. They rose into the hills, until they stopped in a small clearing enclosed by wide-trunked trees with wattled rings around their perimeters. There was no place else to go.

"We're here," she announced, and led him into the jungle. They hiked for an additional hour and arrived at an Indian village. It felt like a diorama at the Museum of Natural History come to life. Naked toddlers crawled in the dirt while naked women squatted and suckled naked babies. Half-simian men dressed in strips of hide that barely covered their genitals peeked at Max and giggled. Yet something was anachronistic about the diorama; most of the men held rough wooden spears, but a few held guns.

Max surreptitiously clicked the shutter on his camera. Graduate school, hell, postdoc, nada; this was the top, the acme, the heart of the heart of darkness. The natives poked at him to see if he was real and chattered in a language that must have been an amalgam of Spanish and local dialect.

"Twenty years ago," Maria said, "this was a happy village. It was poor, but there was enough food, and there was even the beginning of prosperity." She pointed to a rusting television antenna stuck into the ground. "Then came Somoza."

"Isn't that an Indian bread?"

Exasperated, she sighed. "That too, but I'm referring to Anastasio Somoza, ruler from '63 to '79."

Max knew his dictators like boys—the boys in Xualtapec— knew baseball heroes. He knew their dates and their stats, numbers of opposition assassinated or disappeared, numbers of hundreds of millions stashed in Swiss bank accounts, but all of his heroes were current. Aside from the legendary Papa Docs and Idi Amins who created the sport, he had no sense of history.

"After Somoza was killed in an automobile explosion, we thought Daniel Ortega and the Sandanistas would make things better. They didn't. No one ever makes things better for these people. Only now that we've adopted Western guns and separated ourselves entirely from what you call civilization has it gotten better."

A hush came over the crowd.

Maria whispered in his ear, "Whenever the chief talks to you, turn your back on him."

"Why?"

"To show respect, gringo. Do it if you want to live."

Max had never thought in these terms. Of course he wanted to live, didn't he? He recorded death, but couldn't imagine that he might be in as much danger as those whose deaths he recorded. After all, he was just a photographer. Nobody hurt photographers, at least not deliberately. Or did they? For only a second, he felt doubt and wondered how much he wanted to live and how much his frantic gallivanting around the globe had really been a courtship with death, until an elderly man, who, like Maria, wore green and blue feathers around his neck, hobbled up from behind the crowd. The old man stared at Max for a good five minutes, then reached forward and touched the several cameras that hung around his neck like mechanical jewelry. Then the old man spoke, and Max turned around.

Maria, the only one who had not turned at the sound of the feeble voice, said, "He wants to know how you are known."

Max thought about what answer might make sense to this primitive. "Maker of images," he replied.

"Your name, asshole."

"Oh, Max."

She spoke and the chief spoke again.

"He wants to know if you come from beyond the seas."

Strictly speaking, Max could have driven from the East Village, but he thought it was best to agree. "Sure."

The chief spoke again, more animatedly.

"He wants to know if you have a Polaroid."

"What?"

"The nearest lab is too far from here. He'd like to have a photograph taken. I told you that we weren't always so isolated."

"But I can't take a photograph if I can't turn around."

"You only have to turn around when he talks."

The chief was silent.

"Well, then, yes, I mean for a portrait I'd have to use the Leica, and it would be better in my studio, but—"

She interrupted him. "You may turn."

Max did have a Polaroid, which he used mostly for preliminary photos to gauge composition, but he would give the chief what he wanted. He made an unnecessary ritual of showing everyone his light meter, holding it up like a chalice of eucharistic wine along with several other contraptions from his kit bag. Finally, he clicked the shutter, which he had attached to an unnecessary flash because he thought it might be impressive. Fire from a box heap big trick.

Formula-coated paper slid out of the camera.

Together with the tribe, he watched the image develop on the raw stock. A miracle.

The chief smiled and slapped Max on the back in an apparently universal language of congratulations. Max took several more shots of the village elders, who lined up in order of whatever savage hierarchy they lived by. By then the sun had started to set and even the flash-enhanced images grew dim. It was time for dinner.

Everyone gathered in a circle around a crackling fire, and passed around a charred wooden pot filled with some gooey and fetid meat. Max didn't ask what it was, because he didn't want to know. He knew enough to eat and smile. Then the chief took a sip of liquid from a rough tin cup of military provenance and handed it to Max. Worse than the meat, the liquid smelled like industrial cleaner, but Max didn't need to check with Maria to understand that it would be best to drink it and like it. Heck, the stuff couldn't be worse than some of the cheapo champagne Loco stole from Astor Wines, so he smiled again, tilted his head back and said, "Cheers!"

A second later he heard the cup drop to the ground and then felt himself slump to meet it. One of the elders propped his head on a log, and an apparition appeared.

It was Maria, who cooed, "No one drinks it straight."

"No one told me."

"Sure, you Western pig."

"But you're Western too."

"But I'm not a pig."

"What sort of animal are you?"

She knew enough English to answer, "I'm a bitch."

Max took a deep breath. "You don't look like one."

"I have a nose like one. I can smell so well that I know what you want."

"What?" he gasped.

"The volcano."

It wasn't the answer he expected, but, slurring with the alcohol, he said, "Shurrr, the volcano. Thas what I want."

Silently, she stood and circled the fire, once, twice, three times. Max remembered the game of Duck-Duck-Goose he had played as a five-year-old in a sunlit suburban kindergarten. His head had spun then, while he watched a little girl named Laura who had a charming speech impediment that made her pronounce her own name Lauwa, and it spun now as he tracked Maria, but he staggered to his feet and followed her back to the car, where he collapsed into the passenger seat as her foot hit the pedal and they ripped backward through the vines that seemed to have grown to envelop the car during dinner. Half a mile backward, she hit the brakes and took a fork he hadn't noticed when arriving. Now they jolted off into the jungle.

It was nearly dawn when he awoke, alone, a warm breeze rustling through the open door. Outside, the trees and vegetation had disappeared. Moonlit footprints led into the distance through a fine black sand glittering with flakes of mica.

"Catherine," he thought, for only a second. "If you could see me now."

He was on top of a mountain, and could perceive the glow of the Indian campfire in a clearing way below. He followed the footprints, but sank into the soft black sand. He noticed that the prints were barefoot and took off his boots. The sand was warm.

Maria stood silhouetted on a ridge by the first flares of sunlight rising from the distant east. He walked up beside her and looked down—miles, it seemed—into a simmering cauldron. The volcano looked like a giant pizza. "Is it alive?" he asked.

"As you and I," she replied. "Seismologists believe the last explosion took place sometime in the thirteen or fourteen hundreds, but it might explode again at any time without warning. Aside from our momentary advance when the Somozans and

Sandanistas thought we had strategic value, my tribe never developed much beyond its discovery of fermented grain because we could be destroyed at any moment. The knowledge of imminent oblivion puts a crimp in belief in progress. That's why my father wanted a photograph, so that something might be left after doomsday."

"Your father?"

"You can call me princess."

Max stood on the edge he had always yearned for.

Maria removed her gun from its thick leather holster, and for a second he thought he was finally in the right place at the wrong time. Then the princess dropped her weapon, which landed with a small thud and a puff of gray dust, and removed all of her clothes except for the feather necklace. As she stepped forward to meet him, she said, "*Aqui es tranquilo.*"

CATHERINE WAS OUT when Max returned home for the last time. Scattered across the desk where his blown-up prints and miniature contact sheets once riffled in the breezes that slid over the loose windowsill like fish, he saw renderings and blueprints, cross-sections and schematic diagrams of electronic transmission boards. Almost but not fully identical, they were labeled "Rabbit Number One," "Rabbit Number Two" and on until "Rabbit Number Twenty-four."

Of course, this was Catherine's big day, and Max wanted to share it with her. For the first time since he could remember, he was at ease, *tranquilo* indeed. He had peered into the volcano, thinking it might be his last sight on earth, and then, well, what happened happened. *Quien sabe?* He would keep the memory of Maria from Catherine as a kindness to them both. He felt as free as a bird on a sunny day, purged of the need to take stupid risks ever again. From here he could settle into a compassionate middle age, taking pictures of rock stars or bar mitzvahs. He might even investigate dry cleaning, shop around for a house with a built-in pool, live like his mother said, "like a human being."

He ran joyously down the stairs and hailed a cab to Midtown—a real New York City taxi, with a driver who spoke as much English as a Chechan—and gave directions to the reviewing stand in front of the Metropolitan Museum, where the parade was scheduled to begin. Blocks away, the traffic came to a halt, obstructed by families crossing the street, all heading in the same direction, so he paid the driver and continued on foot. "Sorry, sorry, passing through," he excuse-me'd through the crowds that lined the parade route, as dense with humanity as the jungle was with trees. Some people had been waiting for hours because publicity had done its job as well as production.

If the Thanksgiving show relied upon variety, it was uniformity that Catherine sought to wow the world with today. Of course, there would also be the usual floats and marching bands without which a parade wouldn't be a parade, but the main act was a radical departure from tradition. People would gape and stare, eyes bulging, mouths slack, as one after another, after another, after another, after twenty other giant rabbits marched proudly forth from the hangar-sized inflatable warehouse Catherine had received a permit to erect behind the museum in Central Park.

Max could see her on a platform next to the reviewing stand, a fancy name for the pink and baby-blue bunting-swagged athletic bleachers where the mayor, various councilmen, store officials and other dignitaries sat beneath a row of television cameras that would bring the spectacle to the Easter morning homes of those unable to attend. She was like the captain of an ocean liner leaving the dock on its maiden voyage, standing proudly at the helm while her mate and subordinates scurried around her, making sure everything was shipshape.

Across the sea of upturned faces, she caught a glimpse of her boyfriend. Max waved wildly and she pierced him with her glare as fixed as a harpoon.

He cringed backward.

"Daddy, that man pushed me," a child in a red felt bonnet cried.

"Sorry, sorry," he muttered to get through the crowd to tell Catherine about his wonderful discovery that life was worth living, just as a blare of trumpets harkened the first band and the first of the rabbits emerged from its enormous plastic hutch.

Amid the delighted "oohs" of the crowd, Max was the only one who failed to participate in the fundamental rapture caused by the oversized creature whose nose wiggled endearingly as it stepped, hopped, stepped and hopped onto the rough macadam of Fifth Avenue.

Not in the slums, not in Chechnya, not in the Liberian desert or the Nicaraguan jungle, had he ever felt such fear. As perhaps everyone from the dead man at the bank on Avenue A to the last dead peasant in Xualtapec might have received one sliver of an iota of a premonition that his next breath would be his last, Max suddenly knew that Catherine knew about Maria and the volcano. And worse than his sexual betrayal of her, he understood that he had done a far, far worse thing than he had ever done before. He had reneged on the unspoken contract, which, though she often mocked and disdained it, nonetheless united them. Max had turned his back on death, while Catherine had silently, secretly, pursued him into the dark realm, which now belonged entirely to her. The pupil exceeded the master.

Rabbit Number One—code-named Annabelle—squatted in the middle of the intersection of Fifth Avenue and Seventy-ninth

Street and deposited a freckled egg the size of a Volkswagon from somewhere within her capacious reproductive tract. Half a thousand people along the curb broke into spontaneous applause.

More amazing, the egg seemed to have a mind of its own. It circled Annabelle clockwise, then reversed direction and circled her counter-clockwise. She blinked down, her eyes as watery with maternal bliss as any human mother's.

And before the crowd could wipe their own empathetic tears from their cheeks, the first float, sponsored, of course, by the store, rolled into the street. Drawn by a white Rolls-Royce convertible, it was festooned with six miles—Catherine had done the math—of lavender streamers and bore a log-cabin-sized replication of the square-block store itself, the children of the major stockholders waving from its windows.

Nothing could be finer; the day was splendid, and brass filled the air as fifty members of a high school band outfitted in kelly-green uniforms, bright gold-colored epaulettes, military kepis and black satin shoes swept around the corner along with Rabbit Number Two—code-named Barnaby—who wagged his scut to a jazzed-up version of:

"In your Easter bonnet, with all the frills upon it . . ."

But as Annabelle hopped past Seventy-eighth Street, the egg she had deposited at Seventy-ninth remained behind. It rolled with an adorable wobble toward the curb, and toddlers reached out to stroke its smooth surface. It seemed to be examining the crowd with distinct volition. Suddenly it stopped, did an ovoid version of a double-take, pivoted and began to roll in a more specific direction. It was rolling toward Max, starting to pick up a little speed.

He looked at the tower to see Catherine wielding a joystick that, when she shifted her hand left, informed the egg to shift left. He felt like a solitary pin at the end of a bowling alley.

Just before the egg would have rolled into—and probably crushed—him, he leapt off the curb into the street. A policeman reached after him, but when the egg likewise veered away from the onlookers, their pas de deux seemed to part from the festivities. Max slipped between the ranks of the band.

Their cheeks as bloated as if, well, eggs were stuffed into their mouths, the acned marchers from New Tremont High glanced sidelong while trying to maintain their order and the beat of the music, blaring out,

"Here comes Peter Cottontail
Hoppin' down the bunny trail . . ."

The egg maneuvered as well as Max, between the trombones, around the piccolos, until the last row of snare drums passed and Max and the egg were alone in the street before the second float, sponsored by Charter, the "official" bank of the parade, came by.

Max zigged and the egg zagged, and parade watchers laughed at their unique clown act.

But unlike the other acts which followed in swift succession, another band, this one with baton twirlers, and another gigantic float sponsored by the "official" airline of the parade, Max and the egg never advanced down Fifth Avenue. He kept trying to make his way upstream toward Catherine, but was cut off time and again by the egg's increasingly ominous surface every time he made any headway.

The fireman's band, which, unlike the high schoolers, maintained its ranks, nearly blocked the egg as it played:

"Seventy-six trombones . . ."

Max was getting as tired as a bull in a ring faced with a relentless matador. He dashed in front of the float representing the Hebrews crossing the Red Sea, but tripped over the undulating red silk. The egg was nearly upon him. He rolled away, swiftly but not swiftly enough, because the egg bumped over his left foot, breaking several small bones.

Luckily the bump threw the naturally lopsided thing itself off balance. As Max hobbled to his feet, the egg hit the side of the float, jarring Moses—played by Hiram Halliston, star of *Bet a Batch—Win a Bundle*, into an array of spear-waving Egyptians.

A crack appeared on the egg's thin shell, and it started to leak a clear, viscous fluid, which further slowed it down. Max couldn't help but marvel that Catherine had been so diligent in her plans that the egg, in addition to whatever silicon control mechanism it contained, must have been filled with a simulated albumen solution. She had always been a stickler for details.

At that moment, giant Rabbits Number Three and Four, code-named Carla and Donbey, appeared from behind the museum. They stepped and hopped, stepped and hopped along the fountains and in front of the reviewing stand, and loomed over Max and the egg that had been abandoned in the wake of the Hebrews, who had escaped disaster one more time in their disaster-filled history.

Donbey shook his head sadly, and a tear, of sorrow rather than sentiment, seeped down the matted furrow beneath his left eye. He raised a paw to wipe at the tear, which dropped and formed a yard-square puddle next to Max. Then a steely, unrabbity resolve entered Donbey's eyes. It was that of a loving father whose offspring has been hurt. He raised his paw threateningly.

Max was trapped between the rabbit and a hard thing when

the egg's shell finally burst along its seam, and a geyser of thick viscous yolk and slimy translucent albumen gushed out along with a hail of shards, which instantaneously shredded his clothes and cut a three-inch gash along his forehead.

Okay. At least Max didn't have to worry about the egg anymore, but Donbey was now clearly enraged, his expression beadier and more rodentish. Instead of the step left, step right, cute little hop, step left, step right, cute little hop he had been programmed for, he bore down on Max. Fortunately, Donbey, like his human prey, lost traction in the foul slick his firstborn had left behind. His feet, mounted on treads from demilitarized tanks, no longer rose and fell, but glided like the blades of a novice ice skater who can propel himself quite well, but can only stop his motion by crashing into the wall of the rink. He hit the curb, tilted off his hind legs, to gasps from cowering onlookers, who were saved only when he ricocheted off an awning behind the presently arriving and also sliding Rabbit Number Five, code-named Evelyn. The two enormous creatures crashed into each other amid a tangle of floppy ears, and sparks burst from her head, and one of his mechanical eyes popped from its socket, bounced twice and crushed a hotdog cart and its vendor, a recent immigrant from Pakistan.

Now that there was blood on the streets, the crowd's pleasure turned into the same terror Max already felt. Those in the front-row positions they had been so happy to obtain pushed back against the second row, which pushed against the third row in a rapidly escalating panic.

Police tried to keep order, but the people who couldn't escape backward rushed forward and toppled the rickety sawhorses designed for the mildest form of crowd control. The band from Teaneck dropped its instruments and littered the streets with tubas and trombones mangled by a rapidly developing rabbit stampede. Following Donbey and Evelyn, Franklin and Giselle, neither of whom responded to the signals from authority, cruised out of their hangar. Giselle battered herself against the facade of an apartment building, smashed a picture window and tore away the already loosened awning, which fell on and suffocated several teenagers and a family from Des Moines, while Franklin hopped over a stone balustrade into Central Park, aiming for open territory.

The yells and shrieks took on a wave effect as one block conveyed its terror to the next block which had not yet been assaulted by the rabbits, joined now by Helen, Isaiah and Judy, who, unable to advance past the impasse created by Barnaby through Evelyn, turned on the reviewing stand. The mayor stood on his seat and waved his hands until Isaiah nudged him over the edge, twenty feet to the pavement.

Further fleeing dignitaries were jolted out of their seats and fell between the bleachers' terraced rows, as Max, forgotten for a moment, climbed toward the tower overlooking the chaos, where Catherine's assistants helplessly punched the buttons of their control boards, which further short-circuited as Kelley and Leonardo led a charge of the remaining rabbits. Jostling each other like rush-hour commuters, rabbits from Marcia and Neville to Tamara and Usher ripped through the plastic walls of their hutch and split off in every direction. Olivia went straight through the plate-glass rear wall of the Metropolitan Museum into the Polynesian wing, trailing fetishes and wooden masks and chomping on a bark canoe as if it were a carrot.

A police helicopter tried to shoot down the marauding rodents, but one of Neville's huge ears flapped up and swatted it from the sky like a pesky insect. Already a phone call had gone out to the National Guard, but it would take hours to gather and contain the pandemonium. Streets from Seventy-ninth to Fifty-ninth were scenes of mass hysteria, and some of the rabbits had already taken Madison Avenue, while others advanced on Park. Still, Max felt sure that there was one fail-safe switch and that it was in Catherine's hands. She alone remained on the control platform, mistress of her universe, watching with placid satisfaction. Had she planned this all along, or only seized the moment—like a photographer who knows exactly when to press the shutter? It didn't make a difference. Whether she had only followed Max's lead or had been transformed or always had it in her, there she was, death's own dark deity, Queen of Thanatos, dressed entirely in black. Ms. Greenjeans, hah!

Max ascended the emptied bleachers, desperate to reach her and stop the mayhem. Their eyes met, and she reached down to finger her joystick.

Out from the the obliterated hutch came the last and largest rabbit, Xenon, who towered over the other rabbits as they towered over the tiny people. A malevolent stare in his mechanical eye, he bore down on his prey like a fox on a country rabbit. He extended a giant fuzzy paw as Max gripped ahold of the rim of Catherine's platform.

Fortunately, the rabbit's mechanism was fairly crude, so the human prey eluded his predator's grasp, but Xenon's gleaming and grinding front teeth loomed, each the size of a tombstone. They seized his foot and tenderly chewed off his shoe.

"But, but," Max, barefoot as he had been on the volcano, babbled to Catherine, who stood calmly no more than three feet away, "aren't they vegetarians?"

"Not these rabbits."

"Just fact-checking."

"Your facts have always been wrong, Max."

"Okay, okay." He would say anything to satisfy her as Xenon's rubbery lips tickled up his calf, knee and lower thigh.

"Whatever you want. Just stop it," he begged. "You can stop it," he repeated himself. "Whatever you want."

"Actually, factually, it's what you always wanted," Catherine scoffed with a somewhat rodentish expression herself.

"No!" he screamed, as he felt his belly and chest being sucked farther into the awful creature's ravenous mouth, as it prepared to bite down, tooth to tooth, straight through his heart.

"Oh, yes," she replied, lifted the strap of her boyfriend's treasured Leica off his shoulders, steadied the camera, aimed, adjusted the exposure, and, just before she took his picture, said, "Smile."